DRAGON FREEHOLD

T.M. BAUMGARTNER

SPECULATIVE TURTLE PRESS

CHAPTER I
A TERRIBLE IDEA

This is the problem with secret plans, Lisette thought to herself as she jammed her fingers into a crack in the stones and inched her way up the tower wall. Far below her, the waves crashed against the sea barrier. *There is nobody to talk you out of it when you have a terrible idea.* She blew out a breath through the mask hiding her features and found a toehold that moved her a little higher.

Back in the cozy little room above her watchmaker's shop, this had seemed like the perfect idea. Taxes had been rising sharply for the last few years, and nearly everyone in the freeholder quarter was in danger of having their shop seized by the duke's men for non-payment. So why not borrow the coins from the duke's own tower to pay the taxes?

Another fingerhold gained her another hand-span toward her goal. Her shoulders burned from the effort.

She knew she wasn't the first to come up with this solution. That was why the entryway was guarded, and the first three floors of the tower were warded. A thick layer of

1

magic kept anyone from getting a handhold to pull themselves up. More wards inside protected the duke's trophies
— rumor had it that at the top of the tower waited the
magical items that helped him communicate and control
the city's dragons. But Lisette didn't want anything with
magic. Those would be too easily tracked and worthless for
paying her taxes besides. She wouldn't be able to use them
herself; she could see magic just like everyone else, but
she'd never been able to make it do anything. No, what *she*
wanted was the currency kept in the local treasury office on
the fifth floor.

Her foot found a protuberance, and she pushed herself
up. Surely she had to be close to the window by now.
Whether she'd be able to unlock the shutters to get inside
was a different matter. Her normally nimble fingers felt like
sausages after all the abuse she'd put them through.

Back in her bedroom, she'd come up with the perfect
plan. She wouldn't be able to get inside through the
guarded entrance, but the walls were a different story. The
uncles in the shop next door had procured a box of magic
trinkets at some sale or another. They had handed the
whole box off to her to see what she could make of them. It
had taken half a year of playing, but Lisette had finally realized the wrist and ankle cuffs clung to nearby magic unless
they were rolled away. A few nights of discreet practice at
the burned-out mage's lookout on the hill had left her
proficient at scrambling up above eye level between the
regular rounds of the guards. It had seemed like fate.

The part she hadn't really considered was how she
was going to climb the wall *after* the third story. The
mortar between the tower stones had crumbled with age,
which made finger holds easier to find. Unfortunately, it
also made the stones loose. She'd nearly plunged to her

death when a stone under her foot had fallen, and then she'd almost been caught when the stone had cracked into the pavement next to the guards walking below. Only her dark clothing, blending in with the grey stones, had saved her from arrest and forced labor on one of the duke's ships.

Lisette sent a quick prayer to the gods. She might be able to handle the galleys, but the seasickness would do her in.

She peered up into the darkness. One more body length and she'd be at the window. Then she would unlatch the shutters, fill her pockets with coins, and walk down the interior of the tower and out the entrance without the guards even noticing. Her fingers and shoulders just needed to make it a few more minutes. Gritting her teeth, she thrust her hand into the next hold and dragged herself up.

When she reached the window, she nearly cried in relief. Instead of a complicated lock holding the shutters closed, there was just a wooden bar on the inside, meant more to keep them from flapping in the ocean breezes than to keep anyone out. Lisette pulled the thin blade from her belt, worked it between the panes, and pushed at the bar until she felt it fall away. Then she hauled herself through the open window into the dark room and collapsed on the stone floor inside.

This really was a terrible idea. Now that she had made it into the tower, she could admit it. But she was here now, and as soon as her breathing settled a bit she was going to pick the lock on one of the strongboxes piled in the corner, take just enough to get the freeholder quarter past this current crisis, and head for home.

An alarm bell rang in the level above her.

"Gods take it," she whispered under her breath. She'd

been careful. How had they seen her? And why ring a bell instead of coming into the room?

She heard guards shouting to each other as they ran past the closed door.

Interesting.

So they *didn't* know where she was. Maybe she could find a place to hide. If they couldn't see her, maybe they would assume she had run off. Lisette looked around in the dim light. By rearranging the strongboxes, she could make a space behind them. That would be better than nothing.

"Stop him! Thief!" More footsteps ran by in the corridor.

Lisette stared at the door in disbelief. There was a *second* person breaking into the duke's tower tonight? Of all the bad luck...

The door opened. A lithe figure slipped inside. He was clad in black, with a half-mask shaped like a fox covering his eyes and nose. He locked the door behind him, then paused when he saw her. "Huh. Well. *You're* new."

CHAPTER 2
MEANS OF EGRESS

The alarm bell above continued to ring, and the sound of boots running down the hallway spoke to the chaos outside, but inside the room, everything was calm.

Everything except Lisette.

"You're ruining everything!" Her voice was halfway between a growl and a whisper.

The man in the fox mask looked from her, to the strongboxes, and then back again. "Ah, I see. In my defense, I wasn't planning on getting caught. And it's not as if you had reserved the tower for the evening."

Was that a thing that criminals did? She was a watchmaker, not a thief. How was she supposed to know the etiquette of the profession? "Did *you*?"

His wide mouth curved into a grin beneath the mask. "Can't get anything by you, can I?" He held up one finger when she would have spoken. The door handle rattled. "I don't suppose you had planned a magical means of egress?" When she stared at him, he clarified. "A way of getting out of here. How were you planning to get away?"

"I *know* what egress means. I was planning on walking out the front door, but then you went and messed everything up." Shoulders already twinging, Lisette glanced out the window. Going down would be easier than climbing up, but she wasn't sure her fingers would support her. "What was *your* plan?"

"I was going to go out the window, but two floors down and on the other side of the tower. The ground's a little softer there." He joined her by the window and looked down. "Oh well. I guess there's nothing for it. I'll just have to remember to roll when I land. That's the secret, isn't it? Or is it bending your knees? I always get confused about which one applies when." He unslung the satchel from his shoulder and began rooting around in the contents. "Guess I don't need this anymore." He held up a mirror, then shoved it back. "Now where is the... Aha, here, hold on to this end."

Lisette stared at the rope in her hand, then looked back at the satchel. "What was the mirror for?" Even if he could tie the rope to the window shutters, it was only long enough to get him less than two stories. That left a three story jump.

"So you *haven't* been in this business very long, have you? I thought not. If you'd seen the inside of the Duke's prison, you'd never let your hair grow that long. Too many rats would get tangled in it, you know?" He knelt and started tying the rope to the leg of the desk. "It's quite lovely, by the way. Your hair."

Lisette blinked. "Are you *flirting* with me?"

"Of course I am. This might be my last chance." He tugged at the rope to test his knot. "The mirror is to set off the spell of concealment, which was *supposed* to get me back down from the seventh floor without being seen." He paused and looked at the remaining coil of rope. "Don't suppose you know any knots that take up less rope... No, you don't look like the sailing type. Here, help me move this thing closer to the window." He went to the other side of the desk and started pushing.

A heavy blow rattled the door in its frame, making Lisette jump. She dropped the end of the rope and helped shove the desk until it crashed into the outside wall.

He threw the end of the rope out the window and jumped onto the desk. "Excellent. Are you ready?"

Lisette looked at the door, which rattled but seemed sturdy enough to hold everyone out for another minute or two. "You go on ahead. It was nice to meet you and all, but I need to do some things."

"But that's not..." The man in the fox mask blew out a breath. "You seem like a distrustful person, which is quite an attractive trait, but right now..." He jumped down from the table. "You understand that normally I would let you find this out for yourself, but we're a little pressed for time." He removed a pry bar from his belt, swung it into the nearest strongbox, and levered the lock off. He yanked up on the lid.

With a creak of leather and wood, the top opened, and the man in the mask stepped back with a flourish. Lisette rushed forward. She'd been planning to pick the lock so nobody would know she'd stolen anything until after taxes were collected, but she supposed that didn't matter anymore. Once they finished breaking down the door, the guards would be idiots not to count the coins in the strongboxes.

She paused with her hand outstretched. All that met her eye was sand. "That's..." She dug a hole, expecting to find coins under the top layer. "But..." She eyed the other strongboxes.

"All sand, I'm afraid."

"But how could... The duke..." Lisette pulled herself together. "Where is the *money*?"

"If I knew the answer, I might tell you just to see you smile. Alas, I think it may not exist." Another crash came from the other side of the door, but this one carried a different tone. "It sounds like they've found an axe. Perhaps now would be a good time to leave."

Lisette was still fixated on the sand. She'd climbed the entire crumbling tower and it had all been a *lie*. "But they've been collecting taxes from us..."

"My guess is the money has gone straight to pay for his debts. But if we could just discuss the financial improprieties at a later date..."

An axe head came through the splintered wood of the door.

"Right, that's it. I apologize in advance, but we really *are* in a hurry."

Lisette found herself lifted onto the desk. The masked man jumped up next to her, holding the rope in one hand. He was digging in his satchel again, crowding against her. She tried to shift away from the window. "Why don't you go first?" The last thing she wanted to do was get down to the ground and have him fall on top of her. It didn't matter whether he rolled or bent his knees when he fell — she'd end up with broken bones.

"Hold tight." He slung one arm around her waist and climbed onto the window ledge, leaving her dangling.

Lisette threw her arms around his chest and clutched him convulsively. "What are you...?" His shirt felt like sailcloth, sturdy and a little rough under her fingers. He smelled of pepper and vanilla, an intriguing combination she resolutely ignored.

The masked man let go of her so he could pull something out of the top of his satchel. "Mind your eyes." He backed out the window, tossed something into the room, and took two steps down the wall, holding onto the rope with both gloved hands. "And off we go."

CHAPTER 3

WELCOME TO THE PROFESSION

Dangling five stories above the ground, Lisette felt the man in the fox mask throw something into the tower and heard it hit the floor. Two seconds later, a white flash illuminated their surroundings, as if phosphor had been lit and then doused at every window of the tower.

"What was that?!"

Inside the tower, the screaming and yelling increased in pitch, but to Lisette's ear, the tone was anger, not pain.

"Can't very well leave hair behind for the mages to track me with, can I? Unfortunately, the spell isn't very specific."

"They can track hair?" Lisette knew mages could find any item containing magic, and then trace its history to see who had touched it, but hair didn't hold magic inside it. Her death grip around his chest had to be restricting his breathing, but he didn't seem bothered as he held the rope and steadily walked down the building.

"I *thought* you seemed new at this. Welcome to the profession, by the way. Don't be discouraged by the sand. I promise that rarely happens." His foot slipped and they swung into the building. "They're going to be lucky if this tower doesn't fall down someday soon."

"The mortar does seem to be in terrible condition," Lisette agreed. She made an involuntary noise as something twitched against her side. "Your bag is moving."

"Is it? Oh, good." He flattened against the side of the tower, on purpose this time, and an empty strongbox went crashing to the ground behind them. "Sometimes she gets bored and wanders off, and that's always a hassle." He maneuvered them to the side, a little out of the range of items dropped out the window. "Where was I? Oh yes, the sand is a bit of a disappointment, but at least you didn't end the evening by losing all your hair, so I'd say you should be quite proud of yourself."

Lisette glanced down. There was still a long way to fall, and they hadn't reached the wards. "I nearly killed myself climbing up there for no reason, and now the guards will be after me, and I *still* can't pay my taxes."

"If you don't break your ankles jumping down, you'll have a very good chance of outrunning the guards. I find it takes them a few minutes to get over suddenly losing their hair, and their boots make it hard to run very fast. Plus, that spell might have blocked the entrance until they've sorted out which magic is theirs. But how did you... No, never mind, it's rude to ask. Forget I said anything." He looked over his shoulder. "But I'm afraid we're going to have to bring this evening to a close. We're at the end of the rope, and any moment now they're going to figure out how to cut through it. So if you don't mind... If you jump first, I'll try not to hit you if you're still there when I land."

The wards shimmered just half a body length below. Lisette could have climbed down the tower, but not with the masked man's body between herself and the wall.

However... "If you hold still for a bit, I think I can get us both a little closer to the ground before we need to jump."

Loosening her grip on his shirt took effort. She climbed down his body, not stopping to think about the propriety of her hands sliding over his hips and down his thigh and calf. Dangling from one thin-soled boot, she sighed in relief as her own magical ankle cuffs gripped the wards. Then it was just a matter of picking the right handholds until she was low enough to get the wrist cuffs in play as well. Above her, she heard the masked man climbing down the wall above the wards.

"This next bit might be a little tricky." Lisette eyed him as he climbed. "If you can lower yourself and hang on to me, I can get us down to the ground." She was *fairly* certain the cuffs would hold their combined weight. And if she was wrong, well, she'd just have to remember to roll.

"What? Oh, I see. Clever! I'd have never thought to use those for something like this." As he spoke, he crouched just above the start of the ward, worked on finding the perfect handholds, then slowly lowered himself until he was next to her. They stared eye to eye, his mask concealing the upper part of his face, and hers concealing the lower. Then he let go with his right hand and gripped her right shoulder, and let go with his left hand, swinging behind her and slipping his arm around her waist in one smooth gesture. His low voice next to her ear made something flutter in the pit of her stomach. "Shall we?"

Lisette forced herself to concentrate on her movements, rolling each limb to free it from the wall, then placing it lower and letting it grip again. She'd never practiced climbing down, certainly not with another person hanging on, but she was forced to admit the real problem was the distraction caused by his arm around her waist. Still, there were guards shouting out nearby windows, and she couldn't afford to get caught.

They were still one story from the ground when the first two guards came running down the alley.

The man in the mask made a little sound. "I believe this is my stop." He loosened his grip and slid, landing on the ground in a crouch. Running straight toward the guards, he waited until they saw him and then ducked into another alley while Lisette continued her ungainly descent. For a moment, she thought one of the guards was going to ignore the masked man and concentrate on her, but he skidded around the corner, shouting to his comrade.

Lisette got her feet on the ground and freed herself from the ward just in time for another pair of guards to appear, bald heads shining in the lamplight. "Oi! Stop!" She took off in the other direction, scrambling to think of a new plan as she ran.

To get to the freeholder quarter, she needed to head northwest. But the last thing she wanted was to lead them straight back to her watchmaker's shop. If she ran north and angled to the east, she could circle around the dragon warrens. That would give her time to make sure nobody was following her. The only downside was if someone was brave enough to go straight through the warrens, they might make it to the other side and cut her off.

Lisette decided to take that chance.

She sprinted along the waterfront, weaving among a flock of revelers in matching parrot costumes. It always took a while for the masquerade spirit to take hold — costumes worn on the last day of the Festival of Secrets would be far more elaborate. But at least having her face covered didn't make her stand out. If she could stop for a moment, she could fashion something from the bright banners flown from the balconies and leave in plain sight, but the guards were still on her heels.

She ran north, up the hill toward the dragon warrens, her breath coming quickly now. The man in the fox mask had said the guards' boots would slow them down, but she wasn't gaining any ground. She needed to cut off to the east, to go around the warrens, but she heard shouting in the parallel street to her right, a cry of "Copper, copper, ai-yo!" from the street children, warning each other to scatter. The guards had counted on her turning to avoid the dragons and had sent someone in that direction. Probably to the west as well, but the rag market didn't attract the pickpockets and thieves who needed the warning.

That left two options. She could climb up and run along the rooftops, but she hadn't done roof running in years, and she didn't know this area well. She was more likely to get trapped than to get away.

So... through the dragon warrens it was. Lisette, having a healthy fear of huge beasts breathing fire, had never gone beyond the wall. Even the street children stayed away. Aside from the duke's servants, who were tasked with driving cattle through the gates, only the wealthy and bored ever went inside, daring each other to race through. Most of them arrived safely on the other side, laughing and out of breath.

But at least a few times every year, a noble's child would be lost, and no matter how many city guards were sent in afterward, nothing was ever recovered other than charred jewelry, or some clothing. Some of the city guards would also go missing, but that was considered the price Harbor Crag had to pay for the magic of the resident dragons.

The survivors passed along tips — rules that claimed

safety if only a runner's footsteps were even, or as long as the left side of the path was used. Lisette had heard all the advice over the years, most of it contradictory, and none of it backed by any logic.

Lungs burning, Lisette clambered over the bricks that had once been the wall encompassing the dragon warrens and staggered north along the path. Here and there, piles of dirt and rock rose in the moonlight. Some were the remains of buildings that had been abandoned when the dragons had moved in; others were evidence of underground excavation by claws longer than Lisette was tall.

She glanced over her shoulder to see two guards pull up to a stop on the bricks. Yes! She was going to lose them in the dragon warrens. They wouldn't be able to get around to the other side before she exited.

Then the ground beneath Lisette's feet gave way and she plummeted. Plunging down a steep slope, she scrabbled at the dirt and rocks with her abused fingers, trying to find purchase, but the angle was too sharp and she picked up momentum as she fell.

She tumbled to a stop at the bottom of the slope. Beneath her hip, something delicate and wooden crunched.

But it was the giant eyes in front of her that made her gulp. Orange and gold irises nearly as large as her torso glowed and swirled. As her own sight adjusted, she picked out the rest of the gigantic head. Delicate ears flicked forward as Lisette sucked in a breath. Beyond, the immense body of the dragon stretched across a massive earthen chamber. A wave of magic rippled along his scales.

The dragon blinked and cocked his head. "And what do we have here?"

CHAPTER 4
A NEW CURIOSITY

L isette stared at the dragon looming over her, her heart pounding harder than it had when she'd been running uphill to get away from the guard.

"Do you not speak?" The dragon's voice was impossibly musical, making her eyes water with the beauty and sadness of it. It would be so easy to lose herself in that. But something sharp poked her leg, and her self-preservation kicked in.

She scrambled to her feet. "I do. I just..." She straightened her clothing and dusted herself off, coming up with a handful of splintered wood with figures painted on it. Standing within the halo of magic being given off by the dragon, it was hard to tell, but she thought the slats of wood were imbued with spells as well. Her brain finally put it all together. "Gods preserve us, I've smashed your zoetrope." She clapped her hand over her mouth. She hadn't meant to point that out. "I'm so sorry."

"Hmm." The dragon lowered his head back down to the ground. "So they've sent me a new curiosity who has broken an old one."

"I could..." Lisette picked up the rest of the cylinder — or what had once *been* a cylinder — from the ground. No, there was absolutely no way she could fix that. In her shop, she worked in metal and glass; this delicate woodwork and painting was beyond her. Plus, even though she didn't understand the magic that would have projected the lighted images on the wall, she could tell the spells were frayed and misshapen now. "I'm so terribly sorry about this. If I could fix it, I would." Then her brain replayed the dragon's last sentence. "Oh. Um. Actually, nobody sent me. I was running away from the guard and I fell."

Had it been wise to admit that to the dragon? Surely dragons, protectors of the city, would side with the guard. Maybe she should have kept her mouth shut. Except, the dragon's ears flicked forward again. "So. A new curiosity *not* sent. Interesting."

Only a fool would be flattered by a dragon's interest. Lisette had to admit to herself that she was a bit of a fool. But then, only a fool would end up in front of a dragon in the first place. Even so, that note of possessiveness worried her. Lisette glanced behind her at the slope that had carried her there. Given enough time, she could get back up, but one fiery breath from the dragon would kill her instantly.

"Murderer or thief?"

"Me? I'm a watchmaker." As Lisette's eyes continued to adjust to the light in the chamber, she picked out details. Gold coins were scattered around the edges, more wealth than she had ever seen in one place, but they looked as if they had just been tossed there. In contrast, dozens of items made of less precious components rested in niches or on shelves, some of them glowing from magic within.

A tiara made from preserved greenery — or metalwork so delicate it mimicked the color and texture of freshly collected oak leaves — rested in an alcove hollowed out by a giant talon. A sculpture of a dragon sitting upright caught her attention, and she peered at the clock set into the breast. Lisette suspected it would move somehow when the hour chimed, and curiosity suggested she delay her departure so she could see what it did.

The purpose of some treasures wasn't clear to her. Her fingers itched to get a closer look at the box with visible gears resting on a shelf. Next to it, a shimmering hourglass held magic instead of sand. And was that a dragon scale mounted on a chain? If so, it was from a different beast, for this dragon's scales were black and amber, not the blue of a sunny day edged with the green of a stormy sea.

And books... Shelves and shelves of books waited at the other end of the cavern, some bound in leather with silver inlay, others stitched together with no outer protection at all. A stack of tubes on its own shelf presumably held scrolls.

"Of course. I have seen many a watchmaker chased to their ends." The dragon's voice, still lovely, felt sharp enough to slice her open.

Lisette pulled her attention away from the books. "Well, yes. I did break into the treasury. That's why they were chasing me. But technically, I didn't steal anything."

At the far end of the cavern, the tip of the dragon's tail raised and fell. Lisette had seen that movement in cats stalking prey. She hastened to explain.

"I broke into the treasury to steal money for taxes, but the strongboxes just held sand." The unfairness of the evening rolled over her. "All that work, for nothing! And now half the freeholders will lose their shops, and what is the duke even doing with all the taxes he collects?" Her voice dropped as she no longer addressed the dragon. "He's surely not spending it on the city, as he claims, or the roads would be smooth enough not to break an ankle."

"The *duke*." A hot wash of dragon's breath blew around Lisette, smelling of charred meat and dry wood.

Lisette nodded. "He's raised the taxes for the third year in a row. Business has dropped off because only the nobles can afford to shop in the freeholder quarter, so more and more of the buildings are being forfeited to the duke." She frowned. "If I didn't know better, I'd say he's *trying* to bankrupt the quarter. Malice and stupidity can be hard to distinguish." She'd never heard the duke described as stupid, but his pick for chancellor of the treasury left everyone wondering.

"The *duke*," the dragon repeated.

Lisette's pulse, which had started to regulate itself now she had a chance to catch her breath, stuttered and sped up again. She didn't want anything to speak about her in the way this dragon said the noble's title. "You seem to dislike the duke even more than the freeholders. I don't suppose you'd consider letting me leave since we have a common enemy —"

The dragon cut her off. "Move." His tail twitched again.

"Pardon me?" Lisette's voice came out as a squeak. She'd seen cats toy with mice, waiting for the prey to move before pouncing on them again. Perhaps if she held perfectly still, the dragon would lose interest.

"Move!" The dragon's head raised, and his body rippled as powerful muscles bunched.

All rational thought fled. Lisette threw herself sideways into the cavern, and the dragon roared and launched himself up the slope where she'd been standing. His progress came to a sudden halt. For the first time, she saw the chain, thick with magic, tethering him in place. The final link seemed to be embedded in the rock of the wall itself, as if the chamber had been placed here because of the chain and not the other way around. Now it was stretched to its full extent, and she could see the shackle around the dragon's leg, the skin on either side blistered and oozing.

The dragon roared again, and reflected heat warmed Lisette's skin. Up at the surface, a man screamed in pain, then abruptly fell silent. The smell of roasting flesh wafted down, making Lisette's stomach turn. At least two more men screamed in terror, their voices getting dimmer as they ran away.

The dragon backed down the slope and crouched, both chain and cuff hidden again. He swallowed and then burped. "That ought to keep them away for a while," he said with satisfaction. "Now, where were we?" He cocked his head and looked at Lisette again. "Oh yes, you were explaining how a watchmaker turned into a thief who found nothing to steal. So tell me, are you more successful at watchmaking than you are at thieving?" He towered over Lisette, eyes glowing, waiting for her answer.

"I suppose I am." Lisette moved her foot so she wasn't standing on a rock, only then realizing a thick gold coin worth enough to pay the quarter's taxes many times over had been beneath her sole.

The dragon snorted. "Too bad. I could use a thief, but I have no need for a watchmaker." The smell of charred meat filled the area.

CHAPTER 5
A BARGAIN

The dragon loomed.

Lisette cleared her throat and continued speaking as if she hadn't paused. "Though in my defense, I would have been successful if there had been something in the treasury to steal." And if the man in the fox mask hadn't brought the guards down on both of them. A rush of indignation rolled over her at the memory. He had ruined *everything*. She wished he was with her now. *He* could be the thief the dragon needed. He also seemed like the type of person who was good at talking his way out of difficult situations.

"You haven't bothered to pick up any of the gold in my burrow." A long claw reached out to adjust the coins she had slid over when she jumped. "I question your dedication to thieving."

Lisette stared at him. "Who would be stupid enough to steal from a *dragon*?"

He harrumphed, a trickle of smoke leaving both nostrils, but it felt like a pleased sound. "At least you have *some* sense."

Lisette thought she was gaining an understanding of the dragon now. He appreciated honesty and directness. "Besides, even if I..." She almost said *escaped*, but that didn't seem like the right thing to bring up. "Even if I made it back home with a gold coin or two, I wouldn't be able to use them. Where would a watchmaker get gold? I'd have to find someone to change it into silvers and coppers, and I don't have the contacts for that. I'd probably just end up dead in the harbor."

He snorted again. "A thief unable to sell gold."

Lisette looked around the room. "But also the only thief here."

The dragon turned his head to regard her, and she was very aware of the heat coming from his nostrils. "A bargain, then?"

"I'm listening."

"I will give you the sum you need in coins suitable for paying these *taxes*, and you will have one day to return with the Dagger of Aarat."

Haggling over a deal was something she could do. "Seven days." When wisps of steam erupted from his nostrils, she hastened to continue. "I haven't slept in a day and a half, and I'll need my wits about me. Plus, I'll need to figure out where this dagger is."

"Three days. The dagger is held in the *duke's* main residence, somewhere close at hand where he can get to it at a moment's notice."

Lisette hesitated. The chances of her getting away with breaking into the duke's home and stealing a knife without getting caught were slim. She was almost certainly signing up for a life of forced labor on one ship after another. But at least everyone in the freehold quarter would be able to pay their taxes for another half-year.

Besides, did she have a choice? If she agreed to this bargain, the dragon would have to let her leave. If she didn't... She remembered the gulp that had disposed of the guard.

Lisette raised her chin. "Very well. I agree to your bargain. What does this dagger look like?"

"You've seen me, so you will recognize it when you see it. This will help." Fast as lightning, his claw whipped out, one talon piercing the skin on her forearm.

Lisette cried out, first in shock, then in pain as a line of fire trailed up her arm. It traveled over her shoulder, into her chest. For a long moment, she felt her heart stop and her lungs freeze. Her whole body was on fire. She would have screamed, but she couldn't draw a breath. Couldn't move at all. The light of the cavern dimmed.

Then, a moment later, the fire contracted into a pinpoint behind her breastbone, and her heart fluttered to life. She strangled the scream that had been forming, but she couldn't stop herself from moving away. A thin trickle of blood dripped onto the floor from her arm.

"Three days," the dragon repeated. "If you have not returned by then with the Dagger of Aarat, the dragon fire will consume you." He settled his head back down on the ground. "I do not recommend telling others about this bargain. The duke has listeners searching for such news, and if he hears of this, it would not go well for either of us." His back leg reached out, snagged a small leather bag, and launched it through the air. It landed at her feet. "The coins, which should be enough to pay your debts, and no inconvenient gold among them."

Lisette stooped to pick up the bag, opened the drawstring, and looked inside. Mostly silver, with a few coppers to break up the pale shine. She dug out the coins needed to allow all the residents of the freehold quarter to pay off their taxes, then added a copper to make up for the lost revenue she would have over the next three days as she worked out how to steal something from under the duke's nose. She transferred the coins to her belt, and then pulled the drawstring and set down the bag, still heavy with coin.

When she looked up, the dragon regarded her. "Just those few?"

Lisette's irritation at the question surprised her. "The bargain was for the sum I need, and this is what I need. Now, is there a safer way out of here? If the guards catch me on the way out, we both lose."

The dragon stared at her a moment longer, irises swirling faster. Then he blinked and looked at the opening to a tunnel on the other side of the cavern. "If you follow the widest path, it will open near the north wall."

Lisette nodded her head and walked across the room, ignoring the metalwork that called to her, and entered the tunnel hewn out of the rock. This passage wasn't big enough for a dragon, or at least, not *that* dragon, but there were signs that large claws had done the digging. Without the magic and the hidden lighting of the dragon's chamber, she was walking in the dark after a few seconds, so she let her fingers trail along the rough wall to guide her.

Behind her came the dragon's voice. "And you owe me a curiosity to replace the one you broke."

"I remember." Her voice was just above a whisper, but somehow she knew he would hear her anyway.

Lisette stumbled along in the darkness, one hand on the stones to guide her, and the other curled up against her chest where banked dragon fire waited to destroy her.

Three days.

CHAPTER 6
BETTER NOT TO ASK

By the time Lisette made it back to the freeholder quarter, dragon fire still burning in her chest, the light of dawn was sending tendrils down to the cobblestone streets, illuminating the community the original freeholders had fought so hard to create. With buildings covering an entire block at a time, the shops were separated from their neighbors by interior walls.

Years of remodeling allowed access between shops, testament to the changing relationships of the neighborhood. Maintenance was the responsibility of everyone together, forcing a cooperation unseen in other parts of the city, where tenants depended on absent landlords to fix leaky roofs and sagging walls.

Lisette stopped a moment to admire her shop. Gold script proudly proclaimed *Allinde Watch Repair* on a window displaying a rack of pocket watches, clocks, and other small mechanical devices. The street children didn't usually smash windows in their thieving — rich men's pockets being easier to target — but nothing in the window was worth much to anyone other than Lisette.

The brass pocket watch, its numbers faded into illegibility, had belonged to her grandmother, who had used it to teach her mother the intricacies of repairing devices, and then her mother had used it to teach Lisette.

The cuckoo clock had a dragon that emerged and spit out wooden fire every hour; it might have been worth more if the dragon had looked more like a dragon. But it had been commissioned by a long-deposed duke to bear his likeness, so within the year, the clock had been politically fraught as well as ugly. It still drew a crowd of children and strangers outside her shop on a daily basis.

Using her scratched bronze key, Lisette opened the door, stepped inside, and then locked it behind her. If she stood with arms outstretched, she could almost touch both walls, but the shop was home.

Three days. She had three days to figure out how to break into the duke's palace, find the dagger, steal it, and bring it back to the dragon. Gods preserve her, she'd talked with a *dragon*.

Ignoring the narrow stairs that led to her tiny bedroom, she ducked through a doorframe carved into the plaster, and pushed aside the velvet wall hanging obscuring it from the other side. Fine furniture greeted her eyes, some of it showing a bit of wear, but everything repaired and polished.

"Uncles, are you awake?" Rye and Barlow would never still be asleep at this hour, but freeholder manners were ingrained in her.

A full-length mirror on the opposite wall reflected her image, and she took a moment to straighten her clothing. Her hair was a lost cause, dirty and tangled from her adventures. *Quite lovely*, the man in the fox mask had said about it. What an infuriating cad. Still, she probably should be grateful she wasn't bald. If she'd been caught up in that spell, she'd have a hard time arguing her innocence; her hair would take years to grow back. Lisette pulled her curls into a loose braid and hoped the uncles weren't awake enough to notice.

"Good morning, Lisette!" Rye's voice came from behind the three-paneled screen that separated the carefully curated shop-front from the maze of inventory piled high in the back. "How did your mysterious errand go?"

"Mysteriously, uncle." Lisette grinned as she made her way through the shop. Rye and Barlow had helped care for her since she was an infant, and keeping secrets from them would be impossible if they really wanted to know, but they were careful not to pry into her private life. In turn, she had been very careful not to give any hint about the true nature of her plan the previous evening; they would have had the excuse of true ignorance if she'd been caught. She withdrew the coins she'd bargained for from her belt as she walked.

Rye, still straight-backed and handsome despite his years, grey hair contrasting with brown skin like a painting from *Arnatha's Book of Portraits*, sat before a table holding an intricately carved wooden frame. He held a rag in one hand and a tiny brush in another as he freshened the paint on the figures cavorting around the frame. During the day, he would be immaculately dressed in a fresh shirt, vest, and pressed trousers, but now he wore a comfortable old tunic, ripped at the hem and showing signs of past painting projects. He looked up, took in her disheveled state, and raised an eyebrow. "Oho, so it was *that* sort of errand, was it?" He winked.

Lisette rolled her eyes. "Definitely not." She put the coins down carefully at the edge of his workspace.

For the first time since she'd entered the room, Rye

looked his age. He raised his voice without turning around. "Barlow, quit fondling the old junk for a moment and come out here, please."

A thump greeted his words, as if someone had stood up suddenly, forgetting there was another crate stacked above him, and Barlow appeared from around the corner. Even during the daytime, he never managed to appear anything other than slightly rumpled, but now he had devolved into his natural state, streaks of grime standing out on pale skin, and packing straw embedded in his brown hair. His favorite pastime was digging through crates of household goods bought at auction.

Most of it would be nearly worthless, suitable only for firewood or the rag market, but he had a keen eye. Between the items Barlow found, and the furnishings Rye restored, they made a comfortable living, one that helped them support their neighbors in the quarter during bad years. But now the duke had raised taxes yet again.

Barlow suppressed a grin when he looked at Lisette. "Good for you! I thought you'd given up on that completely after that..." He trailed off as Rye tapped the table next to the pile of silver, and all humor fled. "Creatures of the deeps, Lisette, where did *that* come from?"

Lisette wanted nothing more than to unburden herself to these two men whom she had known since birth, but doing so would only make them worry more. Besides, what had the dragon said? The duke had *listeners*, but he hadn't specified whether that meant mortal or magical means. Lisette would trust the uncles with her life, but she had no way to defend from a spell of listening. "Better not to ask. This should be enough to get the quarter through until next tax time."

Barlow looked at the coins, then at Lisette, and then

enveloped her in a hug. "As long as you haven't agreed to marry that gorro just to get us out of this mess." He stopped talking and leaned back to stare into her face. "You haven't, have you? I'd rather lose the shop than have you stuck with him."

"No, uncle, I haven't seen Lord Hanley in months." She'd spent a lot of energy *avoiding* Lord Hanley. Considering how much time she spent in her shop, avoiding the noble and his unwelcome importuning was an exceptional feat. Lisette would gladly feed him to the dragon if she could figure out how.

With her luck, the dragon would probably just spit him back out.

Barlow looked from Lisette to the coins, then tightened his arms briefly and stepped back. "You should take that over to Jacinda now, before it gets lost in the stock back here."

Scrunching up her face, Lisette stared at the coins. "Well... She's going to ask where I got them." Her plan had started and ended with breaking into the tower. Now that she had the money, she realized giving it to the speaker for the quarter was going to require a whole new plan unless she wanted wild rumors circulating.

Rye had been separating the coins into stacks. "Most of these haven't circulated in hundreds of years. Where...? No, don't say anything." He wiped his paintbrush off on the rag and nodded decisively. "Barlow, we found the coins in the amphora you unpacked in that crate this morning."

Barlow raised one bushy eyebrow. "The gods have truly smiled upon us. Especially since that amphora is a cheap replica that is — at most — fifty years old." He raised his hands in surrender when Rye glared at him. "But what better hiding place for old coins? Whoever left it there must have died before they needed them. The freeholders will burn candles to their spirit."

Pushing his chair back, Rye stood up. "*I'll* take these over now. The two of you would let something slip before Jacinda even opened her door."

Barlow winked at Lisette even as he clapped both hands over his heart. "You wound me. Just because that *one* time I..."

Lisette cut in before he could explain, yet again, why it wasn't his fault he'd ruined three days of increasing bids from two buyers. "Thank you, uncle." She stood on her toes to kiss Rye's cheek.

Rye held her gaze. "I hope it's worth whatever you had to do."

Lisette hoped so, too.

CHAPTER 7
ABOUT THE DUKE'S PALACE

After Rye had changed his shirt and left with the coins that would keep the freeholders in their shops for a while, Barlow tugged at Lisette's sleeve. "Come see what I really *did* find in a crate this morning."

Lisette wanted nothing more than to wash up and go to bed. But she needed information about the duke's palace, and Barlow would have it. Barlow loved to talk to everybody about everything, often ignoring customers while gossiping with the old man the quarter paid to keep the streets swept. If he'd had to run the business by himself, it would have failed within a month; with Rye there to handle the practical tasks, Barlow's ability to absorb information was an asset that had kept the shop flourishing for decades.

Barlow would know how to get her into the palace; she just needed to get it out of him without having him volunteer to come along.

Lisette followed Barlow between the stacks of open-sided crates piled up to the ceiling. To her, it appeared to be a random assortment of old furniture, lamps, fancy costumes, and a hundred other things that people might want. But Rye and Barlow knew exactly where each wall hanging and footstool waited, and they were very good at knowing what people might be looking for.

As for Lisette, if she ever added something else to her tiny bedroom, she would need to find somewhere else to sleep.

Instead of the ability to chat with customers, Lisette's talents lay entirely in fixing anything mechanical. Barlow entertained himself by eavesdropping as she dealt with patrons. If she said something particularly blunt, Barlow's laughter would ring out from next door. Rye was more circumspect, but occasionally he would shake his head and sigh after a demanding client had left her shop. It could have been annoying, but it made her feel safe, knowing they were right there and paying attention.

"What's the latest word about the duke's palace?" she asked as she squeezed through a gap into the very back of the shop. "Have you heard anything about the masquerades?" Tufts of packing straw covered the floor, and Lisette picked up the pry bar about to be lost under the mess. She placed it on the edge of the battered table.

Barlow had been right. The amphora was a replica, and not particularly well done at that. Even Lisette could tell it wasn't worth anything. The table also held a stack of weathered and stained ship's logbooks, a bundle of clothing, some chipped crockery, and a pouch that she would bet held molding tobacco, given the smell.

There was also half an almond-honey pastry on a plate, and Lisette's long night caught up with her. She broke off a corner and ate it while Barlow moved a chair to the side in a futile attempt to create more space for them both.

He frowned and turned. "Where did I... Oh, that's

right." Barlow slipped by her and opened a drawer in the cabinet crammed under the table. "The duke's palace? I make it a rule to stay away from there myself, but Margueritte's man, not the sailor, the other one, the trader who broke his leg in the spring, has a daughter — it might be the daughter of a third cousin, or possibly both, who knows with those traders? Anyhow, the daughter is working at the parties all throughout the masquerade season. The duke wanted animal acts, but when they showed up with a tiger, the kitchen staff threatened to leave, so they've been scrambling to get entertainment. And scrambling to replace the servers who weren't willing to dress up as animals." He stood up with metal gewgaws in both hands and frowned at her. "Why do you need to know?"

"I need a way inside."

"If you just want a tour, I know the sister of the man who cleans the tiles there. I'm sure he could bring you along some day. He could call you his new apprentice."

Lisette wrinkled her nose. "I need it to be a little more discreet than that. And soon." Her three-day limit was already wearing on her.

Barlow eyed her. "Unless you can come up with a trained dog on a moment's notice, your best bet is to go in as a server. They're supposed to be vetted by the agencies, but my guess is they'll be too disorganized to check. If you show up and act surprised you aren't on the list, they'll just wave you through. Do I want to know what's going on?"

"I need to do a favor for someone I know." She tapped her nose. "Keep it quiet for now?"

Barlow gave a heavy sigh as he set the items in his hand down on the table. "You know how much it hurts me to keep secrets. But yes, I'll keep it quiet. Other than Rye, of course."

Lisette nodded. "Of course." Barlow and Rye didn't keep anything from each other.

"Does this someone you know have anything to do with those old coins?"

Lisette looked at him archly. "You mean the coins you found in that horrible amphora this morning?"

Barlow rolled his eyes. "Fine. Keep your secrets. You know I'll eventually find out who has you braiding your hair to make it look less like you tumbled down a hill."

Lisette felt her cheeks heat and resolutely turned her attention away from that infuriating man in the fox mask. "What do you have for me?"

CHAPTER 8
KRAKEN TAKE HIM

Barlow seemed amused by her blush, but followed her change in subject and described the items he had kept aside for her. "A music box, something I think may be related to a sextant, and the other piece I have no idea." He lined the three things up on the table.

Lisette wiped pastry crumbs off on her trousers and examined them. The comb and pins of the music box were covered in rust, and it was missing the winding key, but she thought it wasn't so far gone that she couldn't salvage it. Depending on the tune it played, it might be worth nothing or a fair bit.

The second item did indeed look like it was a sextant wed to some sort of battered clock, but even in a casual appraisal she could tell it was no ordinary timepiece. Traces of magic clung to it, still strong enough to make her believe it had once done something of great note. If it required a mage for its original function, she wouldn't be able to make it work, but she could at least fix any parts that kept time.

The third item was about the size of her fist and shimmered with magic, though it was corroded so badly she almost couldn't make out the individual pieces of metal. She lifted it. "I'll have to clean this up to get any idea of what it is. It looks like it spent some time in the sea." Barlow would understand her unspoken concern; items with powerful magic that went into the ocean were often dumped there because they were dangerous. "Where did you get these?"

"The usual. Contents of a warehouse abandoned twenty years ago. The new owners didn't want to pay someone to go through it all, so they auctioned everything off, sight unseen. They delivered it this morning. We already got some nice tapestries out of it to make back our investment. I haven't even opened the other two crates." He cocked his head to the side as he tapped at the nails of the one on top. "Though it looks like someone else might have. I suspect anything that was of value in that one is long gone."

"Plus..." Lisette prompted and waited.

"What?" He frowned at her, then his face lifted. "Oh yes, plus we found an ugly replica amphora with some old coins packed inside." He shook his head. "But the tapestries really are quite nice. I'm airing them out upstairs — I'll show them to you tomorrow." He waved at the table. "Do you want to take a crack at those, or shall I send them out for scrap?"

"I'll give it a try." When Barlow found broken mechanicals, he gave them to Lisette to fix and then the two shops split the payment. Lisette enjoyed the challenge, and Rye's customers would pay far more than Lisette would ever dare ask. Lisette's customers just wanted a watch fixed; Rye's customers wanted to own pretty things that nobody else had.

Lisette pocketed everything but the sextant. While Rye used the pry bar on another crate in the stack, she examined the clock attachment to see how it would come apart. "So they're scrambling for entertainment."

"What?" The squeak of nails being pried from wood paused. "Oh, the duke's palace." Barlow resumed his task. "Yes. Margueritte's man's daughter said they've been trying to hire acrobats to come dressed as animals, but it's still a mess. Anyone with any talent has been booked since last year or the year before. The duke may be the duke, but contracts are contracts."

"Indeed." Lisette scraped off a bit of rust with her fingernail. There. The slot was cleverly hidden, but there would be a button within that would let her pop the back off. Once she did that, she might have a better idea of what this was meant to do. "Did she say —"

Her question was cut off by Barlow's whispered "Kraken take him!"

When Lisette looked up, Barlow was holding a handful of packing straw and a ring that glowed with magic. His normally pale skin had drained of all color. Lisette shoved the sextant in her pocket and reached out to touch his shoulder. "Uncle, are you well? Do you need to lie down?"

Barlow jerked away from her. "Don't touch it!" His voice lowered. "There's no point in both of us getting caught up in this." He held up the ring so she could see it better. "It has the duke's crest and it stinks of magic. You need to get out of here. Find Rye and..." Barlow looked close to tears. "Hang it all, there's no way to keep him out of this, is there?"

Rye and Barlow had been set up. The guard would be here, probably quite soon, ostensibly tracking the ring by magical means, though Lisette was certain someone with them knew exactly where it was. They would find the ring, arrest Barlow, Rye, and probably anyone else who might ask questions, and the shop would be forfeit.

If Barlow hadn't touched the ring, he could have just dumped it somewhere for someone else to find. But he *had* touched it. Once the ring was recovered, a mage would be able to see who had handled it recently.

At the front of the shop, the door rattled, and someone pounded on the wood. "Open up in the name of the law!"

Lisette grabbed a dusty rag from atop another crate. "Give it to me." She used it to protect her hand as she scooped up the ring.

Barlow tried to stop her. "No, Lisette. You hide. There's enough room for you in the big lacquered cabinet. If I bring the ring out to them, they won't search the shop, and you can go home after they leave."

Lisette rolled up the rag and shoved it into her now bulging pocket. "Listen to me! Stall for a bit. Make a big show of trying to find the key to open the door, that sort of thing. Rye will be back soon." Rye would certainly have seen or heard about the guards and already be on his way back. "And then you keep your mouth shut. No jokes. No funny remarks. Nothing. Let Rye do all the talking." Barlow's pallor and nerves could be chalked up to seeing the guard on his doorstep this early in the morning.

Barlow grabbed her arm. "They'll be at the back door, too."

Lisette nodded. "But they won't be on the roof." She kissed his cheek, stuffed the rest of the pastry in her mouth, and ran for the stairs.

CHAPTER 9
'WARE THE GUARD

As Lisette ran up the stairs, through Rye and Barlow's room, and then to the slats bolted to the wall in place of a ladder, she heard Barlow's querulous voice talking to whoever was on the other side of the door. She touched the pocket holding the ring. If the guard found her with the duke's property, she would never be free.

Barlow's voice floated after her. "Well, of course I'm going to open the door. I just have to find the key. I'm all alone in here right now and I'm not usually the one who opens up in the morning. Can't you come back when my partner is here?" His voice strengthened. "If you break that window, we'll never sell to the guards or anyone related to them ever again, and your mother will curse the day you were born, guard leader."

That threat must have worked because Lisette didn't hear glass breaking. Instead, Barlow's voice became more pleasant. "Ah, here it is. I don't know why I didn't think to look there first. Getting older, you know."

By that point, Lisette had climbed the slats and

unlatched the portal onto the roof. As she pulled herself up, her shoulders reminded her of all the climbing she had done in the past night. For a brief moment, she thought she might fall back down into the shop.

Images of being discovered with the duke's ring in her pocket, and then Rye and Barlow being arrested, made her grit her teeth and push harder. She kicked her feet to propel herself sideways. Then she was up and lying on the sloped roof, breathing a sigh of relief.

Walking lightly, Lisette headed to the west end of the building, picking up speed as she moved away from shops the guards might be inside. In her teens, she and her friends had run on the roofs for a dare, but she hadn't been up there — aside from patching a leak — in the seven years since her mother had died and Lisette had taken over the shop. Once, she would have remembered all the dips and ridges of the roof, and known whose repair jobs shouldn't be relied on enough to walk over, but now she just had to trust that if she started sliding, she'd be able to catch herself before she went over the edge.

The guards would expect to find the ring in the crate, but Lisette thought they would also have someone with them capable of tracking the ring, if only so they didn't have to find one small thing in a room filled with hiding places. How long did she have before they were after her?

At the end of the building stood a pine tree, bent and twisted from exposure to the ocean breezes. Lisette scrambled down the branches and dropped to the cobblestones in front of the amused gaze of a tea vendor stoking the fire under the urn on his cart. He recognized her, of course, or he'd have been waiting for her under the tree with the stout branch he kept near his feet.

Lisette waved. "'Ware the guard, uncle." She hoped

there wouldn't be trouble, but the guards had gone to the shop expecting easy prey. The type of person drawn to that sort of life might take out their frustration on the first person they saw.

The tea vendor tapped his nose. Letting her stride loosen, Lisette pulled her mask up, looking for all the world like a masquerade reveler who was just now walking home after a very wild night. The freeholders would know better, but news of the guard's raid would be spreading through the quarter like wildfire. Nobody would say anything to the interlopers.

At the edge of the freeholder quarter, she headed south on butcher's lane — already busy with householders shopping for the day — down the hill and toward the sea. The coppery scent of old blood rose from the streets. If she could throw the ring into the water, hopefully it would be carried out to sea and not washed up on the shore for anyone to find.

One of the street children, a little girl with brown hair and a scar breaking up her left eyebrow, kept pace with Lisette on the other side of the street. Though she was tired and worried, Lisette kept an eye on her. If the girl stole the ring from Lisette's pocket, it would be sold back to the duke's men before Lisette noticed it was gone — nobody was stupid enough to keep something like that.

But the children were also experts at judging their marks, and the girl would have noticed things about Lisette the average person didn't. Lisette walked like a reveler, but she was heading the wrong direction. Her mask made her look like she had been at a masquerade party, but her clothes weren't quite fine enough when seen in the light of day. She looked more like a decoy sent by the guard to identify pickpockets than a reveler; Lisette might be more likely to have a tendon slashed than her pockets picked, but she was relying on the fact that nobody would want trouble, especially during the masquerade season.

The faint scents of vanilla and pepper stopped Lisette in her tracks. Two women walking behind her exclaimed and narrowly avoided her. "Apologies," Lisette called out by reflex even as she scanned the street. Was the man in the fox mask *here*? She thought she would recognize his build even if she hadn't seen his face, but nobody on the street seemed familiar. She must have imagined the smell.

From this angle, she could see two schooners anchored in the deeper water of the harbor. Smaller boats bobbed alongside, loading or unloading cargo. For as long as Lisette could remember, the duke and his council had been talking about dredging the center of the harbor to allow the larger ships to anchor next to the dock. The magical cost would be enormous, but it would cut down on shipping time and bring more business to the port.

The magical cost... Walking again, Lisette thought back to the dragon, shackled in the warrens. Butcher stalls gave way to vegetable stands, mostly root vegetables stored since winter. Onion and garlic made her eyes water. Everyone knew the dragons were there, providing magic for the mages of the city, and offering protection. But somehow Lisette had never heard that the dragons were being *held* there. Had it always been that way?

One nursery song her mother had sung talked about dragons flying over the city and burning a plague ship in the harbor. Granted, the verses of dialog between the watch commander and the dragon likely had some artistic license, but the city *had* been spared the last plague that had ravaged the coast.

A dragon held in chains couldn't fly.

The ember in Lisette's chest reminded her the dragon would still burn her alive in less than three days if she didn't do his bidding, chains or no chains.

She stopped again, staring at the beach in the harbor.

The tide was out.

Antipathy toward boats had made Lisette ignore almost everything to do with the harbor, but even she knew how the tides worked. If she threw the ring now, the incoming waves would wash it further up the shore. And that was if she could even get it into the water. She would have to either walk on the dock or past all the beached fishing boats to get there. Either way, she would be noticed. With her luck, someone would immediately dive for the ring after seeing it descend.

She could wait for the next high tide, but that would give the guard hours to track the ring. To keep safe, she would have to keep moving and her sleepless night was already catching up with her.

Could she hide it in a caravan traveling along the inland route? She dismissed that thought immediately. It would depend on a caravan leaving at the exact time she showed up. If it didn't, she would just be pulling more people into the guard's net.

An orange tomcat dashed across the street, dragging a carp nearly as big as he was.

There was only one place she could go where the guard wouldn't follow. Maybe if she'd had some sleep, she could have come up with a better plan, but it was all she could think of, and she had to keep moving.

Turning east, Lisette headed toward the dragon warrens.

CHAPTER 10
NO SENSE AT ALL

Walking in through the tunnel instead of falling down a slope, Lisette's entrance into the dragon's cavern was more graceful this time. Even so, the dragon wasn't any less intimidating. When Lisette rounded the last turn, she found him crouched and waiting, black and amber scales gleaming. Magic glittered from his books and treasures behind him.

"Ah, my curiosity returns." His voice pulled at her, but she resisted, reminding herself of how much was at stake.

"Lisette." That hadn't been what she'd meant to say, but something in the possessive nature of his words irritated her. "My name is Lisette. And I'm not *your* anything." She'd had enough of powerful people trying to own her — she didn't need that from a dragon, too.

Steam trickled from his nostrils. "Have you no sense at all?"

The question caught her by surprise, forcing a nervous laugh from her. "Possibly not." Her scalp prickled from fear.

"Are the children no longer taught? Your name gives me

power over you." He shifted, and the links of the chain rattled.

Had that been in the nursery rhyme? Lisette didn't think so, at least not in any verse she remembered her mother singing. Still — did it matter? "Dragon, you're a hundred times bigger than me and breathe fire. And you're faster. How much more power over me do you need?"

The dragon blinked. Magic trickled along the edges of translucent scales, then disappeared. "Lisette."

His voice was barely louder than a whisper, but the fire within her chest expanded, curling around her thoughts until she didn't know who she was anymore. Nothing mattered aside from the beauty of dragon fire. She lived to serve the dragon. She would die if he turned her away.

Then the dragon blinked again, and abruptly she was back in her own body, now standing right in front of the dragon's head. Heart pounding, she attempted to swallow, but her mouth was too dry.

The dragon withdrew a step. "Now do you see why only a fool freely gives their name to a dragon?"

Lisette nodded her head rapidly.

The dragon rested his head on one forearm. "Why are you here? You don't have my dagger."

The part of Lisette's brain that still worked noted that it had gone from the *Dagger of Aarat* to *my dagger* and that might be useful, but mostly her brain was busy howling at the sky and telling her to run. She cleared her throat. "I have a ring that belongs to the duke, and this was the only place I could think to bring it."

A snort of smoke erupted as she mentioned the duke, but the dragon didn't otherwise move. "And what would I want with *his* ring?"

Lisette blew out a long breath. "Honestly, I didn't think

that far ahead. This was just the only place I could think to take it where the guards wouldn't be able to get it back." With a few sentences, she told him of the discovery and the arrival of the guard, though she left out Barlow's name. Surely it couldn't matter if the dragon was given his name by her, but she didn't want to take the chance. "As long as the mages don't have the ring, they won't be able to prove my friend ever had it. So I was hoping I could give it to you to keep it safe."

"And what would you give me in return?"

Lisette's shoulders sagged. The only thing the dragon seemed to care about was bargains, and she had nothing left to offer. "A favor?"

"A favor."

"In the future, after I bring this dagger back, I'll owe you a favor. You get to choose."

"Very well, I will protect the ring for fifty years, and in return you will owe me a favor, to be specified by me in the future..." He trailed off, lifted his head, and dropped it to the ground. "Have you not learned anything yet? If you specify no limits to this favor, I could choose something impossible, then declare the bargain invalid and give the ring to the *duke* for my own gain."

"Ah." Lisette wiped her sweaty palms on her trousers. "What sort of limits should I add?"

The dragon's eyes turned toward her, though he didn't move his head. "You want me to determine both sides of the bargain?"

She had, but it didn't sound as if he was going to do the work for her. "How about: a favor within my power." She frowned. "That won't automatically lead to my death." She nodded.

"And if I ask you to dig a hole for the next twenty years?"

"Why would you...?" Lisette shook her head and tried to keep her thoughts in order. "A favor within my power that I can accomplish within... seven days... that won't automatically lead to my death. Or serious injury." She cocked her head. "Is that better?"

The dragon blinked again and let out a long breath, but there was almost no steam. She thought he might just be sighing. "Very well. The bargain is made. Now, where is this ring?"

Lisette emptied her pockets onto the nearest shelf while she tried to calm her trembling body. Surely the dragon wouldn't kill her while she owed him a favor. The ring, in its rag wrapping, had migrated down under everything else she'd been holding. By the time she uncovered the ring, the shelf held a variety of items, from a small folding knife to the mechanical trinkets Barlow had passed on to her earlier that morning. She held the ring up, careful not to touch it with her bare flesh. "Here."

But when she turned to show the ring to the dragon, he was focused on the shelf. "Where did you find *that*?"

The objects were so small — and the dragon so large — that she couldn't tell which item he was staring at. "Which one?" She pointed at the mechanicals, since there was nothing particularly odd about the other items. "These three came from the crates my friend opened. The only history he had on them was that they were in a warehouse that had been abandoned. He bought the crates unopened." She held out the ring. "Where do you want me to put this?"

In the blink of an eye, the dragon plucked it from her hand, only the fluttering of the edge of the rag showing his passage.

With one enormous talon, he carved a small niche in the wall near her head, and dropped the ring into it. Dirt and pebbles rained down on the floor and her feet. "There. Now you may see it always and ensure the terms of our bargain are being kept."

Lisette looked at him in disbelief. Did he think she was going to just casually drop by a dragon's lair to look at the ring? "Thank you."

"You are most welcome." He turned back to the mechanicals. "The concentrator, on the end. I had thought they were all destroyed and the knack of making them lost. Aside from those the duke and his friends keep."

Lisette picked up the corroded mechanical on the end, the one that neither she nor Barlow could identify. "This one is more than halfway to being destroyed, if you ask me. It looks like it spent some time in salt water, and that's never good. I was going to clean it up and see if I could figure out what it did and then give it to R— my *friend* to sell." She was having second thoughts about that now. If someone had gone to the trouble of making sure nobody knew how to make them any more, having one sitting in Rye and Barlow's shop window for all the world to see was a bad idea.

"If you can fix it, I will trade coins for it. What price will you take?"

Had it been up to her, Lisette would have taken a few coppers, and those only to cover the time she wouldn't be spending fixing watches and clocks for other customers. The satisfaction from analyzing and fixing something new was worth more than coins.

But that was why Lisette lived in the tiny room above her shop, and had needed to take extra custom just to scrape up the money for taxes the last time they were due. Rye was far more practical; he would be the one to set the price. "I'll ask my friend. And I won't have time to start on it until after I find that dagger, unless..."

"The terms of the bargain cannot be changed."

Lisette sighed and transferred everything but the ring back to her pockets. She'd thought that might be his answer. "I need to go. If the guards got frustrated trying to find the ring, I might have to spend the next day tidying up." Rye and Barlow's shop might need to be straightened, but nothing made an angry person feel quite as powerful as watching tiny gears fly around the room, and Lisette's shop was full of things to be broken.

"Go in safety. I would not have my favor unredeemed through your death."

"Yes, that's what I was worried about, as well." Lisette made a slight bow and went back into the passageway.

Five steps away, she heard a snorting noise. The dragon was laughing.

Now she just needed to break into the duke's palace, steal the dragon's dagger, find some curiosity to replace the zoetrope she'd broken, fix this concentrator — whatever that was — and after all that, accomplish some as-yet-undetermined favor she had agreed to perform for the dragon. If things kept going like this, she was going to need to write it all down or she'd forget something.

But first things first — the dagger. She had an idea of how to get into the palace, but she was going to need some help.

CHAPTER II
NAMING THE BLACK FOX

B ack in her shop that afternoon, Lisette waited until Rye had sent the last customer out the door (with the painting of improbable sea monsters that Barlow had rescued from the trash heap at an estate sale and Rye had aggressively discounted) before she pulled back the hanging that connected the two shops. The street had been quiet when she'd come back from her second bargain with the dragon, and Rye had given her the all-clear sign, so she had headed to her tiny room to get what sleep she could.

Now it was time to get ready for the evening.

Rye saw her first. He swept her up in a hug and whispered, "Thank you" into her ear before he stepped back. Though he was smartly dressed, his collar was wrinkled and he had a hint of stubble on his chin, both reminders of the turmoil of the morning.

"Jacinda paid the quarter's taxes?"

He nodded. "And the *thing* Barlow touched?" Rye paused, uncharacteristically hesitant. "How likely is it to be found? Should we buy passage with the traders?"

"It's safe in a place where nobody will be able to get to it for a very long time." When Rye opened his mouth to ask questions, she shook her head. "I'd tell you if I could." She looked around. "Doesn't look like they caused too much damage in the search."

Rye smiled, though he still looked worried. "Half the quarter was on the street watching them before I got back. They hadn't brought enough guards for a riot, and when the mage showed up, *he* said it wasn't anywhere nearby." He huffed a laugh. "Lord Hanley wasn't much pleased with that."

"Hanley was behind this?" Lisette winced. She'd assumed the blow had been another attempt to weaken the freeholders by removing the most prosperous shop, but now she wondered if it was retaliation for helping her. Neither Rye nor Barlow had been subtle in their dislike of Lord Hanley when he had been importuning Lisette. "Maybe I'm the one who should buy passage with the traders." She shrugged and added it to her list of issues. That was a problem for another day, one after she had dealt with the dragon fire in her chest. "I need a costume."

Rye didn't move. "Let me guess. An animal costume."

Lisette smiled. Barlow had told him about the information she'd been seeking. That made things easier. "Yes. I figure there must be something in all the junk back there." She waved a hand at the screen hiding the stock in the back.

"Junk?" Rye sniffed. "If I'd known you were going to be insulting, I wouldn't have restrained Barlow and Tiffany when they wanted to start sewing you a peacock costume that wouldn't have fit through the doorway."

Lisette clapped her hand over her mouth. Of course, Barlow would have involved Tiffany. Tiffany was Lisette's oldest friend, another freeholder who did fine leatherwork in a shop across the street. Barlow and Tiffany were wonderful people separately, but when they got together, they lost all sense of proportion.

Lisette needed a costume that would blend in, not one that would make everybody who saw it stop and stare.

"Lucky for you," Rye continued, only the faintest twitch at the corner of his mouth betraying his awareness of her realization, "I told them we needed to make sure all the new crates were unpacked first, and they got distracted."

"Thank you, uncle."

"But they went off to get dinner a while ago, so they might have started up again."

Lisette rubbed her face.

The door to the shop opened, and Barlow and Tiffany came in. Barlow held two bread bowls of stew, which he handed off to Rye and Lisette. Tiffany — short, stout, and somehow even more attractive after bearing three children — carried two enormous bags with fabric spilling out over the top.

After they had greeted each other, Tiffany pointed toward Lisette's bedroom. "Let's go. We have things to accomplish."

Barlow laughed.

Lisette ate as she climbed the steps. "Where are my nieces?" If Tiffany had to get back to her children soon, Lisette wouldn't need to worry as much about reining in her excesses.

"With my mother, so they aren't going to save you." Tiffany laughed. "Don't bother looking guilty. You're transparent." She paused to reposition the bags so they would make it through the narrow doorway. "Whew! I don't know how you live in such a small space."

The room held a narrow bed, covers neatly pulled up,

and a cushioned chair in the corner, with a desk shoved in alongside the bed. To Lisette it didn't seem particularly cramped, because she'd spent the first seventeen years of her life sharing the same amount of space with her mother. "I don't have six people in my room, so that's part of it."

Tiffany laughed and set the bags down on the bed. "We wanted to make you a peacock costume, but Rye said that would be too much."

"Thank the gods for Rye," Lisette muttered as she sat on the corner of the desk and kept eating.

"And then I wanted to make you a pony, with a little cart behind you, but Barlow seemed to think you were going to be working at the duke's party, so that would be inconvenient."

Lisette saw this as the probe for information it almost certainly was, and stayed silent.

"So we went back and forth a bit, because it's not easy to come up with something alluring and yet also practical." She raised her eyebrows. "Barlow said there might have been a *man* involved in whatever you were doing last night."

Lisette choked on her stew and coughed. "Barlow has a vivid imagination."

"Does he really?" Tiffany waved a hand. "Fine, keep your secrets. I'm just happy you haven't given up on them entirely after that thing with Hanley. Anyhow, you're going as a dog. Mostly because that was the mask we had. But we'll dress you up a bit and I'll do your hair, and we'll see how it looks." She started pulling things out of the bags. "First off, dress or leggings? I have a dress that would be perfect, though we might need to pad things a bit."

Lisette thought about the climb up the tower. The whole point of working at the party was to get into the building easily, but getting out might be another thing entirely. "Leggings."

"Finish your dinner while I get things ready. You missed all the excitement on the street this morning. The guard showed up to search Rye and Barlow's place for the ring the Black Fox stole. Though why he would bring it here, nobody would say. And then it *wasn't* here, of course, so Lord Hanley had egg on his face." Tiffany was concentrating on organizing the things she'd brought, and thus missed the incredulous look Lisette was giving her.

"Who... The Black Fox?" Lisette knew exactly who Tiffany meant, though she hadn't realized he was famous.

"Darling, we have to get you out of this hole in the wall more often. The thief who has been stealing from all the nobles for the last month or two. He wears a black mask in the shape of a fox. It's all very romantic. He stole the duke's ring from the tower last night." She held up a tunic with brown and black stripes, then put it to the side. "I say we should throw him a party, the Black Fox, not the duke, of course."

"But..." Lisette took another bite to keep from talking.

Even if the man who had climbed down the tower with her had stolen the ring, she didn't see how he would have had time to get it into the crate that had been delivered to Barlow, even if he had wanted to.

No, it made much more sense that the ring had been planted in the crate before Lisette and the thief had even been inside the tower. Knowing the Black Fox had broken into the tower had just given the guard a better story for their search.

"It does make me wonder what Lord Hanley is playing at," Tiffany continued, still pulling clothing out of bags.

"Now does your mystery man like to keep everything hidden, or is he more of a flaunt it all sort?"

Still thinking of the Black Fox and whether he *could* have been involved in hiding the ring in the crate, Lisette answered absently. "Hidden." Then she raised her head. "What? No, I promise, I'm not doing this to meet someone. I just need to do a favor for a..." She trailed off. In no circumstances could she imagine a way the dragon could be considered a friend. "For someone," she amended.

"Uh huh." Tiffany raised one eyebrow, clearly not believing her. "How do you want me to do your hair?"

Lisette pulled out a strand and looked at it, trying to be objective. He probably flirted with all the women he ran into during his thieving. It hadn't meant anything, and she would certainly never see him again. "As long as it's out of the way, I don't care."

Tiffany dropped what she was holding and leaned closer, peering at Lisette's face. "Are you *blushing*?"

"Absolutely not. It's just hot in here." Lisette cleaned her hands off and stood up. "What am I putting on first?"

Handsome thieves who might or might not find her hair lovely were not something she had time to deal with. She had to get inside the duke's palace, steal the dagger, and figure out how to do some other favor for the dragon so she could go back to her nice, safe life.

CHAPTER 12

TEACH YOU A TRICK
OR TWO

By the time Lisette reached the duke's palace that evening, the service entrance line wrapped around the side of the building. It didn't seem to be moving very quickly. In front of her, a large brown-skinned man, whose grey beard hung nearly to his waist, looked her over and shook his head. "Lo, how the mighty have fallen, am I right?" He spoke with the careful enunciation and projection of an actor used to performing in crowded tents and open fields. His wooden tiger mask had been pushed back to rest on his head, but in the cape and striped leggings, he still cut a dashing figure. "I haven't held the role of a beast on stage since I was a small boy." He shrugged. "So it goes. The coin is good, and perhaps I'll find a new patron."

The woman in front of him, dressed as some sort of rabbit, turned to face him. "Not even the most embarrassing thing you've done in the past year, is it, though?" She winked at Lisette. "Once a week he plays living furniture at the house of horrors."

56

The tiger-man shrugged. "They pay reliably *and* they feed the performers well."

Lisette nodded in appreciation. If she lost the shop, maybe she could be paid for holding still. Her mask itched, but she couldn't take it off without damaging the hair style Tiffany had decided upon. Her curls had been gathered up on both sides of her head, with the ends flopping free in an approximation of dog ears. Combined with the dusty half-mask Barlow had pulled from a closet, and the strips of fur wrapped around her tunic and leggings... She still didn't look anything like a dog. But seeing the others in line, in their equally unrealistic outfits, made her feel slightly better.

The tiger-man made a show of looking at her costume. "Not bad, but you might get better tips if you shortened the sleeves and made the tail more obvious."

The woman in front of him raised an eyebrow. "And you would know all about it, Harlison, wouldn't you?"

"Yes, I would, thank you very much. A patron is a patron, no matter how they notice you." He leaned toward Lisette and dropped his voice. "I could teach you a trick or two, if you want."

From behind Lisette came a high-pitched laugh. She glanced back and saw a middle-aged woman in zebra stripes. "Not that old 'teach you a trick or two' line, Harlison!" She giggled again. "Has he tried his 'Lo, how the mighty have fallen' production yet? Our Harlison made it up to the third pikeman on a traveling production of *Death of The Duchess*, so don't let him fool you. He's just like the rest of us — he's made more as a professional mourner in the past ten years than he has on a stage."

The tiger-man shrugged. "Can't blame me for trying,

can you? How have you been, Carline? Still with the old stick-in-the-mud, or has his mother finally driven you off?"

"She popped her clogs last year and he chucked me out so his sailor could move in. Not a surprise, mind you, but I thought he'd have the decency to wait until after the funeral. I'm staying with a friend for a bit. I'd be playing the part of a standing lamp once a week if my back didn't play up. Brown throws a gig like this my way every once in a while, so I manage."

"Brown supports half the actors in the city. For his cut, of course, but the man has to live. Did you hear how much the actual animal performers are getting paid?"

Carline fanned herself. "Enough that I spent yesterday trying to catch a gull down by the docks. I never knew how hard they bite." She held up her hand and pointed to a red mark. "Finally decided it wasn't worth it. Who wants a bird flapping around near their food? They'd probably station me and the gull out near the privies. Oh, did you hear what happened to Guillome last week? Caught with both producers' wives at the same time."

Lisette stayed silent as the two actors caught up on news about each other and old friends while the line slowly crept forward. The less they knew about her, the less they could tell if anyone connected the theft to a woman in a dog costume. Besides, their stories were amusing.

The best part about the line moving so slowly was that by the time they reached the front, Lisette's nerves had mostly given way to boredom. She hadn't been contracted for this job, and she'd expected to need to talk her way in, but the man with the sheaf of foolscap papers in front of him merely looked up, made three check marks in various areas on the diagram in front of him, and shooed them along. "Dog to the kitchen, lion and zebra to the main ballroom. Gather in the ballroom at the end of the evening to get paid. Next!"

Carline leaned toward Lisette as they walked inside the palace. "Bit of luck for you! They say the servers aren't allowed to eat anything until the end of the evening, but who's to know? The passageway between the ballroom and the kitchen is long enough that you could eat half the tray!" She straightened up and nudged Lisette toward a side door that rang with the clatter of metal trays. "That's you. Hey, Harlison, what do you think about putting on a show?" She and the tiger-man followed a giant woman trailing cloth tentacles up a wide staircase.

The kitchen, or rather, the staging area just outside the kitchen, was a hive of activity. The permanent staff, wearing just the briefest felt masks as a nod to the occasion, trotted in and out carrying cloths, glasses, and silverware. Lisette joined the group of animal-costumed people trying to stay out of the way in the corner. Their garb ranged from one woman in a snake mask and not much other than green body paint to a man with butterfly wings. The only thing they all had in common was they all looked young and fit.

Lisette was glad she'd spent the afternoon napping.

A staff member in a slightly more elaborate mask hurried into the room and pointed at them. "Next group! You will be taking food to the guests." He mimed picking up a tray from the empty table in front of him, settled it on his shoulder, then turned and disappeared back into the hallway.

After a moment of confusion, the entire group sprang forward and hurried after him.

Still bearing his imaginary tray, the man turned to face them while walking backward down the poorly lit, unfurnished hallway. "Performers do *not* eat the food before guests and don't think we don't notice empty spots on the tray when you arrive in the ballroom. There's a reason you don't get paid until the end of the evening." Just when Lisette opened her mouth to warn him about the stairs behind him, he twirled and ascended. "Careful of the second step. The stone is worn and it's easy to slip."

Lisette glanced down as she started up the stairs. Hundreds of years of people walking up and down the steps had worn them all, but the middle of the second tier looked more like a ramp than a stair step.

"Keep moving!" The man in front of them wasn't visible anymore.

As a group, they ran up the stairs, the butterfly-man cursing as his wings slipped. At the top of the steps, they followed their guide down another dimly lit corridor, turned the corner and...

A huge ballroom appeared in front of them, lit up bright as day. Crystal chandeliers hung from the ceiling. The ceramic floor sparkled, with grey tiles on the edges of the room, and a black and blue pattern in the middle — Lisette suspected that delineated the dance floor. On the far side of the room stood the drinks station. An ice sculpture of a dragon, wings extended in flight, hovered over an enormous punchbowl. In another corner, chairs arranged in a semi-circle showed where the musicians would sit.

The impossibility of the light nagged at Lisette until she looked harder. No, the lighting wasn't coming just from the candles in the chandeliers — the entire dome of the ballroom was lit up using magic. The effect was stunning, but she couldn't even begin to calculate how much magic that would take.

Lisette had never felt any desire to attend the

masquerade parties hosted by the wealthy nobles, but this was a sight she wouldn't forget.

"You there! Dog! Quit gawking and keep up!"

With a start, Lisette realized he was yelling at her. Behind the mask, her face heated, and she was glad nobody could see. She trotted to catch up with the rest of the group.

Still holding the invisible tray, their guide offered it to an imaginary reveler. "You will do exactly two laps of the room, always moving in this direction. Be very careful of the dancers. Let me repeat that. Be very careful of the dancers. Every year, someone doesn't pay enough attention and gets knocked down. Do not let that happen to you." He waited, looking over the group until they all nodded, then continued on his way, offering the invisible tray to invisible people and weaving among a crowd that didn't exist.

The edge of the dance floor left enough room for at least two people holding trays to pass alongside it, so either the servers had been entirely off course, or the dancers weren't staying on the darker tiles.

"Remember, you are dressed as animals, so stay in character. No talking to the guests."

They finished the circuit of the ballroom and headed back into the dark tunnel. Lisette dropped to the back of their group so she could look at corridors which branched off along the way. One of those had to give access to the upper floors.

Performers with animals came out of a side corridor, heading for the ballroom. Parrots, cats, dogs, and even a pony were carried or led by masked performers, all heading toward the light. Lisette was getting an inkling of the pure chaos the night would entail.

The pony swung wide on the turn, making Lisette step

back to keep from getting pushed. She bumped into someone behind her.

"Pardon me," a familiar voice said.

Lisette whirled. His black fox mask had been traded for a cat half-mask that matched the coloring of the calico cat in his arms, but she knew his build and the faint vanilla and pepper scent. "You!" Her voice was accusing.

"You!" He sounded delighted.

The kitchen leader's voice cut through Lisette's dismay. "Dog! Keep up!"

Lisette ran after the rest of her group, seething. This was going to be hard enough without *him* there to mess it all up again.

Somehow she had to get rid of this thief so she could steal the dragon's dagger.

CHAPTER 13
MAKE AN EXCEPTION

By the third tray of spiced meat strips, Lisette was ready to leave. If quitting had been an option, she would have walked right out the main ballroom entrance where guests were still being announced on arrival. The tray was heavy, the stairs got higher every time she went up them, and the masquerade guests were rude.

"I don't normally let dogs in my bed, but I'd make an exception for this one," said a slight young man with the broken-veined nose of a chronic drinker. His companions laughed and made little howling noises.

The comment had been obnoxious, but almost clever... the first time she'd heard it. This was the sixth time, and she didn't expect it to be the last.

Thankfully, given the rules about staff talking to guests, she didn't even need to pretend to smile at their wit. In the multiple laps Lisette had made around the room, she'd also discovered the tray made an excellent defensive weapon; she could twirl around as if she were just doing her job, and that meant the nobles couldn't get close enough to put their hands on her.

One man had snuck up behind her, and she'd knocked the edge of the tray into his throat. It had been an accident. But when he reeled back coughing, she'd been glad staying in character meant she couldn't apologize. She had managed one "Arf!" that sounded more like swearing than barking. The man's companions had laughed and gathered him back into their group, and he'd started to think the thing was funny even before she'd moved away.

Duke Gerard himself, the fourth of that name in his line, wandered through the ballroom early in the evening. Lisette recognized him mostly by the gold medallion hanging on his chest. Otherwise, he was indistinguishable from all the other rich young men whose families expected them to attend the ball. Lisette had seen the duke riding in a few parades, but he never seemed to project any power or charisma. If she'd had to pick one word for him, it would have been *forgettable*. Even his mask, mottled white and black, and shedding tiny feathers every time the duke turned his head, seemed unremarkable.

The three advisors who accompanied the duke, all older men with trappings of wealth, were a different sort. Lisette noted how they greeted certain people, snubbed others, and tightly controlled who got within speaking distance of the duke himself.

After they all made a circuit of the room, and the duke had stiffly escorted one determined young woman on the dance floor, they retired to the card room. When Lisette peeked in a while later, the duke was sitting at a table with people she identified from their garb as a ship's captain, a trader, and a mercenary commander. Most of the chips were piled up in front of the mercenary. The advisors were standing, talking to a crowd of other grey-haired men in expensive masks.

Lisette had always imagined the dancing at the duke's masquerades would be... She didn't know what she'd imagined, but it wasn't the chaos she was seeing in the middle of the room now. The waltzers seemed energetic enough, but they bobbed about like unmoored boats in a harbor on a stormy day, couples tripping and crashing into each other. She watched as one couple slammed into the wall while trying to stay upright. Now she understood how servers and dancers collided every year.

The zebra, Carline, ran across the dance floor, threading gracefully between the couples, pursued by the tiger, Harlison. He caught her arm in the center of the floor, and their chase turned into a waltz for a few seconds, and then the zebra pulled away again, pursued by the tiger. Lisette smiled. They'd found a way to stand out in this crowd of performers.

Of the actual animals, the pony had been swiftly relegated outside, and its manure cleaned up as the first guests arrived. The other performers moved around the room, the animals performing tricks — or not, in the case of one parrot. All that parrot did was swear, loudly, which had made it a favorite until someone had complained. Then it had been sent outside to perform with the pony, though a few of the younger guests had followed.

Lisette kept a close eye on the man with the calico cat. She'd intended to sneak upstairs later in the evening, when guests would be more full and less sober, and a server leaving wouldn't be noticed as quickly. But if this man disappeared, she would have to change her timetable. She couldn't allow him to mess up everything again. This was her one chance to get the dagger and not be consumed by dragon fire.

The thief watched her, too, smiling and winking when

she passed him on her endless laps around the ballroom. His cat could sit, jump on his shoulders, roll over, and do various other things on cue, but what made his act appealing was the humor.

"Simi, sit down." He shook a finger at the cat, as if he were upset. "Sit down right now." The cat turned and sauntered away. The man in the mask leaped to be in front of the cat. "Now, now, Simi, we talked about this. You know what happens to cats that are naughty!" The cat fell onto her back, closed her eyes, and put all four feet in the air. "Ha ha ha, no, she's kidding. She just won't get extra treats," he said to the laughing audience. He stage-whispered angrily. "Simi! You stop that right now." The cat stood up and faced the other direction, and as he moved around, pleading with her to look at him, she continued to move so he was always facing her tail.

In spite of herself, Lisette found the act amusing. When she looked closely enough, she could see the hand signals he was using to get the calico to perform the tricks she was really doing. The cat must have been what was moving in the satchel as they climbed down the wall. What kind of thief brought a pet along to break into the duke's tower?

The night wore on, moving forward two laps of the ballroom at a time.

By midnight, Lisette's trays were coming back to the kitchen with nearly as much food as she'd left with. Every new tray held treats freshly made, or newly out of the coldstore. She wondered what they did with the extra; it would have fed the street children for weeks.

On her second lap of the room after the midnight bells rang, the man with the calico cat was gone. Lisette turned in the middle of yet another guest's dog joke to look around the room. The thief had taken breaks before, but during those he had wandered around the room, cat on his shoulder, watching the other acts.

Suddenly, he was gone.

Lisette gave up on offering her tray to drunken guests and headed for the tunnel. She paused to let two dancers pass in front of her, then moved forward again. At the guest entrance, two ceremonial guards waited with the seneschal for late arrivals who needed to be announced. Lisette offered them food to cover her attempts to see beyond the ballroom. Neither man nor cat was in sight.

Back in the tunnel that went to the kitchen, Lisette waited until no other server was in view, and ducked down a side corridor. She kept the tray since it gave her an excuse if anyone saw her, but she increased her speed.

The first tunnel led outside. A peek through the door showed the pony bowing to a distracted audience, a swearing bird clutching its mane.

Lisette went back to the central tunnel and chose another corridor. This one curved around and started going down, so she abandoned it and went back. She needed to get upstairs.

The third tunnel ended in a set of stairs and a small food elevator powered by a hand crank.

After hiding her tray inside the conveyor and sliding the outer door shut, Lisette crept up the stairs.

CHAPTER 14
MISS ME?

The servants' staircase was nearly as worn as the one leading from the kitchens, but it was clean and obviously used. Hopefully, it went where Lisette needed to go. The dragon had said the dagger would be somewhere the duke could quickly get to. She was betting on that being either his bedchamber or study. Since she'd never heard anyone mention a special dagger, it likely wasn't displayed in any of the public rooms.

On the second floor landing, Lisette opened the door just a crack and listened. She could hear the sounds of the orchestra, and the hubbub of hundreds of people talking in the distance, but nothing closer to her. Shoulders back, she opened the door wide and stepped out, ready to bluff her way through if anyone was there. The alcove she found herself in, which held stacks of linens and blankets, was vacant.

Lanterns were lit in the hallway, casting a warm glow onto a myriad of paintings of chickens. Despite her need to hurry, Lisette stared at them, trying to figure out if there was some deeper meaning. Maybe Rye or Barlow would have the discernment to judge the first one a masterpiece, but to her it just looked like a wildly unrealistic buff-colored chicken sailing a ship. The next painting showed a black and white speckled hen in front of a table holding bread and a wineglass. Giggles threatened to overwhelm Lisette, brought on by the stress and the sheer absurdity of *this* art being in the palace. She had to force herself to stop looking at them.

Intricate molding covered the ceiling, telling her she hadn't accidentally strayed into the servants' quarters. This had to be the right place, chickens or no chickens. The duke's chambers would likely be at the end of the hall, but she forced herself to check behind each door along the way. She found nothing but unused bedrooms, and a library nearly bereft of books. At another time, she would have perused his small collection, but the ember of dragon fire in her chest had started throbbing.

Besides, if it turned out the only books on the shelves were treatises on keeping chickens — or worse, chicken poetry — she wasn't sure she could keep her hysterical laughter at bay any longer.

The door at the end of the hall was locked. Lisette retrieved two hairpins from behind her ear, quickly bending them into more useful shapes. From the time she had been old enough to sit on her mother's knee, Lisette had been putting together intricate mechanical objects, often more by touch than sight. Barlow had capitalized on that ability for years by having her open locked chests and cabinets that he had acquired without the matching keys.

The lock in front of Lisette opened with disappointing ease; part of her had been hoping to learn something new.

After listening briefly, she opened the door and went inside, using the key hanging from the knob on a red ribbon to lock it again. There. Now she should have a few minutes to find the dagger, hide it under her costume, and sneak back out without needing to worry about someone coming inside.

She was in a tiny entryway, with four doors to choose from, all closed. She started with the one on the right, though even before she opened the door, the smell of turpentine told her what she was going to find. Morbid curiosity made her go inside.

Stacks of canvases leaned against the walls. In the center of the room stood an easel. Lisette couldn't help herself. She took a step to the side so she could see the waiting canvas and bit her lip when she saw a partially filled-in grey hen. A few stray feathers on the floor confirmed the painter had been using a model.

The duke — for surely only the duke would be using an art studio so close to his bedchamber — had painted all the pictures in the hallway. How had she never heard of this obsession of his? Servants talked. There was no way to stop them, short of instilling a compulsion magically. This should have been fodder for gossip in every pub in the city.

Cold prickled along her spine, smothering the last of her amusement. Lisette wasn't sure which bothered her more, magic being used on the servants in the palace, or magic being used for a purpose this banal. The magic of the dragons was meant for the defense of the city, not to prop up the ego of the duke by ensuring nobody laughed about his hobby.

She backed out of the room and opened the next door, which turned out to be a washroom. Two more doors.

The third door opened into a spacious chamber with a large canopy bed and two end tables, both covered by small glass bottles holding liquids and powders. The bed was covered by a huge green quilt. At this point Lisette wasn't surprised to see the covering had chicken scenes embroidered on it. Those chickens were more realistically proportioned and had been done by someone with genuine talent, so she assumed he had purchased the spread. The walls, of course, were covered with chicken paintings, and even the rug on the floor had lines resembling the tracks of fowl.

A cat's inquisitive meow drew Lisette's gaze up to the canopy. "So you *are* here, gods help us all." She'd been hoping he was in a different part of the palace.

A masked face popped up from the other side of the bed. "Miss me?"

CHAPTER 15

THE DAGGER OF ΛARAT

L isette frowned at the masked man kneeling on the floor across the duke's bed. "Why are you here?"

He stood up and brushed off his knees. "They aren't cleaning as well in here as you might expect, but I suppose the chickens throw them off." He leaned to peer behind the headboard. "As to what I'm doing here, the same as you I'd imagine. And once again, we both forgot to make a reservation." He frowned at the floor near his feet. "So far, all I've found is a sketchbook and an entire pharmacy of sleeping aids."

Lisette reached up to scratch the cat's chin while she scanned the room. The dragon had said the dagger would be kept close to hand, but she'd expected it to be in a container or drawer, and there was nothing like that in the bedchamber. She dropped down to look under the bed and found nothing but a thick layer of dust and the face of the man looking at her from the other side.

"See? The housekeeping is shockingly bad. Which is interesting, because the rest of the palace seems perfectly in order."

Lisette climbed to her feet, her actions mirrored by the man on the opposite side of the bed. "Perhaps they don't let the servants in these rooms."

The man's nose wrinkled as he surveyed the clutter. "This place is filthy, but I don't think it's filthy enough for that."

Lisette shook her shoulders to release some tension and headed to the door. "Maybe the compulsion on the servants keeps them from doing their jobs properly."

In three steps, he had dashed in front of her, arm held out to arrest her motion. "Compulsion?" The calico cat jumped down from the canopy to land on his shoulder.

Lisette used one finger to push his arm out of the way and went back into the antechamber. "I've never heard a hint about these chickens, have you?"

"Well, no, but..." He trailed off and Lisette wondered what he'd been about to say. "You're telling me nobody in the city is laughing about this?"

If he didn't know that, he hadn't spent much time in the city. That was an interesting fact all on its own. "Not laughing, not talking about, not even renaming their shops to encourage his business." Having spent years watching pubs trying to steal each other's customers, Lisette was certain every public house trying to attract the duke would be chicken-themed by now if anyone had known about his paintings.

A quiet laugh greeted her words. "Red Rooster Glove Shop. Speckled Hen Pies. Or perhaps, Bantam Boots?"

The glance he threw her way offered her a clue to his words. He was trying to figure out her profession. There weren't enough watchmakers in the city to hide her identity if he tricked that out of her. "Not that I've seen. Hence my assumption of a compulsion."

"Probably not a compulsion." He put a hand on the doorway to the fourth room, the only one Lisette hadn't opened yet. "It would be far easier to accomplish by a spell of amnesia, or even one of ignoring..." He opened the door and they both stopped moving. "Oh my."

In front of them lay a small room, almost austere in its simplicity, with just a small wooden table and a row of shelves lining the far wall, and initially notable only for the complete lack of chicken paintings.

But every item on those shelves practically glowed with magic. The Dagger of Aarat had to be one of them.

A trickle of unease kept Lisette from moving forward. "We should have been able to sense these from the hallway."

The man next to her hadn't entered either. "You have a point." He pulled his satchel forward and rummaged through it, finally pulling out a leather pouch that fit in the palm of his hand. Loosening the drawstrings, he took a pinch of the powder within and puffed on it.

The doorway lit up with a web of magic lines.

Lisette took half a step back. "What is that?"

"An alarm. I don't suppose you're a strong enough mage to disable it?"

Lisette wasn't *any* kind of mage. "No. You?"

"I think we'll have to use alternate means to keep the guards from noticing." He reached onto his shoulder and picked up the cat. After a quick caress to the top of her head, he tossed her gently into the room. The cat landed on the floor and walked forward, fluffy tail held straight up.

Lisette watched in fascination. "Your cat evades magic?"

The man clicked and the cat jumped onto the first shelf. "What? Oh. No, she's a living creature, just like the rest of us. But all buildings have mice and other vermin that get into spaces you'd rather they didn't. You can't have your alarms causing a panic every time a rat gets into the room, or you'd be forever on edge. A smart mage limits his alarms to notice people."

"*That's* why you brought your cat to the tower." Another thought occurred to her. "Can they really track hair by magic, or did you just need to make sure they didn't notice the cat fur?"

"Determined to leave me with no secrets, I see." He clicked to the cat again, and she jumped to the next shelf and began weaving through the items. When she got near a tiny leather book, he whistled. The calico delicately bit the corner, picked up the book, and hopped down to the ground. "But that does leave the question of what I'm going to do with you." He crouched down to retrieve the book from the cat, offering her a small dried fish in exchange. The little book went into another drawstring pouch, this one with a crackle of magic running around the edge. "If I leave now, you're just going to go in there, set off the alarm, and grab whatever it is you came to get, aren't you?"

Lisette leaned against the wall and crossed her arms. "Can you give me a reason why I shouldn't? If half the guards are chasing you, my odds of getting out of here increase."

His eyes narrowed. "And if I hit you over the head and leave you here, I'll be gone by the time anyone finds you, but you'll have a lot of explaining to do."

Lisette didn't move. "Head wounds are tricky. You might kill me by mistake. And a dead body in the duke's chambers? That might set off alarms on its own."

She had no idea if that was even possible. Lisette knew

next to nothing about magic other than it was something to be avoided.

He eyed her, and then the room with all the objects. "Did something specific catch your eye, or would anything do?"

"A dagger." Lisette pushed off the wall and stood at the doorway, feeling the warmth of him against her shoulder. The dragon had said she would recognize it, but she had never learned to fight. One dagger looked like another to her.

But as she stood there peering at the items on the shelves, she realized she *did* recognize it. Or, at least, she felt it. The burning ember in her chest sensed... a kinship to something on the far end of the third shelf.

She pointed, careful not to break through the web of magic whose glow had faded. "Over there. Third shelf."

The man looked at her for a moment, then reached down to pick up the cat and send her into the room again. In a few moments, the cat knocked the dagger off the shelf, and then picked up the end and dragged it after her.

Watching the calico come forward, Lisette had a moment of doubt. Surely a weapon with a name would look more impressive. This looked blunt and tarnished, like the cheap knives sold down by the docks.

Then the cat crossed the threshold and traded her bounty for another dried fish, and the man started in surprise as he grasped the dagger. "Oho, you don't play little games, do you?" He stood up, still staring at what he held.

Lisette reached for the dagger, and he pulled it out of reach. "Not yet, unless you want them tracking you from the start." He dropped it into the drawstring pouch with the book. "I assume you have some way to store it?"

Lisette thought of the dragon. Once she had brought it there and fulfilled the terms of that bargain, the dagger was the dragon's problem. "Yes."

He closed his satchel and picked up the cat. "Someday I would very much like to hear who you work for and what they're involved in, but perhaps now isn't the best time."

Back in the main hallway, Lisette kept her gaze away from the chicken portraits and concentrated on watching the man next to her. If he tried to get away... She didn't know what she would do, but she couldn't let that happen. At least not while he had the Dagger of Aarat.

Suddenly he swore under his breath, shoved the cat into her arms, and pushed her against the wall, covering her body with his own. "Guards," he whispered.

For a moment, Lisette froze. Then she realized what he was trying to do. She giggled somewhat convincingly, tipped her head back, and brought one leg up to curl around his waist. She kept her voice low. "Aim for the bedroom to your right?"

His breath was hot as he nuzzled her neck. "It might work. They've probably been running into couples all night." This close to him, there was a sweetness to the pepper scent. She felt the raised line of a scar over the muscles on his shoulder.

But even as they bumped along the wall, hopefully looking like lovers in the throes of passion trying to find an empty room, Lisette heard the guards running forward.

"You there! You can't be up here!"

Lisette and the thief stopped moving. With the hand not holding the cat, she could feel his steady heartbeat under her fingers. That gave her courage.

As the other guard came to a stop nearby, he pulled manacles from his belt and sighed. "If we make an example of these two, maybe we can keep the nobles from trying to sneak up here all night."

Lisette met the eyes of the man pressed against her. He whispered, "Take good care of Simi. I'll be right behind you." Under his mask, she could see one eyebrow lift as he waited for her response.

She gave a tiny nod, and his lips twitched. Then he took a breath and swung around with the exaggerated movements of a drunk. He plowed straight between the two guards, wrapping his arms around them and dragging them back with him as he stumbled. "But you are ruining the *best* evening of my life!" All three of them tumbled to the floor.

Holding the cat firmly in her arms, Lisette edged around the men and fled.

CHAPTER 16
LOCKDOWN FLAGS

At dawn, Lisette admitted defeat and headed home, calico cat still in her arms. The thief had said he would be right behind her, but he wasn't. She had stayed as close to the palace as she could, trying to find out what had happened to him. She hadn't seen anyone dragged out toward the prison beneath the old keep. Either she had missed it, or he had escaped.

Or he'd died. That thought made her clutch the cat tightly enough that Simi mewed in protest. No. The thief must have escaped.

Lisette climbed the hill toward the freeholder quarter and tried to figure out what to do next. The thief, who was definitely *not* dead or in prison, had the dragon's dagger. She had his cat. But she had no way of contacting him, and he didn't know her name or even what she did.

Why hadn't she told him she was a watchmaker when he'd been guessing? If she had, he would have known where to find her. The only connection they had was breaking into the same buildings two times in a row. While she would have gladly broken into a third building to get the dagger back from him, she didn't know which building to choose.

Would he even *try* to find her? True, he had seemed attached to Simi. But Lisette had seen his surprise when he'd picked up the dagger. He had recognized its value. Maybe he would just get another cat.

Simi purred in her arms.

Lisette opened the door to her shop, climbed up the stairs, sat down on her bed and stared at the calico cat. "I suppose I ought to find some things for you if you're going to stay." Cats lived on the street all over the city, drinking from puddles and catching rats in the alleys, but Lisette wasn't about to let Simi out of her sight. The cat was her only bargaining chip in getting the dagger back.

Lisette had less than two days, and now she had no idea where the dagger was. She tried to pull the mask off over her head, but the ties were threaded through the ribbons holding her hair in place.

Tiffany's voice floated up from the shop below. "I'm coming up. You have five seconds to tell me to go away if you've someone with you."

"You saw me come in alone." Lisette's friend must have been waiting by the window to show up so quickly after she got back.

"I could have missed something." Tiffany's footsteps came closer, and then her head popped around the doorframe. "The dance at the palace was over hours ago." She looked at Lisette's lap where the cat was purring and making biscuits. "You stayed out all night and came home with a cat."

"The last couple of days have been a little odd," Lisette agreed. She tugged at the ribbons holding her hair in place, only succeeding in making them more knotted. "Can you...?"

Tiffany came forward. "Stop messing with it. You're making it worse." She began unraveling the ribbons. "How did it go?"

"Your disguise got me into the palace." Lisette thought back to the evening. "The ballroom itself is amazing. But the rest of it..." She bit her lip to keep from laughing at the chicken portraits. She couldn't tell anyone about that. Rumors were too easily tracked back to the source, and the palace would definitely be looking for someone who had been in that corridor. "How do I find someone if I don't know his name or where he's from?"

"Aha!" Tiffany untangled one last tie and lifted the mask from Lisette's face. "I *knew* there was a man involved. But the whole point of the Festival of Secrets is not knowing someone's name. At least until the last night," she added, continuing to remove the hair ribbons, "at which point you find out he's a baker's assistant whose mother promised him to the god of the depths when he was born."

Lisette tilted her head just enough to see her friend's face. "You've had three children together. I think it's time for his mother to admit the truth." Those dedicated to the god of the depths were protected on the water, but could not have children. "I'm serious. I need to find someone. In less than two days."

"Well, the good news is that you don't need to worry about him leaving the city. They have the lockdown flags flying on the hill." Her quick fingers released one of the dog ears and then her hands stilled. "Why do I have the feeling you might be involved in that?"

"How could I be?" Lisette tried to relax her shoulders.

Locking down the city, which kept the traders' caravans from going in or out and trapped any boats in the harbor, was only done for emergencies. Avoiding the plague ravaging the area and searching for the assassin of the then-duke's son were the only reasons she had ever heard about. Exactly how important *was* that dagger? Or was it the book?

"There's an answer that's not an answer." Tiffany's fingers started moving again. "I'll pretend I never noticed. Anyhow, your man is still in the city somewhere."

"But how do I find him? I need to get his cat back to him."

"You don't know his name?"

"No."

"Or what he does?"

Lisette doubted the Black Fox's profession was listed as *thief*. "No."

"Or what part of the city he's from?"

"No."

"What do you know?"

Lisette thought about it. She'd never seen his face. He'd — arguably — saved her from the guards twice. His cat liked him. He was polite even in times of stress. "He smells like vanilla and pepper."

Tiffany laughed as she removed the final hair ribbon and shook out Lisette's hair. "You might need to let him find you. Let me think about it." She put the mask and ribbons on the desk. "I'll find some things for the cat. You get some sleep."

CHAPTER 17
BENEVOLENT GARGOYLE

Too worried about the loss of the dagger to sleep more than a few hours, Lisette spent the day working at the back of her shop. The few repairs she had waiting for her — a pocket watch that had been over-wound one time too many, another pocket watch that had been dropped and the crystal cracked, and a little device similar to a music box using magic to move the dancing mannequin into different poses as the cylinder went round — took a few hours. Then she started working on the corroded mess the dragon had called a concentrator.

She'd been worried the cat would try to get into everything, but Simi had eaten the food Tiffany had brought for her, done her business in the box of gravel, and then leapt up to the highest shelf in the shop and settled down to observe, looking for all the world like a benevolent gargoyle.

For this new item, Lisette opened to a fresh page in her logbook, drew a rough sketch of both sides, and labeled the pieces she could see. With a pocket watch, she wouldn't have bothered. They all worked more or less the same way, and any minor variations were quickly obvious to her. But she didn't yet understand how this concentrator worked, and the last thing she wanted to do was take it apart and not know how it went back together.

Once the first sketch was done, she began disassembling it, using oil and gentle pressure to free pieces that had been stuck together for decades. With tweezers and her screwdriver set, she gently removed the first set of screws and placed them in a holder. Then she flipped the piece over and pressed the recessed release. When the device was new, that movement would have been smooth, but now she felt the grit of sand and rust as she pressed.

The smell of oil and the process of examining each piece to see how it could be removed calmed her in a way she couldn't describe. The dragon fire in her chest and the lost dagger weren't forgotten exactly, but that stress had been temporarily put aside. *This* was her purpose in life, and she had known it since she'd sat on her mother's lap and watched her mother repair a pocket watch. Lisette stopped every few minutes to update the logbook, absently wiping oil off her hands on the rag she kept at the bench for that purpose.

A few pieces had been so delicate, there was nothing left of them aside from a higher concentration of rust in the area. For those, she drew what she saw and continued. Once everything was cleaned and ready to be put back together, she would see what she could fashion from pieces she had available.

When all the parts had been documented and separated into individual holding containers, she submerged everything in the solution chamber of the cleaning box and wound the dial. The box would vibrate the solution, gently agitating all the pieces and removing as much of the dirt and corrosion as it could. After the cleaning box finished, she would need to address each individual piece, grinding, sanding, or replacing as necessary.

Lisette turned back to her bench and tidied the workspace. Like a switch had been flipped, all her worries flooded back. What did it matter if she refurbished the concentrator and figured out how to get it working again if she couldn't return the dagger to the dragon within the next day? Her stomach ached.

She had just closed the logbook when Tiffany burst through the door, her two-year-old daughter held on one hip and a broadsheet in her other hand. "I think I have the answer!"

Joints stiff from sitting so long without moving, Lisette stood and stretched. "Which answer?" When her niece stretched her arms out, Lisette picked her up and kissed her forehead. "And how is the wickedest little girl in the quarter today?" She drew back so she could see the child better. "Are we bathing in dirt instead of water now?"

Her niece giggled, and Tiffany sighed. "She followed some of the older kids into the tunnels and I spent half the day trying to find her."

Lisette caught Tiffany's eye and grinned. The tunnels under the freeholder quarter had existed longer than the freeholder buildings. Rumor said they were smugglers' connections leftover from the old city. If that were true, Lisette thought they would have extended down to the beach, which they didn't. But she didn't have a better idea of their original purpose.

Lisette and Tiffany had spent a lot of time in the tunnels, thinking they were exploring the unknown. Every generation in the quarter did. There wasn't anything particularly dangerous down there, and it was safer than playing in the streets, with their heavy carts and careless riders.

The girl pointed upward. "Kitty!" She straightened her body to slide down, and Lisette lowered her to the floor.

"No touching Auntie Lisette's things," Tiffany warned her. Then she handed the broadsheet to Lisette.

"Black Fox strikes again. City locked down while guard searches for brazen thief," Lisette read aloud. She didn't look up. Surely Tiffany hadn't made the connection between the Black Fox and Lisette's mystery man that quickly.

"Not that. Turn it over and look at the ads on the back."

Lisette obediently flipped the sheet over and skimmed the boxes of text. A warehouse near the dock was having an auction in two days. A caravan had open spots for passengers. There was a reward for a necklace lost at a masquerade, no questions asked. Someone was searching for their friend who had been the second mate on the Aurora three years ago.

Tiffany leaned over and pointed at a box near the bottom, so Lisette skipped down to that section. *For the mystery girl with the lovely hair — you stole my heart along with my cat. Meet me at midnight one block north of where we first spoke. Let's see what happens.*

Lisette's heart leapt, and the knot in her stomach untangled. The thief wasn't dead or captured. If the Black Fox had been caught and the guard was looking for his accomplice, this wasn't the kind of trap they would set. The location depended on the recipient knowing they'd first met at the tower. Even if someone connected the cat with the palace, they wouldn't know where to look.

"That has to be you," Tiffany said when Lisette didn't speak for a moment. "How many other cats could people be looking for? Not so sure why he couldn't meet you in a cafe or a restaurant, but I'll give him points for style, at least."

"It's not like that. I told you — I just need to get his cat back to him." At midnight, she would get the dagger, go by the warrens on her way home, and aside from one as-yet-unspecified favor for the dragon, life would be back to normal. She would never have to deal with this irritating thief again.

Midnight couldn't come fast enough.

CHAPTER 18
A BAREFOOT GIRL IN A YELLOW DRESS

As she hurried through the lantern-lit streets packed with revelers, Lisette pulled her cloak around her, both to keep it from snagging on anything, and to hide the calico cat in the crook of one arm. Simi didn't seem at all bothered by the people or the noise. Lisette supposed a performing cat would be used to all that.

Lisette, on the other hand, was a bundle of nerves. She couldn't wear the dog mask again, in case someone connected that with the theft of the dagger, so she had borrowed Tiffany's shimmering gold headdress adorned with feathers and beads.

Lisette had wanted something less noticeable, but her friend had insisted. "You want to stand out so he can find you." She handed Lisette a simple hooded mask of black cloth. "And if you decide you want to ditch him in the end, slip this one on instead. It will hide that lovely hair of yours. And it's a different color."

The gold headdress had a matching gold cape. The number of lingering glances Lisette attracted made her uncomfortable. There was a reason she didn't go to the masquerade balls during the Festival of Secrets. She would have given anything to be back in her shop, working on a pocket watch.

Simi purred in her arms.

The waterfront was chaotic, with nobles in expensive carriages stuck in traffic, and intoxicated partiers in less extravagant costumes walking or drinking in the thoroughfare. The street children darted here and there, one occasionally falling to the ground and crying in apparent pain while others took advantage of the distraction to remove the valuables of watchers in the crowd. Sailors from the ships stuck in the harbor passed by in groups of two or three, rags with eyeholes their only nod to the dress code of the occasion.

Other than one patrol — which seemed more interested in being visible in the streets than stopping crime — Lisette hadn't seen the guard.

Everyone appeared to be ignoring the veil of magic around the city, just visible at the edge of the harbor. The lockdown flag flying on the hills was a signal, but the veil surrounding the polity enforced the decree, the city's ancient defenses activated by the duke and the council. No fishing boat could get beyond the harbor. Not even the smugglers who had secret paths to the overland route could get out.

The duke's reaction to the Black Fox kept everyone in the city.

Interestingly, fox masks had exploded in popularity overnight. Tiffany had spent the afternoon sewing one after another, using stiffened fabric instead of her usual leather to cut down on the time it took. Now it seemed every fourth reveler wore some version of a fox, though few of them were black.

One block north of the tower, a line of carriages waited to drop off nobles at a residence flanked by two huge stone dragons. Sweat prickled along Lisette's spine as she saw the crest carved into the statues. Of all the places Lisette didn't want to be, outside Lord Hanley's home was high on the list. The only two places that would be worse would be *inside* Lord Hanley's home, and locked in the prison beneath the old keep.

Lisette reminded herself that Lord Hanley would be busy with his duties as host, and he wouldn't be paying attention to the hundreds of people in the streets near his home. Besides, she was wearing a mask.

She looked around, trying to spot her thief without being too obvious about it. Dozens of people in the street were the right size and build, but she didn't know what mask he was wearing this evening. Only a fool would wear the black fox mask out on the street tonight, and he hadn't struck her as a fool. The calico mask he had worn at the duke's party would be out as well. So she knew two of the masks he *wasn't* wearing, but that wasn't helpful.

What if he had meant a side street? Or literally one block north from where they had first spoken, which was five stories up in the air. That would mean he was waiting for her on the top floor of Lord Hanley's residence.

The idea left Lisette light-headed.

Someone bumped into her hip, and Lisette looked down. A little girl in a yellow dress, her face painted to look like a duck, danced next to her, barefoot on the cobblestones. The scar through her left eyebrow gave her a look of sardonic amusement when she smiled. With a start, Lisette recognized the street girl she had seen pacing alongside her through the butcher's market the day before.

Dancing closer, the girl demanded, "Do you have a cat? The man said I was to find the lady with the cat." Her voice blended in with the noise of the street.

Lisette kept her cloak pulled close around her. "What man?" If someone had recognized the note in the broadsheet for what it was, the guard could have employed the street children to look for her.

The girl shrugged. "A man." Her voice was flat, as if one man was indistinguishable from another. "Smelled nice, though."

Lisette opened her cloak to reveal Simi in the crook of her arm. "Where is this man?"

The girl twirled away, pushing her way through the people in her path. Lisette suspected more than a few of them would be missing valuables at the end of the evening, but that wasn't her problem. She hurried after the girl, trying to keep her in sight. They went past the main entrance to Lord Hanley's residence, a carriage blocking her view of the entryway, and turned the corner to a slightly quieter blind alley with balconies overlooking the street.

Every residence was brightly lit. Laughter and talking spilled out from within. A few people called between the balconies, but none of them took note of the street. A vendor had set up a grill at the corner nearest Lord Hanley, selling skewers of chicken and beef. Once Lisette made it past the customers queued up for food, the crowd in the alley thinned out.

It suddenly occurred to her that even if the Black Fox had hired this girl to find the woman holding the cat, that didn't mean the girl hadn't set up an ambush with the other street children. Lisette's steps slowed and she moved closer to the wall.

The girl with the scarred eyebrow whistled sharply. A few revelers turned, saw nothing out of the ordinary, and turned away.

A low voice near her ear sent a tingle down Lisette's spine. "You're not an easy person to find."

CHAPTER 19
NOT AN EASY PERSON
TO FIND

L isette whirled, cape billowing with the movement. Simi purred more loudly and wrapped her paws around Lisette's arm.

Her thief, wearing a gold fox mask, leaned nonchalantly against the wall, grinning at her confusion. Where had he come from? There *hadn't* been anyone there a few seconds ago. He pointed up. Lisette tilted her head back. There was no balcony, but the building was only four stories. He'd climbed or jumped — or who knows, maybe flown — down from the roof.

Before Lisette could say anything, he held up a finger and turned to the girl. "This is the one. Thank you." Metal clinked as he put something in her palm.

The girl whirled away, immediately lost in the crowd around the grill.

"Shall we go for a stroll?" The thief offered his elbow.

Strolling would make it harder for anyone nearby to listen to their conversation. It would also get her farther away from Lord Hanley's estate. Lisette took his arm, feeling the muscles under a tunic deceptively tailored to

93

hide his athletic frame. They skirted the crowd around the smoky coals and walked away from the stone dragons guarding the entrance to the estate.

"You said you'd be right behind me."

"I did, didn't I?" He guided her around a closed carriage stopped in the street, the coachman brushing the horse in front. "Unfortunately, the palace guards were just a bit too quick, and it took me until dawn to find a way out."

"How did you? I thought..." Lisette stopped talking. She wasn't about to tell this thief she'd been worried about him.

"A little misdirection here, a little trickery there. I would have tried it earlier, but my diversions only worked because everyone was tired of searching." He nodded at her arm where the cat was still hidden under the cloak. "Did Simi behave herself?"

Lisette kept a firm grip on the calico in her arms. Simi was her only leverage to get the dagger back. "You know the whole city is locked down to find you."

"I wasn't about to leave before I found you again, was I? The mask suits you, by the way."

"And you wouldn't leave your cat."

"Of course. Though Simi is pretty good at finding her own way back. Eventually."

They turned and headed up the hill, dodging groups of merrymakers. Musicians wandered by, playing a lively dance on lute and flute, with a woman circling them and holding out a cap for payment. The Black Fox withdrew a coin from his belt and tossed it in the cap.

A few seconds later, there was a spark of magic close by, followed by a high-pitched yelp. Lisette looked down to see a young street child, a boy no older than five, sitting on the cobblestones, clutching his hand. The Black Fox shook his head. "You're going to have to learn faster than that if you don't want to end up in chains on a ship." He crouched down. "If you ever feel a hint of magic, apologize and back away. You don't want to mess with magic." He stood up and offered his arm to Lisette again. "Or, you could learn to use it," he said to her, more conversationally. They walked forward, leaving the child still sitting on the street. "Is that what you did?"

Lisette wondered at the question, then realized this was his way of asking about the dagger. "All I know about magic is to stay away from it. You *do* have that thing I picked out last night, don't you?" If he'd had to discard the dagger in the duke's palace while he was escaping the guard, she needed to be working out a way to get into the palace again, not spending time with this irritating thief.

"Of course I do. How else am I supposed to get Simi back? I can give it to you now, if you have a suitable container for it." He glanced over at her. "I hope you have some way of hiding it. You said the whole city was locked down to find me, but they're also looking awfully hard for that thing *you* wanted."

Lisette blew out a breath. "I just need to keep it long enough to hand it off." Another few blocks and they would be at the wall surrounding the dragon warrens. The thief had been picking up on subtle cues and letting her lead the way. She supposed it didn't matter. He wouldn't follow her through the dragon warrens, so it would be as good a way to lose him as any.

"Ah, a job for hire. An ambitious choice for someone without much experience. You did well."

Lisette huffed a laugh. "Two places in two nights and I didn't get anything from either of them. I'd hate to see your definition of failure."

He grinned and guided her around another waiting carriage. "You're alive and not in chains or bound over on a ship." He cocked his head. "Ah, you get seasick, do you? It would be good to avoid that, then."

Lisette shook her head at how much he picked up from her. "This is it. I'm done. After this, I'm staying..." She'd almost said she'd be staying in her shop, but even that would reveal too much. "I'll be staying home."

"Ah." He waited for a band of drunken sailors to run past. "That's too bad. You have a certain cleverness I could use. I could make it worth your while...?"

In her surprise, Lisette stopped walking, dropped his arm, and stared at him. He wanted to *hire* her? To help him *steal* things? The unlikeliness of it all made her laugh. The sound was swallowed up by the chaos around them, but she felt him shift away. Under the cloak, Simi dug her claws into Lisette's tunic to keep her balance when Lisette reached out.

Lisette closed the distance and took his elbow again. "Sorry. I wasn't laughing at you. It's just... This isn't me. I just needed money to pay taxes, and then..." And then it had all gone wrong and she had ended up here, but she couldn't explain that without telling him about the dragon, and that seemed like a terrible idea. "I'm not who you think I am."

"Not yet." He pulled his elbow — and her hand — closer to the warmth of his body, and started walking uphill again. "But I think you could be if you wanted to." He glanced over at her. "No? Ah well, everyone has their own path to follow." He pulled his satchel forward and opened the drawstring, then opened the bag within, the one that crackled with magic. "Shall we trade?"

Lisette reached in and grasped the hilt of the dagger.

She gasped as the spot of dragon fire nestled in her chest expanded. Fire raced up her hand from the hilt. Then the two sources of flame met. She braced for the pain of being burned from within.

Nothing happened. The dagger had gone back to being just inert metal in her palm. And the dragon fire within her settled, leaving her with a sense of exultation that wasn't her own.

Lisette drew a cautious breath.

The thief coughed. "At some point I might cease to be surprised by you, and that will be a sad day indeed."

Lisette wanted to protest that none of that had anything to do with her, but it wasn't something she could explain. Instead, she tucked the dagger in her belt and wrapped a tie around the hilt to hold it in place. She let the cloak fall open and handed over Simi.

The calico cat butted his nose in greeting, then hopped into the satchel, circled twice, and settled. He slung the satchel back over his shoulder. "I hope she behaved herself."

"She was the perfect guest." Lisette's arm felt chilly without the weight of the cat. She pulled the cloak around her again as they continued climbing up the hill.

"In the festival of a different year, I would ask your name and beg to meet you again, but this year..." He shrugged. "Regrets are useless things that weigh us down."

From this point on the hill, the city glittered in light and magic below them. Another block and they would be at the dragon warrens, and she would never see this irritating and distracting man again.

"In the festival of another year, I would make plans to meet you." She would have, too, in past years. But that had been before Lord Hanley, before she'd decided it would be easier to ignore that part of life than risk someone else getting hurt. Now she was not *that* person, either. "Perhaps next year when — Creatures of the deep."

Lisette stopped walking and stared.

The guard surrounded the dragon warrens. Swords and armor flashed as they reflected lantern light.

Lisette had the dagger, but she couldn't get inside to fulfill her bargain with the dragon.

CHAPTER 20

MAKE A RUN FOR IT

L isette stared at the end of the street, forgetting the chaos of the revelers and carriages around her. If she couldn't get past the guard to get into the dragon warrens, she wouldn't be able to fulfill the terms of the bargain. If she couldn't fulfill the terms of the bargain... The dragon fire within her burned at the thought.

"I take it that was indeed your destination." The thief's voice was quiet in her ear.

"I *need* to get in there." Lisette's heart raced. She was so close, but to try to run past the guards would be suicidal. If she hadn't had a deadline, she could have put the dagger back in the thief's magical pouch and waited a few weeks. Eventually, the guard would be needed elsewhere. But she had less than a day. Nothing would make them leave before then.

The Black Fox offered his arm again. "Perhaps we might go closer. Just two people out for a stroll during the Festival of Secrets."

Lisette took his elbow, but this time it felt as if she were drowning and grasping at a lifeline. "But why are they here?" The guard didn't patrol around the dragon warrens. What would be the point?

Only a fool would go past the outer wall. Lisette was proof of that.

"At a guess, I'd say the duke doesn't want that thing you have at your belt going in *there*." He guided her around another carriage, leaving them in the darker part of the street next to the buildings.

Lisette thought about it. Perhaps something about that dagger made it possible to hurt a dragon. Maybe the duke was worried someone would kill the dragons and harm the city. She wasn't going to *do* anything with it, other than hand it over, but she couldn't very well tell the duke that.

"Or," the thief continued when she didn't say anything, "maybe the duke is worried about something in the book I borrowed. I don't suppose it matters much."

Lisette's heart dropped as they moved closer. This wasn't just a patrol stationed near the entrance. A guard stood every few lengths along the wall as far as she could see. Even without circling the warrens, Lisette knew she would find the guards along the entire circumference. There was no way through.

The thief backed Lisette up against the wall and leaned one shoulder on the bricks next to her, where they could both observe the guard and anyone seeing them would assume they were otherwise occupied. "I don't suppose waiting a few weeks is an option." When she shook her head, he nodded. "I thought not. That certainly does leave things in a difficult state."

Lisette stared at the dragon warrens. They were *right* there. But there weren't any buildings overlooking the walls that she could use to jump off.

The thief pulled his satchel around and rummaged

through it. Simi mewed softly. "I propose a trade." When Lisette didn't say anything, he continued. "I help you get past the guards, and in return, you agree to help me for one evening."

"Help you do what?" This was exactly how she'd ended up owing the dragon so many things, but Lisette didn't see she had a choice. At least the dragon had shown her the importance of finding out what she was agreeing to first.

"Help me steal something, of course. I know you might not believe it after the past few nights, but sometimes a second person makes things easier." He sobered. "I won't ask you to harm anyone. And of course, there's no way I could hold you to this promise, but you seem an honorable person."

Ignoring the guards for the moment, Lisette looked at the thief's face, just a few inches away. Would he help her? Or would he just bring the guards down on her so the city would stop looking for *him*? Except he already had his cat back — he could turn her in easily enough, even without her consent. "I agree."

He smiled, a genuine smile this time. "Keep an eye on the broadsheets." He looked out and the guards then touched her cloak. "You might have to leave this behind. It's nice, but a little eye-catching. Wait until the third explosion and make a run for it."

Then he was gone, threading through the crowds until he disappeared behind a carriage and she lost sight of him in the throng.

Still standing in the shadows, Lisette unclasped her cloak. Tiffany had prepared for this possibility as well — a seam in one section of the lining opened to a pocket of black fabric that could be inverted, and the rest of the cloak folded inside. When Lisette was done, the cloak was gone and she had a simple black bag slung over her shoulder. She swapped out the headdress for the black mask as well.

Then it was time to wait.

The part of her that missed spending entire days in her shop, only talking to a few customers and friends, despaired at her growing list of entanglements. Somehow, trying to pay the taxes for the freeholder quarter had led to becoming a thief for real.

But another part of her, the part she admitted to only in the late hours of the night, rejoiced. If he needed her help, that meant she would see him again.

Lisette sighed at her own idiocy.

A flash of light followed by a boom of thunder came from the northwest. Was he blowing up a section of the wall? Surely he hadn't carried enough with him for that. But if it wasn't explosives — that meant magic.

The guards tensed and called to each other, but stayed at their posts. The revelers in the street either didn't notice or clapped at this new entertainment.

Aligning herself with a thief was bad enough. But a mage? That was exactly what the duke and the dragons protected Harbor Crag from. Who was she helping?

A second explosion rocked the ground under her feet. Two guards left their posts to run toward the sound. On the street, the clapping stopped, and there were sounds of confusion. A woman screamed. Drivers stopped lounging and jumped back up to their seats, slapping their already nervous horses into motion. The carriages all started moving down the hill, snarling traffic as a wave of panic went through the crowd.

Lisette edged closer to the end of the building. There were fewer guards now, but still too many to avoid.

"You there!"

Lisette turned her head to see a guard captain walking straight toward her. She froze. She had the dragon's dagger on her belt. If they caught her now, her life was over.

A third explosion shook the ground and lit up the sky near the northwest gate. The guard captain turned to look over his shoulder.

Lisette ran. She dashed toward the wall, then zagged to the left to make it through the ruins of the gates.

At her back, she heard men yelling for her to stop.

Now she was on the packed dirt paths of the dragon warrens, but she needed to get to *her* dragon before the guards caught up. The last time she had come this way, she'd fallen into a hole going straight down to the cavern. But she'd been looking over her shoulder as she ran. She wasn't sure where that opening was.

Heart pounding in her ears, she kept running. The only other entrance she knew about was on the north side of the warrens. There were two problems with using that. First, at least one of the guards behind her was catching up. And second, there were other dragons in the warrens. If she fell into one of the *other* caverns along the way, that dragon might destroy her before she could speak.

Lisette grabbed the dagger at her belt to make sure it hadn't fallen out while she was running. She leaped over a branch, hitting the dirt on the other side with enough force to knock the breath out of her.

A fountain of flame erupted from the ground behind her.

CHAPTER 21

CONTROLLING A DRAGON

A gust of burning air accompanied the flames. Lisette stumbled and fell, sliding on the packed dirt. She rolled over to look back and saw her pursuer on the other side of the flames, arm thrown up to protect his face.

Lisette scrambled to her feet and hesitated.

If that was *her* dragon down there, he had just shown her the entrance to his cavern. She just needed to wait until he stopped exhaling fire, and then slide down the steaming tunnel and hope he recognized her before he roasted and ate her.

If that *wasn't* her dragon, she'd be leaping to her death, and her friends would never know what had happened to her.

The flames diminished, then stopped. She could feel a cool breeze flowing into the cavern as the dragon inhaled.

The guard on the other side of the hole dropped his arm and started forward.

Lisette dove headfirst into the opening in the ground. A

hand caught her boot, but she kicked with her other foot, and then she was tumbling down.

Dirt flew into her mouth. A rock caught her in the ribs as she rolled. Her elbow slid against stone, and she felt the burn of the abrasion.

Then her shoulder slammed into something solid, halting her progress. Lisette opened her eyes and saw a scale-covered leg, black and amber. Lifting her gaze, she looked up into whirling gold eyes and wisps of steam rising from the dragon's nostrils.

"I'm back." She coughed and uncurled, moving slowly in case something was broken. "I guess that's obvious."

"*Move!*"

The command from the dragon overrode every thought she had. Lisette scrambled to the side.

A crossbow bolt buried itself in the ground in front of the dragon's leg. Right where she had been sitting.

While Lisette pictured the bolt slicing through her body, the dragon ran up the slope, gouts of flame going before him. Once again, Lisette saw the chain tethering him to the rock wall, as well as the blistered and oozing flesh in contact with the shackle.

Lisette scrambled over to the other side of the cavern, where she wouldn't be in sight of anyone shooting a crossbow. If the guards knew about the other entrance to the den, she was in trouble — they could sit in the tunnel and shoot bolts at her until the end of time and the dragon wouldn't be able to do much about it. But she'd seen no evidence that any other humans had been in the tunnel recently.

The dragon backed down the ramp and returned to his crouch. On the surface, the guards would be dealing with the wounded and planning their next attack, but underground the silence felt thick.

Lisette wiped sweat from her cheek, only noticing the dark color of blood when she pulled her hand away. She'd hit her head at some point during that fall. "They knew where I was going with the dagger. They were waiting for me. All the guards were waiting."

"And yet you made it through." The dragon didn't sound penitent. Or impressed.

Maybe she should have asked questions earlier. "What does the dagger do?"

The slide of scales along stone echoed through the cavern, and the dragon suddenly loomed over her, his breath hot on her neck. "The Dagger of Aarat controls the dragon called Aarat," he said, as if quoting from a book.

The *duke* controlled the dragons. Lisette had learned that from birth, but she'd never thought about how that was accomplished. She'd assumed there was something special about the duke that made him able to lead the dragons.

But if it was just a matter of the duke owning the right weapon...

"So I give this to you and... he can no longer use your magic?"

The dragon's tail gave an irritated twitch. "The bindings between us will still hold, but he won't be able to renew them. It may take decades for them to fail."

And then, presumably, the city wouldn't be defended against magical attacks. Lisette might be delivering her own death — and the deaths of everyone she knew — the next time a rival city assaulted them, but...

Lisette took a deep breath and thought about this dragon, chained underground, magic siphoned, unable to leave. "You do not wish to be bound to the duke." Somehow, it seemed important to be clear.

"I do not."

Lisette nodded. Perhaps this would doom Harbor Crag. If it took decades for the bindings to fail, the freeholders would have time to work out something. Maybe they could contract with a mage for protection. Or maybe the city would fall. She didn't know.

The only thing she did know was that forcing this dragon to protect the city that chained him was wrong.

She fumbled at the ties on her belt, the blood and dirt on her fingers making the leather slip, but finally she removed the dagger.

She reversed the blade, intending to offer the hilt to the dragon in front of her, but the moment the metal touched the skin of her palm — no, she realized, it wasn't the skin, but her own blood — the magic within it streamed into her.

Lisette screamed.

CHAPTER 22

BREATHE

The dagger's magic filled Lisette, incinerating her from the inside out. She couldn't breathe. She couldn't move. Every fiber of her being cried out. For the first time in her life, Lisette knew what it meant to pray for death.

Lisette. Her name, impossibly beautiful only because the dragon spoke it. *Lisette*, he said again, and she felt all her attention move to him.

A hint of a cooler current lapped against her. The magic began to recede, but there was still so much of it. She wasn't a mage. She had never been meant to hold this much magic.

More of it flowed away from her. This time she felt it leave through the bit of dragon fire in her chest. Somehow, he was siphoning off all this extra power. She wished he would hurry so she could die in peace.

Lisette. Breathe.

Only because the dragon commanded, using her name, she struggled to pull in air. Her chest ached, but it was nothing compared to the pain of the magic still trapped inside her. Something had changed, though. She took another breath, and then another. Her heartbeat steadied.

More magic ebbed away. For the first time, she considered the possibility of living through this.

Lisette opened her eyes, blinked a few times, and recognized the ceiling of the cavern. She was lying on the ground. The lumps under her were probably the gold coins the dragon left scattered around his den. The idea of a bed of gold made her laugh, but it came out as a slightly strong exhale.

Everything hurt.

She turned her head to look for the dragon. He crouched nearby, looking at her, but something looked different. She blinked again, trying to clear her eyes. Instead of his scales being black with amber tips, the warm brown glow extended nearly to the edge where the scales attached to his skin.

The dagger she had spent so much time trying to acquire was in a new niche carved into the wall near the ceiling. Lisette could feel it there before her gaze found it.

Strangely, things had become even more complicated.

Coughing to clear her throat, Lisette opened her mouth, then closed it again. Her throat still burned, but she thought that might be from screaming instead of magic. "What happened?" She considered getting up, but it seemed like too much effort. If the dragon hadn't killed her yet, he probably wouldn't in the next few minutes.

"You bled onto the dagger's blade. That disrupted the existing bindings." The dragon sounded halfway between grumpy and satisfied. "The magic of the bonds tried to return to the wielder of the dagger."

Lisette lifted her head. "You said the bonds would take

decades to break." She let her head fall back. The floor of the cavern really wasn't that uncomfortable.

"You *bled* onto the blade of the Dagger of Aarat."

"Yeah, I got that part." Lisette stared at the ceiling of the cavern and thought about it. "I'm not a mage."

An amused snort of smoke rose through the air. "That was abundantly clear. You also are not a dragon, but you still had my essence within you. And I had your name."

Lisette's head hurt. "So you have your power back. And the city is unprotected."

"The city has other dragons." This dragon whose name — or at least some version of his name — was Aarat didn't sound concerned. "None as old or powerful, but they exist nonetheless."

"I suppose I should be glad I owe you a favor still." Lisette couldn't imagine the dragon having helped her out of the goodness of his heart. And if he hadn't helped, she would be dead now, destroyed by the magic invading her body.

"If you had died before the bonds were broken, the magic would have gone back to the duke." Aarat bowed his head. "I did not intend for this to happen, but I am thankful."

"I don't suppose that favor I owe..."

"Not without breaking the bargain." He paused, and Lisette got the feeling he was trying to figure out how best to explain. "A bargain with a dragon holds magic of its own."

Lisette groaned and climbed to her feet. "By all means, then, let's not mess with it. I'm done with magic." For a moment, she thought she might fall over, but then her body adjusted to this upright position. She'd assumed the dragon fire within her would dissipate after she returned with the dagger, but she could still feel it under her sternum. It didn't hurt, exactly, but she thought it might take a while for her to forget its presence.

"As long as you have bargains with a dragon, you are not done with magic."

"Got it." Bruises from her tumble down the slope made themselves known as she moved her shoulders. "I need to get back to my shop." Another thought struck her. "Will you still be here...? You're still chained." She had assumed the shackles were part of the bonds with the duke, but she could still see the chain going to the wall.

"I do not have the power to break that binding. Yet." The dragon's voice held a venom Lisette hadn't heard before. She really hoped he wasn't planning on taking out his displeasure on the entire city.

"Right." Lisette made an effort to brush off her clothing. She had to look like a mess, with her face all bloody and her clothes showing the effects of her dive into the dragon's cavern.

If the uncles or Tiffany saw her come in, they would have questions. Her only hope was to get home while it was still dark and hope that Tiffany's youngest slept through the night, so Tiffany wasn't awake and looking out her window.

"I'll be back in a few days." She had the concentrator for him, if nothing else. And the sooner Aarat told her what favor he wanted, the sooner she would be free of this magic forever.

"Be well, Lisette." He spoke her name, but it didn't have the power of dragon magic behind it.

Lisette walked along the increasingly familiar tunnel that led to the north entrance, one hand trailing along the wall to keep her place in the gloom. Aarat had confirmed that there were other dragons — younger and less powerful — under the duke's control. Did the smaller branches of this tunnel go to their dens?

It felt wrong to leave the other dragons bound, but she had no means to help them, even if leaving the city unprotected hadn't been a concern.

The opening of the tunnel, still within the walls of the dragon warrens, was hidden from view between a large rock and a tree. Lisette paused there to get her bearings.

Not much time had passed while she was in the dragon's cavern. The stars hadn't moved, though they seemed a little brighter. Brighter, she realized, looking down at the waterfront with its revelers, because the city had dimmed a little. Not as many lights flared, and the colors were muted, shifted more to the orange and yellow of natural torch light. How much magic had the duke been using on such banalities?

The veil of magic enforcing the lockdown was gone.

Lisette headed toward a gap in the crumbling wall. The duke still had other dragons, she reminded herself. Hissing as unyielding stone pressed against fresh bruises, she squeezed through the crack. She probably hadn't doomed the city through her bargain with Aarat.

She really *hoped* she hadn't doomed the city through her bargain with Aarat.

"Stop!" Light flared as a lantern was uncovered. Heavy boots ran forward.

Five guards rushed to surround her.

CHAPTER 23
THE FLAW IN HER LOGIC

Somehow, Lisette had assumed that between the Black Fox hurling explosions and the magical veil falling from around the perimeter, the city guard would be off doing other things. She could see the flaw in her logic now.

"Move away from the wall." The command came from the guard on her right.

Could she make it back through the opening? Probably not fast enough. And if she did, then what? Lead them straight back to the entrance of the tunnel? Could she run fast enough to get all the way back to Aarat's chamber before they caught her?

She stepped forward. She would have to talk her way out of this one. "You have to help me! My friend — He — I think a dragon might have eaten him!" She brought her hands up over her mouth, both because it seemed like the response she *should* have and also because she feared hysterical laughter might burst from her at any second. Lisette knew she had always been terrible at any sort of acting.

"Save it for the magistrate." The guard on her right took her arm firmly. He pulled her into the middle of their group and they began walking. In a few blocks, they would skirt the west wall of the dragon warrens and head down the hill. From there they would take her... where? To the courts? To the duke himself? Or straight to the prison under the old keep?

Lisette no longer had the dagger. That was the only thing that had worked out properly the entire evening. Maybe she could convince the magistrate that she'd slipped into the dragon warrens for a few quiet minutes with a lover. It would be a stupid thing to do, but people did stupider things all the time. And it was the Festival of Secrets, when people might avoid taking a new partner home to preserve the anonymity of the event.

That story could work. If she'd been able to spin a tale like Rye could, it almost certainly *would* work. But she would have to be convincing and not break into inappropriate laughter halfway through.

She was doomed.

They reached the intersection and headed south, down the hill. This had been the area where her thief — her mage? — had been setting off explosions. A group of people holding torches for light examined a section wide enough for a carriage to pass through, where the wall... wasn't. Lisette didn't see any of the bricks that had made up the wall, not even broken fragments. But a layer of fine dirt had been tracked into the depressions between cobblestones along the street.

Bricklayers, clearly pulled from parties and not given a chance to change their clothes, were transferring new bricks from a horse-drawn cart to a wheelbarrow. The guard, or maybe the duke, wouldn't leave the wall open for long.

Contrary to Lisette's expectations, the sudden loss of much of the city's magic hadn't dampened the festivities. If anything, there were more dancers in the streets, with a hint of desperation, as if this might be the last opportunity they had to enjoy the festival. Food vendors still cooked at the corners, and street children wove through the crowds, choosing a parallel path to the guards as Lisette's party moved down the hill.

No, not street children. *One* child, a girl whose face still bore traces of yellow paint. Now in a green tunic and leggings, a red felt mask covering the scarred eyebrow, she skipped, and twirled, and occasionally bumped into people. If Lisette hadn't seen the girl drop something down the top of her shirt, she never would have known she was picking pockets.

Was the Black Fox in the crowd? Lisette looked around at the chaos of carriages and sailors and revelers walking to another ball or just drinking in the streets. If he was there, she couldn't see him. Was this girl there as his emissary, or was she merely working, her presence just a coincidence with no larger pattern?

They had moved beyond the dragon warrens now. From this elevation, Lisette could see three large ships in the harbor. One of them might be her own eventual destination, if the duke didn't just hang her outright. Lisette didn't know the exact penalties for stealing from the duke's own chambers. Nobody had ever dared to do so.

The street girl twirled and danced in front of the guards, making the one in the lead swear as she bumped into him. But instead of taking something from him, she had dropped something in the street, a tiny pouch that sparked with magic.

Lisette had one terrifying second to wonder if this was the same thing the Black Fox had used to obliterate the wall. She looked at the girl and found her crouching in the street with her hands covering her face.

"What —?"

Everything went white.

CHAPTER 24
A TINY GRUBBY HAND

Lisette staggered. In the absolute darkness that followed the flash of light, she couldn't see a thing. Given the screaming of the revelers around her, she wasn't the only one. A horse snorted, and panicked hooves clattered on the cobblestones, with someone yelling "Whoa! Whoa!" and swearing. A crash of wood on stone was followed by the overwhelming smell of ale.

The surrounding guards were made of sterner stuff, or at least quieter. The firm grip on her upper arm tightened, as if the man suspected she would run away. Then he swore in pain and let go. A sword rasped against its sheath.

In the midst of it all, Lisette felt a tiny, grubby hand clasp her own and pull.

Lisette allowed herself to be towed, bumping into people, completely disoriented by her loss of vision. She couldn't even tell if they were headed uphill or down. She just had to trust that girl wasn't leading her into a back alley to slit her throat so Lisette couldn't tell anyone what she knew about the Black Fox.

They moved beyond the crowd of people screaming

about their eyes. When the din quieted, Lisette realized they had turned a corner, putting a building between themselves and the chaos. Cobblestones under her feet told her they were still on a road.

The girl moved faster, skipping now as she pulled Lisette along. Lisette could hear people around them, some running toward the sound of the uproar, but she still couldn't see anything. She kept her voice low with an effort. "Will this wear off?"

The girl continued her skipping. "Fifteen minutes, he said. Best if we're well away from there by then."

Lisette assumed the *he* who had told the girl the length of time was the Black Fox. "What was that thing?"

"Dunno. Fox man gave it and said throw it to the ground and cover your eyes. Worked a treat." She dragged Lisette sideways, and Lisette heard the creak as a heavily laden cart went by. "You're a freeholder, yeah?"

Lisette stumbled over an uneven part of the road. "Why do you say that?"

"Not a noble, or you'd never have seen me. Don't smell bad enough to work at the markets. Clothes're too nice for a workhouse. Least they were earlier tonight. Not so sharp now. And you stand up straight, like you're not afraid to be seen." She twisted, releasing and grabbing Lisette's hand again. "No accent, so you're not a trader. And you're sometimes on the street in the freeholder quarter."

So much for the anonymity provided by a mask. "Yes. But I'd prefer not to have anyone follow me back there."

An outraged snort met her words. "Next you'll be telling me nobles don't keep money in their purses. Anything else obvious you want to say?"

"Sorry." Lisette tried to concentrate on the uneven roadway. With ruts this big, they must be near one of the major streets, where heavily laden carts made potholes inevitable. Perhaps at the butcher's market. "Do nobles *not* keep money in their purses?" A hint of fish greeted her nose, and once again she felt disoriented as her brain relocated her two blocks away in the fish market.

"Hah! Not them. Mostly sand. If they need to buy something with coin, they take it from their belt. You never noticed?" She sounded incredulous, as if everyone should have realized. Then the girl tugged Lisette to the side, and the echoes told her they were in another alley.

Faint patches of light showed in the darkness. Torches? Lanterns? Lisette still couldn't see well enough to distinguish anything, but having a point to use as a guide helped her keep her balance. "I guess I don't get many nobles in my shop. At least ones that buy anything." For a while, Lord Hanley had been a constant presence, and then everyone in his circle who wanted to see the shop owner he was so obsessed with. But while they wasted a lot of her time asking questions about watches they might need fixed, somehow they never brought anything in for her to work on.

"You don't work on credit." The girl twirled, briefly letting go of Lisette's hand again. "I don't either." A faint clink of metal accompanied her words.

Lisette smiled despite herself. Blurry outlines formed. She took a large breath in relief. She hadn't thought the Black Fox would intend to permanently blind her, not when he needed her for something, but she depended on her eyesight for her profession. "I suppose that's a good practice in any line of work. Hold up a minute." She planted her feet and pulled the girl to a stop. "Let me put on my cloak. If they're looking for a woman in dark clothing, this might throw them off."

"Eyes working?"

"A bit." Lisette pulled her hand from the girl's grip, unslung her bag, and inverted it, lifting it up so the gold fabric didn't fall on the street. She kept the elaborate head-piece in her hand to put on next.

"I'm off, then."

"Wait! I didn't bring many coins with me, but let me give you what I have." The girl had done her a huge service, possibly saving Lisette's life and risking her own in the process. Lisette owed her.

A snort of derision greeted her words. "Keep it. Badger takes his cut of everything I bring him, but I'll still make more tonight than you freeholders do in a month. 'Sides, fox man already paid for me to see you safe. Don't like to get paid twice for the same job — folks have different demands."

Lisette slung the cloak over her shoulder and clasped it in place. "Take my thanks, then." She pulled the black hooded mask off, running her fingers through her curls to get them more in order before settling the other mask in place. The cloak would hide the worst of the damage to her clothing, and hopefully the elaborate mask would make the dried blood on her face less noticeable.

By the time she had finished securing the headdress, her vision had returned almost to normal. She was alone in the alley, with no sign the girl had ever been there.

Lisette walked the same way they had been traveling, letting her stride lengthen. When she got to the next inter-section, she would change direction and head back toward the freeholder quarter. The guards wouldn't have commu-nicated a thorough description of her, not yet anyhow, so they would be looking for a woman in black running away from the dragon warrens. A woman in a gold cloak and mask traveling on a path in the opposite direction shouldn't give them pause.

Once she got home, everything would be back to normal. Almost. Aside from the favor owed to the dragon. And if she hadn't doomed the city by breaking Aarat's bonds with the duke. Oh, and now she had promised to help the Black Fox in his thieving. *Keep an eye on the broadsheets*, he had said.

Lisette hurried through the streets, trying to decide if the flutter in her stomach was fear or anticipation.

CHAPTER 25
OPTIMAL SPOT FOR EAVESDROPPING

A bath, a few hours of sleep, and a meal of fruit and honeyed nuts helped Lisette feel almost normal — at least until she moved and all her bruises protested. The cut on her cheek hadn't been too bad, but the skin had purpled and her skill with makeup couldn't completely hide it.

Tiffany might have been able to do a better job of it, but the last thing Lisette wanted to do was listen to her friend exclaim over the damage. Lisette wouldn't be able to tell her what happened, and Tiffany would draw the wrong conclusions.

No, Lisette decided she would just do her best and leave her hair down to fall over her face if someone looked too closely. She waited until she was sure Rye and Barlow were both busy talking to people before she ducked her head through the opening and waved good morning to them. Then she flipped over the sign in the window and unlocked the door.

None of the customers who entered the shop seemed to be talking about the sudden drop in magic overnight. One fisherwoman mentioned the lock down flag had stopped flying. She had come in to see if Lisette could save her pocket watch. Touching the seafarer's protection medallion on a leather thong around her neck, she told Lisette the watch had been submerged in salt water after some creature of the deep had nearly swamped her boat.

She talked as Lisette worked. "No matter what's out there, it's a good thing we're allowed out again. This duke hasn't kept up the food reserves. If we had to keep in place for more than a few days, half the population would be out catching rats for dinner. I always salt some fish and keep it aside, just in case, but I'm doubling my stores now."

Lisette had the watch opened up and the movement stripped, ready to go in the cleaner's bath, by the time the fisherwoman finished explaining the best way to prepare salted fish with rice. Since Lisette didn't have a kitchen, and had never done more than watch as street cooks plied their trade, she let the words wash over her as she worked.

"Mind you, I don't think it was the duke's idea to end the lockdown," the fisherwoman said as Lisette started the cleaner and leaned back. "He was yelling about *something* out there this morning." The fisherwoman had made herself comfortable on the brocade visitor's chair Rye insisted Lisette keep there. He claimed it reminded people they might need to buy something in the shop next door, but Lisette thought it just kept her visitors in the optimal spot for the uncles to eavesdrop.

"This morning?"

"Oh yes. They're searching everything leaving the city, even the trader caravans and the fishing boats, so you can imagine how popular that is. Do I have time to wait for the guards to poke at my nets when I could be on the water?

Nobody does. The duke himself was there for a bit, yelling at someone."

The cleaner's bell dinged, and Lisette started reassembling and oiling the watch. "I'd have thought he'd be too busy with the Festival of Secrets to worry about running the city."

"Ha!" The fisherwoman's laugh was louder than the joke deserved. "It'd be better if he was. I heard the traders had to unpack and repack all their carts. As if the guards are going to find something the traders want to keep hidden. No, all that does is irritate everyone, and the last thing we want to do is have the traders decide it's not worth coming to Harbor Crag." She shook her head. "I like fish, mind you, but even I know there are other things the city needs."

As she worked, Lisette listened to the other woman's list of spices that only the traders traveling the overland route could supply. The watch seemed to be in good order, with no major damage from the submersion in the sea. The timing adjuster gave her consistent readings, another good sign. Once a year, Lisette paid a mage from one of the traders' caravans to keep the adjuster running, but it was a finicky thing. She'd found it wouldn't give the same value twice in a row unless the timepiece was in optimal condition.

Lisette closed the case and stood up. "Here you are. If you have any problems with it in the next few weeks, bring it back, but I think it should be fine now."

The fisherwoman removed coins from her pocket. "Such clever fingers you have. It's a treat to watch you work." She held up one hand, knuckles large and skin rough. "I'd never be able to do that."

Lisette accepted the coin and handed over the watch. "And I'd never be able to pull in a net."

"Ha! Let me know if you ever want to try!" The fisher-woman opened the shop door. "Fair luck to you."

"Good tides," Lisette responded. She waited a few seconds after the door had closed, then raised her voice. "You might as well come in. I heard you laughing over there."

The wall hanging twitched, and Rye poked his head in. "Sorry. It was the thought of you out on a boat that did it." He narrowed his eyes, then came all the way into the shop. "Lisette Allinde, what happened to your face?"

Apparently, her attempt to hide the cuts and bruises had been less successful than she'd hoped. "Fell down a hill. And before you and Barlow start collecting money to pay to have someone knocked out and dumped off the end of the pier, no, there wasn't a man involved. Or a woman."

He sniffed and rolled his eyes. "Oh, please, you think we would hire someone *else* to do that if we found out somebody hurt you?" Rye drew the hair back from her face and peered at the cut. "At least it doesn't look infected." He let her hair fall back into place. "Are you involved in whatever idiocy is happening in the tunnels, or is this a different idiocy?"

"The tunnels? *Our* tunnels?"

"I guess that answers *that* question." Rye adjusted his already perfectly straight silk vest. "Is it connected with whatever you did to get the taxes?"

"Yes."

"And you still can't talk about it?"

Lisette thought about the dragon, no longer bound to the duke. Would keeping that a secret endanger her friends more than talking about it, when someone might be listening for such a conversation? She had no way of knowing. "I don't think so."

Rye nodded. "You'll let us know if that changes or you need help?"

"Yes." Lisette wanted nothing more than to tell him everything that had happened. She circled back to his earlier question. "Now what's going on in the freeholder quarter tunnels?"

CHAPTER 26
HAUNTED

According to Uncle Rye's informants, the freeholder tunnels were haunted.

Lisette laughed. She couldn't help it. "Haunted?"

"So I've been told. By multiple people." Rye waved a hand. "That's obvious rubbish, but someone is going to a lot of trouble to make it look that way. Maybe someone is trying to drive the children out."

"By making it look haunted?" Lisette laughed again. "Are you sure they aren't trying to lure them instead?" When she'd been a child, there had been a building at the edge of the quarter where the ghosts of the first freeholders were said to appear at midnight on a full moon. Lisette and Tiffany had snuck out to see them three different times before giving up. Later, Lisette found out one of the older kids had made up the story in an attempt to scare Tiffany.

Tiffany had always been made of sterner stuff.

"That *would* make more sense, but I don't think so." He pulled the wall hanging between the two shops back so he could keep an eye on his door. "As far as I can tell, last night some of the children in the quarter were woken up by the fireworks and decided it would be the perfect time to go down into the tunnels so they could scare each other senseless." He shook his head at her grin. "Only a freeholder would find that normal."

Lisette's smile widened. "It's tradition." Rye had married into the freeholders, not grown up as one, so he hadn't experienced the safety and stability of the freehold quarter as a child. "Everything looks extra spooky by candlelight, and there's almost nothing down there to burn."

"Except their hair and clothing." Rye shook his head. "In any event, the children were there, scaring each other. But they said almost immediately there was a purple light in one of the chambers. Instead of seeing that as a sign they should go back home, naturally all the kids tried to find out where it was coming from."

A cart went by on the street, moving a little too quickly for safety, but the drayman seemed awake and in control, so she focused on Rye again. "You're saying you would have just gone home and gone to bed?"

"I would never have been silly enough to leave my bed in the first place." At Lisette's get-on-with-it motion, he continued. "But *these* children followed the light around for hours, trying to see who was carrying it until one of them twisted an ankle. At that point, they seemed to realize they should go home. They never found the source of the light, ergo: ghosts." He bowed, as if at the end of a theatrical performance. "And that is the story of the haunting of the freeholder quarter tunnels. A story told by children who tried to scare each other and succeeded."

"But..." Lisette was about to protest the incompleteness

of the story when another thought struck her. "They came home and told their parents?"

"Yes. Apparently, even freeholder parents ask questions when a child sprains an ankle overnight."

Ignoring the jibe, Lisette tried to figure out how to explain the problem to someone who hadn't grown up in the quarter. "There are *fun* secrets, and then there are *bad* secrets. Bad secrets might hurt the community. Bad secrets need to be told to an adult, even if it gets you in trouble. But you would never tell a fun secret, even if someone accidentally got hurt." If the injury hadn't been an accident, it was, by definition, no longer a fun secret.

Sooner or later it would be common knowledge anyhow, because children didn't pay attention to who was around when they talked. But that would take a few days. If this had happened the previous night, some of the children hadn't considered it a fun secret.

A faint crease in Rye's forehead cleared. "So that's why Barlow thought it was important. I thought he just wanted to go tell ghost stories."

Knowing Uncle Barlow as well as she did, Lisette didn't think the reasons were mutually exclusive. "I'm assuming the adults went down there this morning."

"Of course. They didn't stay down there long enough to find anything, but — and I quote — 'it felt weird.'" He rolled his eyes. "I still think it's probably just a bunch of nonsense."

With a sinking feeling in her stomach, Lisette thought about how he'd started his tale. "The kids were woken by fireworks?"

"You had to have heard them. It sounded like they were blowing up half the waterfront."

Sound traveled oddly in the city, but Lisette hadn't

heard any unusual fireworks near the water. But Rye, probably asleep in his bed at the time, might have been woken by the explosions the Black Fox had set off to give Lisette a chance to slip into the dragon warrens. It would be reasonable to assume they were fireworks.

So... the explosions woke up the children. By the time Lisette had made it past the guard with the dagger, they were probably already down in the tunnels, jumping out at each other. Add a few minutes for her to fall down into the dragon's cavern, and a few more while she waited for Aarat to take care of the guard shooting crossbow bolts at them.

That was when she had stupidly smeared blood on the blade of the dagger, disrupting whatever bonds the duke had set on the dragon. And across the city, a mysterious light had appeared in the tunnels under the freeholder quarter.

It couldn't be a coincidence.

"Watch my shop for a bit?" At Rye's nod, Lisette opened the pass-through to get out of her workspace.

She needed to go look at what was under the freeholder quarter, haunting the tunnels.

And she knew exactly where to start.

CHAPTER 27
TURTLE AND POT

A s Lisette had expected, Tiffany was in her workshop, turning out more fox masks to meet the last-minute demand. Leather masks, bags, and clothing in various stages of completion hung on the walls, making it rather like walking into a cave of unfinished creatures. Decorated bags and jackets, made to order and waiting to be picked up, were displayed at a level safe from little fingers. Down near the floor, scraps of leather with uneven stitching and a random assortment of stamps showed the efforts of the next generation. Lisette inhaled deeply when she stepped inside, enjoying the scents of leather, oil, and the faint acrid odor of the dyes.

On a normal morning, her friend would be at the workbench by the window, using the leather punches and stamps and mallets, a plethora of tools placed in exactly the right spot for her to grab without looking up from the piece in front of her.

This morning, Tiffany sat in an armchair, a stack of basic fabric masks, complete with ties, to her left. Baskets of feathers, fabric, and sequins waited on her right. Her nimble fingers moved quickly, adding the touches that made the basic template look like a fox.

Tiffany glanced up without pausing her hands when Lisette came in. "And how did it go last night?" Then she got a better look at Lisette's face and put her work down and stood up. "What happened?" She pushed Lisette's hair out of the way. "I'll kill him, whoever he is."

Lisette waved her hands in negation. "He wasn't there when it happened. I fell. It's complicated."

Tiffany narrowed her eyes and looked at her.

Lisette put her hands down. "I promise. He put himself at risk to help me. I owe him." Literally owed him a favor, but she wasn't going to tell Tiffany that. She walked over to look at the belts hanging from the wall.

Tiffany sighed and sat down. "At this time of life, I'm supposed to be worrying about our children, not you."

One of the belts had a little fold near the buckle, just big enough for a few coins. Lisette put her finger into the gap. "Did you know most of the nobles' purses hold sand?"

Tiffany snorted. "You really don't pay attention when people come into your shop, do you? The ones running around in fancy carriages have less than we do. Most of them don't even own their homes. How do you run a business and not know this?"

Lisette shrugged and let the leather belt slip through her fingers to lie flat against the wall again. "I fix things. I don't give anything back until they pay me. And if they don't pay me, eventually I sell it." As a system, it had worked pretty well for generations. Her family only rarely got stuck with things like the ugly dragon clock.

"Well, don't ever extend them credit. That's my advice." Tiffany picked a black feather from the basket at her side and began attaching it to the mask. "Now, why are you really here?"

"The tunnels. I'm assuming at least one of your kids was involved?" It was a fairly safe bet. Tiffany's children were smaller versions of Tiffany, to the delight and occasional dismay of their baker father.

"Running around in the tunnels with a candle in the middle of the night? Of course they were. Turtle and Pot, anyhow. Ziggy spent half the morning crying because they didn't wake her up when they went."

Turtle and Pot — whose actual names were Clara and Pilar, though nobody ever called them that unless they were in real trouble — didn't always want their younger sister tagging along. And Ziggy, who had never been called Rhiette in Lisette's hearing, was just old enough to feel excluded.

Tiffany put another feather in place. "Pot won't be going anywhere on that ankle for a while, though. Nothing's broken, thank the gods. You never know how a break is going to heal in children that age." She glanced up at Lisette without moving her head. "Why the interest?"

"I need to go look. Do you know exactly where they were?"

Tiffany put the mask down on her lap. "Promise me that someday you'll tell me everything."

"As soon as I can," Lisette agreed.

"Good." Tiffany jumped to her feet and set the nearly finished mask down on her workbench. "Let's go."

Lisette hesitated. "I didn't mean to take you away from your work." She also wasn't sure what she would find down there, and it might be better if fewer people saw it.

"Oh, please. Do you really think I'm going to send you down there on your own? I had to pretend to be the sensible one this morning when the kids came back and Pot was hurt. I've been dying to go look, even though it's probably just something they imagined." She waved a hand at the workbench. "We've cleared enough on the extra masks to put something away for taxes and the emergency fund. I need a break."

Lisette smiled. This was the Tiffany she'd grown up with, unchanged even after three children. "Let's go find out what's down there."

CHAPTER 28

SHIFTING FOUNDATIONS

The tunnels under the freeholder quarter had multiple entrances, some more easily accessed than others. The entrances also had varying sizes, and at least one seemed to have shrunk over the years.

"I don't remember..." Tiffany panted, "...this being so small before." Her face was flattened against the stone as she inched her body through the crack in the meeting hall basement. They'd chosen this access because the gate blocking the official portal had been locked, and they didn't feel like tracking down whoever had the key.

Lisette waited for her friend to get through and move out of the way. The obvious response was that Tiffany had been ten years younger and quite a bit slimmer then. "Foundation probably shifted."

Tiffany gave a breathy laugh. "Good answer." Something scraped against rock and she dropped down into the darkness beyond. "There we go. No problem. Your turn."

Lisette angled herself through the crack. She had always been lankier than her friend, and she hadn't carried three children in the intervening years, but it was still a close fit. She slid into the dark passageway and inhaled the familiar odor of the damp stone.

The flare of a match brought a hint of sulfur, and then Tiffany handed her a small lantern. "Someone else has been using this route. The last time we were here, we still had candles inside glass jars." Tiffany lit a second lantern for herself and blew out the match.

Bringing her lantern closer to the walls, Lisette searched through the inscriptions carved there. It only took a few seconds for her to find their names, shallowly scratched into the stone with a knife that had dulled nearly beyond recovery by the process. The list of names covered the span of her outstretched hands, a monument to all the children who had grown up in the quarter for generations.

Now that she had a reference, Lisette looked to her left and down a little lower, finding her mother's mark. She touched the stone, feeling the indentations under her fingers. Lisette, the shop, and this section of tunnel were all that remained in the world to show her mother had lived. She gave it a gentle pat and then turned. "Which way?"

Holding her lantern out in front of her, Tiffany headed to the right. "Turtle said they were in the 'tunnel with the lines' when it all started, so I think they must have been under the brewery."

Lisette knew exactly which tunnel she meant. Due to some difference in the way the stones had settled, the long tunnel under the brewery had brown striations running through the light grey rocks. She followed behind her friend, almost banging her head as two tunnels joined in a lower section. "Have I really gotten that much taller since the last time we were down here?"

Tiffany turned into another side tunnel, laughing. "Maybe the foundation shifted."

Lisette ducked and followed. Having been in the dragon warrens recently, she recognized some similarities in the way the tunnels were laid out. Though there weren't any obvious claw marks here, even stone could be worn down over time. Had there been dragon warrens in this area before the freeholders arrived? If so, the dragons had been gone before her people had started building — dragons weren't something that people just forgot about.

Given the steep hill that housed Harbor Crag, this section was far below the buildings above, but was on the same level with the buildings three streets over. Tiffany stopped to pick up a wax stub on the ground. "We must be close. Turtle said she lost her candle when the ghost showed up."

The next turn brought them to the tunnel with the streaks of iron ore. In the steady light of the lanterns, it seemed just what it was — a tunnel with veins of color running through the rocks. But Lisette remembered how flickering candle flames on the irregular surface made it seem as if something was moving. This was a good location for scary games in the middle of the night.

Tiffany stopped and faced her. "We're here. Now what?"

"Good question." Lisette turned in a circle, trying to remember what else was nearby. From what she recalled, one direction led to the downhill slope where they'd devised a complicated game involving marbles and targets. The other direction led to a large chamber that had been used by the older children as a meeting place. "Let's look at the big room first."

Tiffany nodded and led the way. "When did we get so grown up? The idea of coming down here to sit on the stone floor and freeze my..." Her voice trailed off as she entered the cavern. "I don't remember all *this* stuff."

At first Lisette thought she meant the furniture; some enterprising children, more unwilling to sit on the stone floor than Lisette and Tiffany had been, had brought down two battered chairs along with a pile of blankets.

Then Lisette stepped out of the tunnel into the larger area and understood.

The last time she had been here, the cavern had just been a plain domed area with fairly smooth walls. Now there were niches carved into the rock at irregular intervals. Most were empty, but Lisette saw the leather spine of a book in an alcove far above her head. A tiny metal vane spun in another. She itched to climb up and find out what powered it.

A flash of purple in the tunnel on the opposite side of the chamber caught Lisette's attention. The ember of dragon fire in her chest burned, and the light was gone. She rubbed at her sternum to ease the sensation.

Tiffany ran forward. "Hurry! We have to catch up!" She disappeared into the tunnel.

"What?" By the time Lisette made it across the chamber, Tiffany was already out of sight, though the light of her lantern coming from a side tunnel made her path clear. "Tiffany, wait! Wait for me!"

The light in front of her dimmed.

CHAPTER 29
BREAKING THE TRANCE

S till not sure what Tiffany was trying to catch up with, Lisette followed the light of her friend's lantern as it grew fainter.

Something wasn't right. Tiffany would never just abandon her in the tunnels and run after something, no matter how much she wanted to get a closer look. The surge from the dragon fire still in Lisette's chest told her one thing.

Magic.

Lisette sprinted down the tunnel, trying to catch up with her friend without knocking herself out as she entered smaller tunnels. Tiffany was moving quickly, but Lisette had the advantage of longer legs.

Three turns later, her friend was in view. "Tiffany! Slow down!" Lisette couldn't see what Tiffany followed, but all of her friend's attention was on one spot just in front of her.

Lisette's words didn't help; she wasn't even sure Tiffany heard.

This was what had happened to the children overnight.

They had followed something for hours until Pot, spraining her ankle, had broken the trance. Lisette hoped she could just delay Tiffany long enough for her to shake off whatever had her in its grip.

Grabbing a handful of the back of Tiffany's tunic, Lisette planted her feet and crouched to lower her center of gravity. At first, Tiffany stopped easily enough. Then she started pulling to get moving again. Lisette slid forward. She set her lantern down on the floor and used her free hand to grab at the tunnel wall. There was nothing to hang onto, but the added friction slowed them down.

If this didn't work, Lisette was going to have to knock Tiffany down. She wasn't looking forward to that. Tiffany had always been a scrappy fighter, and she liked to aim for the nose. Lisette's eyes watered just thinking about it.

Suddenly, Tiffany stopped pulling, and they both went backward. Lisette fell on the ground, Tiffany landing on top of her. Her lantern clattered to the side, but the weighted base kept it upright.

Lisette kept her grip on the fabric of Tiffany's tunic as her friend struggled to get up. "Are you done trying to follow that thing?"

"What? Who?" Tiffany stilled. "What happened?"

"The same thing that happened to the girls, I think." Lisette let go of Tiffany's tunic and wiggled out from under her. "One minute we were in the big room, and the next you were running off after something."

"What are you talking about? We never got to the..." Tiffany trailed off. "The last thing I remember is finding the candle, and then there was that purple light. I had to follow it."

Lisette got up and helped Tiffany to her feet. "We found the candle, and then we went into the big room at the end of the tunnel. Someone brought some chairs and blankets down there. Do you remember seeing that?"

Tiffany frowned. "Maybe? I remember seeing the chairs without remembering where they were." She shook her head with a rueful smile. "Why didn't *we* ever bring anything to sit on?"

Lisette refused to get sidetracked. "And there were niches carved into the walls. Some of them had things in them." Curiosities, she realized. The tunnels didn't just have the *feel* of the dragon warrens. They had the treasures, or some part of them anyhow.

But there wasn't a dragon down here now. The freeholder children couldn't have missed that. And Tiffany hadn't been following a dragon when she'd been entranced.

Tiffany was frowning again. "How could someone carve the rock with no one hearing? Sound carries down here, and there are half a dozen entrances in shops where people would have heard. I'm not sure I could work leather down here without someone checking on the noise. Stone would be even louder." She punched Lisette's shoulder lightly. "And why didn't you get stuck in that thing's spell?"

Either someone had secretly changed the cavern with no one noticing, or the curiosities had been there for years and generations of freeholder children had missed them. Either way, the answer was tangled up in dragons and magic.

Aarat might know what could cause this, if she could convince him to answer her questions, but he was still chained to the wall in his cavern. And even if he were free, Lisette wasn't sure he would fit in any of the tunnels leading to the big room.

"We need a mage."

Tiffany stared at her as if she had just sworn an oath to an undersea god. "Have you lost your mind? You bring a mage down here and the duke will be two seconds behind him. If he finds something he wants badly enough, all the freeholder land rights might as well be ashes."

"We need a mage who isn't beholden to the duke," Lisette amended.

"There's one who travels with the traders, but that caravan won't be here for months." Tiffany looked at the stone walls around them. "Assuming we can even trust him, what are we supposed to do in the meantime? We can tell the kids not to come down here, but..." She caught Lisette's eye and gave a short laugh.

"Yeah." Even if Tiffany could keep her own children away, already a questionable proposition, there were other children in the quarter. Plus, the street children occasionally came through if they were running from someone.

"There's no way to close off all the entrances, and even if it's just the one room, there's no way to block it. How am I going to keep my girls safe until the caravan gets here?"

Was the Black Fox a mage? Or did he just have a lot of magical items? Lisette thought back to how he had exposed the trap in the duke's chambers. Even if he wasn't a mage, he knew about magic.

Did she trust him? If she brought him down here, she wouldn't be able to hide her identity for very long. Though maybe he already knew she was a freeholder. The street girl had certainly figured it out quickly enough.

Lisette realized she trusted the thief more than the mage who traveled with the traders. And the Black Fox was already in the city.

"I may know someone who can help." Lisette's pulse

quickened at the thought of seeing him again. She tried to keep her voice steady, knowing Tiffany would hear any changes. "But it might take a few days to find him."

CHAPTER 30
QUITE THE POET

By the time Lisette and Tiffany made their way out of the tunnels, it was too late to get a notice into the afternoon broadsheets. Even though Lisette had wanted to go back to get a better look at the items she'd seen, she hadn't been willing to chance taking Tiffany through the big room again. And Lisette wasn't about to let her friend stay by herself while she went back alone.

To avoid going back through the magically trapped cavern, they'd been forced to rely on memories of the tunnels they hadn't been through in years, finally emerging at the edge of the quarter, tired and grimy from the adventure.

They stopped to tell the uncles what had happened, and Lisette's plan to get help from the man she had been meeting. Then Tiffany went back to make more masks, and Lisette returned to her shop to compose a message to put in the morning broadsheets. As a method of communication, it was mysterious and alluring, but not very efficient.

Lisette tried again. *To the man with the cat: Noon, same place.* No. That read more like a business proposition than a lover's note. The whole point was to make everyone else believe it was a festival message.

While she considered how to get the thief's attention and specify a place only he would understand, she assembled the bits of the concentrator, now clean and dry. For the missing parts, she bent wire in the shape of the corrosion left behind.

Lisette doubted the concentrator would work on the first try — the pieces could very well depend on a specific type of metal or a precise thickness — but it might be close enough for the dragon to tell her what needed to change. And maybe she would find out exactly what it did.

Assuming the tunnels under the freeholder quarter really had been home to dragons, did that mean whatever magic was luring people away from the big chamber was dragon magic? If she couldn't talk to the thief today, perhaps Aarat could answer some questions about what she had found there.

To my cat man: going to forbidden places was a thrill. Let's do it again. Noon, one block west from where we last met. Ugh. Definitely not. Aside from the blush-inducing awkwardness, that message left the meeting place in doubt. Would it be one block west of Lord Hanley's residence, or the alley? Or even somewhere west of the dragon warrens?

As it turned out, Lisette didn't need to work out the perfect message for the broadsheets — the Black Fox had already placed one for her.

Tiffany burst into the shop, Ziggy on her hip, just as Lisette was thinking of taking a break for dinner. Her friend waved a broadsheet in her free hand. "Your mystery man is looking for you again."

Rye ducked through the wall hanging separating the two shops. "I knew it!"

Barlow crowded in behind him a few seconds later. "What does it say?"

Lisette closed her logbook, where she'd been making a few last notes about the concentrator, and set it carefully aside, out of reach of Ziggy's fingers. By the time she turned to face them, Rye was holding the toddler and Tiffany was carefully flattening the broadsheet on the counter.

"Here we are. 'I miss you, and so does my cat. Do me a favor? Sunset, outside the gates where we first stole a kiss.'" Tiffany looked up. "Quite the poet, your mystery man."

"Quite good at hiding messages in something that looks like a love note," Rye said with a worried frown.

Barlow put a hand on Rye's shoulder. "Why can't it be a message *and* a love note?" He turned to look at Lisette. "Even so, what do you know about this person?"

"Almost nothing," Lisette admitted, trying to ignore her heated cheeks. Telling them what little she did know — that he was this Black Fox whom the broadsheets reported on so breathlessly — would just make things worse. And that would bring in her connection to the dragon, which the duke still might be listening for. "It's the Festival of Secrets. But he's the only person I can think of who might be able to help with that problem we have."

Tiffany was still looking at the broadsheet. "Where you first stole a kiss? First off, what does this man have against a proper location, like a restaurant or a tea stand? And second, you've been holding out on me." She pressed one hand against her heart. "'Oh, it was just business, Tiffany. I was just doing a favor for someone.'"

Tiffany's imitation of her wasn't very good, but it still made Lisette smile. "We didn't actually..." It had just been an act, a showy embrace to provide a reason for being in the duke's private corridor. But they *had* been stealing, and she assumed that was the part meant to give her the biggest clue. "It's just a way to make it look like a festival note."

Tiffany looked doubtful, but she didn't press.

Barlow had been looking at the broadsheet over Tiffany's shoulder. "Is there some egg shortage we should know about? Why are all these businesses advertising with chickens?"

Lisette's stomach sank. She leaned to look at the broadsheet Tiffany was still smoothing against the counter. Barlow was right. Two ale houses and a hotel were touting *Chickens!* Plus, a rug seller had added *Rustic scenes with CHICKENS now available!* to his usual listing.

The duke's hidden passion was no longer a secret.

Rye was staring at Lisette. "You know something about this."

The others stared at her. Even little Ziggy looked up.

"I... I heard a rumor that the duke likes chickens." There. That should be safe enough. Clearly, there *was* a rumor flying around, or the businesses wouldn't be trying to capitalize on it. When everyone looked even more confused, she elucidated. "More of a fascination with chickens, you might call it."

What worried her more was the timing of the rumors. Lisette had broken the bonds between Aarat and the duke, and suddenly news of the duke's obsession, held at bay by the amnesia or ignoring spells for all this time, was out in the open. How much of Harbor Crag had Lisette changed with that one action?

Barlow shrugged. "What's not to like about chickens? They're quieter and cause less damage than goats."

Rye shook his head. "Why would the duke keep chickens *or* goats?"

Tiffany still scanned the other messages. "Do you think

I'd be able to raise my rates for the nobles if I put a chicken on the sign out front?" She shook her head and stood up, letting the broadsheet roll up. "I need to go make some chicken masks. If nobody else has them yet, I can charge a premium."

Lisette felt her eyes widen. "Tiffany, no."

Rye nodded. "That's a terrible idea."

Barlow shrugged. "I think it would be kind of funny. All those chickens out there with the foxes."

Rye shifted Ziggy so she was sitting on one shoulder. "Exactly. It would be funny. And when the duke decides everyone is laughing at him, who is he going to go after? The nobles who own the ships and warehouses that keep the city running? Or the freeholder leatherworker who made a few extra coins on chicken masks?"

Barlow's grin faded. "When you put it like that, it does seem like a bad idea."

Tiffany sighed. "Fine. I'll hold off." She held up her arms to her daughter. "Come on, Ziggy-girl. Let's go pick out some pretty clothes and a mask for your Auntie Lisette to wear."

Ziggy launched herself off Rye's shoulder and he supported her until she was safely in her mother's arms.

Thinking of the climbing she might need to do to fulfill her favor to the thief, Lisette said, "Nothing too fancy. Maybe just a simple mask and a scarf?"

Barlow took Tiffany's arm. "We'll find the perfect thing."

Lisette watched them go out the door. "I'm doomed." She stopped Rye before he returned to his shop. "Uncle? A moment, first?" She reached back and picked up the newly assembled concentrator. "I have a buyer for this, if you name a price."

Rye regarded her, a gleam coming into his eye. "You found a buyer who doesn't care what it costs." The idea of conducting a bidding war lit up his face.

Lisette nodded, thinking of the gold scattered around Aarat's chamber, and the wealth of other coins the dragon clearly didn't treasure. "Yes. But also, I think it would be unsafe to display this." It might be unsafe to have it at all. Her notes in the logbook, with diagrams and suggestions of how the pieces fit together, might be dangerous if anyone thought to look at them. "I think we should sell it to this buyer and keep the whole thing quiet."

Rye's shoulders drooped. He looked at the device in her hand. "Fifteen silvers. That's probably less than it's worth, but if what you say is true, we don't want to call attention to the transaction. Fifteen silvers will give us a nice profit, but it's still an amount we can claim was made from some other piece." He sighed and shook his head.

"Thank you, Uncle."

"Be careful tonight. I don't like how restless the city feels."

"I will, Uncle Rye." Lisette thought of all the magic she had freed by bleeding onto the dagger blade. "I will."

CHAPTER 31

EXITS

The crowd near the gates of the duke's palace was thinner at sunset than it would be in a few hours when the festival balls began. Lisette told herself confidence was everything; if she looked like she belonged here, strolling along the street, then she *did* belong.

With the dying rays of the sun illuminating the buildings, the duke's palace looked tired, stonework crumbling a bit on this corner, paint peeling near that doorway. Either she'd been too nervous to notice the last time she'd been here... Or the duke had been using magic to make everything look better. How much of the city's protection had he been diverting to such uses?

Fidgeting with the ties on her mask, Lisette turned and promenaded in the other direction. Tiffany and Barlow had restrained themselves — slightly. Her mask, a sea creature with tentacles hanging down over her lower face, had fewer sequins than she had expected. Lisette's hair had been loosely braided in sections to match the tentacles.

Tiffany had also sent another two masks with her. "If

you need to lose pursuers, you can switch the masks out and tie your hair up. Plus, the cloak is reversible."

Clearly, the secret messages in the broadsheets had given Tiffany and Barlow the wrong idea about the man Lisette was meeting. Or... maybe it was the right idea, but not the one Lisette wanted them to have. "I'm sure I won't need them, but thank you. Everything is lovely."

Now she was on the street, watching the light fade and starting to doubt whether her thief was going to show up. He wouldn't be using street children to find her here — none of the urchins would dare pick pockets in the street right outside the duke's palace. Carriages went through the outer gates at regular intervals, and messengers on foot. She wondered if there was enough magic to light up the ballroom, or whether this night's ball had been canceled.

Lisette pulled at her mask again and wondered how long she should wait before giving up.

"Pleasant evening for a walk, isn't it?" The warm voice next to her ear made her shoulders relax. A moment later, pepper and vanilla tickled her nose.

"You tend to sneak up on a person." Lisette took his proffered elbow and matched her pace to his. She looked to the side and saw the familiar profile, a black cat mask obscuring his upper face. For once, his satchel wasn't with him.

"Hazard of the profession, I'm afraid." He looked at her and smiled. "My compliments to your mask maker. Whoever they are, they've caught your essence without being too obvious about it."

Lisette huffed a laugh. "I *do* come from a long line of sea creatures. Very discerning of you." She let him guide her around a corner onto another broad street lined by residences of the nobles. "Simi isn't with you?"

"Not tonight. She's enjoying some fish and a warm nap while I'm out working, the ungrateful creature. But I get to see you, and she doesn't, so there are benefits."

The man really was an incorrigible flirt. She needed to get one thing off her chest before she tried to match his light tone. "I appreciate your help last night. If you hadn't sent the girl... I didn't catch her name. Anyhow, if you hadn't sent her to help, it would have ended badly."

He was guiding her toward Lord Hanley's estate. But there were other residences in the area. Maybe they were bound for one of those.

"She's an enigma, that one. If you ask, I'm sure she'll tell you a name, but it will be different every time."

"That would be useful for dealing with dragons," Lisette said without thinking.

The muscles beneath her fingers twitched, the only sign that she'd startled him. "I suppose it would, at that. I guess that answers my question about your destination."

Lisette nodded. There was no point in lying. He'd known she'd needed to get into the dragon warrens badly enough to risk death, so it wasn't a leap to assume she'd been visiting a dragon. And she was going to have to reveal a lot more than that if she wanted his help on the tunnels in the quarter.

As the light faded, more people came out into the streets. The fox guided them around a food vendor setting up his cart on the corner. Lisette's eye was drawn to Lord Hanley's residence, the stone dragons guarding the main gate getting ever closer. "Do I get to know what we're doing tonight?"

"Ah, yes, sorry. How rude of me! You threw me off with your talk of names and dragons. Tonight we are taking the public tours of several of the houses of the nobles."

Lisette stared at him. "Public tours?"

"Oh, yes. It's a time-honored tradition, letting those less fortunate gaze upon the wonders of their betters. The financial aspect is... well, that's also traditional, though possibly not as much acknowledged."

He moved them both to the edge of the street and stopped. "Forgive me for prying, but is there a particular reason you're reluctant to go near this estate, or is it merely the poorly executed gargoyles?"

"I didn't —"

"No, you didn't, but your entire body is suggesting anywhere else would be preferable, even just walking into the sea. So, in the interests of not ending up with a noose around my neck, I'll rudely ask a different question. Are they likely to recognize you there?"

Lisette took a deep breath and regarded him. He waited, not crowding her or seeming the least bit impatient, as if they had all the time in the world. In the street, people dressed in their evening finery walked by, chattering and laughing.

She trusted this thief.

Before she could change her mind, she spoke. "I'm a freeholder." She took his nod as confirmation that he already knew. "I don't know why I thought I could hide it. The girl with all the names figured it out almost immediately."

"Don't feel bad about that." He smiled ruefully. "I couldn't hide my origins from her, either. She's the best I've ever seen at that sort of thing."

Lisette idly wondered if she could bribe the girl to tell her about the thief. Except that would break the trust she was trying to build. She told herself to stop procrastinating and tell him what he needed to know. "I have my own shop in the quarter. And Lord Hanley... fixated on me."

Lisette watched the people going by and told the story. The first time Lord Hanley had come into the shop, he'd accompanied another noble who was picking up a repaired pocket watch. After that, he'd found excuses, one after another, until the point when he hadn't even bothered with those.

"And when I turned him down — politely, which doesn't come easily to me — he just ignored me and kept coming back every day to ask again." Lisette turned to look at the building. "Compliments and flowers. He offered to bring me here to live, let me spend as much of his money as I wanted, all the things he thought I should desire." She shrugged. "He's reasonably attractive, and he's wealthy, and a noble... I don't think anyone had ever turned him down before."

"And that's a good enough reason to avoid him, even if you didn't have any other." The thief blew out a breath. "Though that's often easier to say than do."

"Yes. For a while he was polite to me, just kept offering more things. Maybe he thought we were negotiating the price. Then.... The man I'd been seeing — just a casual relationship, nothing for anyone to get hurt over — suddenly had a broken arm and wouldn't talk to me. And there was a fire in the shop next door." She would never forgive Hanley for that. Rye and Barlow could have been killed.

After a few seconds of silence, the thief spoke. "I've known men to become fixated like that, but I haven't known many to let it go."

"I closed my shop and left the city for six months. I only came back when there were rumors he had found someone else." She still felt guilty about that. The next woman probably hadn't had a community like Lisette's supporting her. She looked over at the Black Fox again. "So, to answer your question, I've never been on the estate. The staff shouldn't recognize me. *He* might, and some of his friends, but probably not in a mask." She steeled herself to walk toward the building again.

"Good to know." The thief didn't move. "I would *like* your opinion on some things inside, but I never meant to endanger you this evening. I doubt we'll see anyone other than the staff assigned to keep the tour moving along, but if you would prefer to stay here, I can leave you to loiter at the tea stand and go on this tour alone."

"No." Lisette raised her chin. "I'd like to see the place." She scowled. "It would be good to know where the exits are in case I ever end up there."

"Practical woman." He offered his arm. "Shall we?"

Lisette took his elbow and walked beside him toward the last place she'd ever wanted to go.

CHAPTER 32
DEVIOUS MIND

After having purchased two tickets, Lisette and the Black Fox joined the group just starting the guided tour of Lord Hanley's residence. Lisette was still outraged at the amount of money that had changed hands. She hung onto that feeling to ward off panic as they walked through the small side gate. "People really pay that much to walk through someone else's house?"

His voice was amused. "They do. And sometimes more."

Coin might buy them all entrance to the house, but not through the front door. Their group shuffled along the side path to the kitchen entrance, while their guide gestured at the stunted rosemary plants and talked about the kitchen herb garden.

In the freeholder quarter, all the buildings shared walls, with only the streets to break them up, so the only growing space was on the roofs and windows. Here, having plants in the ground was a sign of wealth, but with all the tall houses shading each other, not much would grow.

The two women in the kitchen didn't look up from their

work as the group of ten went through. Then the tour members were in a gloomy hallway that smelled of furniture oil and dry rot. Here it felt like the entire house pressed down on them. Lisette's panic bubbled up. She dug her fingernails into her palms.

Her companion spoke in her ear. "The other end of this hallway goes down, probably to the cellar, and there will be at least one way out there. Then there's the kitchen, which has doors and windows low enough to jump from. And from the way the air is flowing, there's at least one chimney around here that you could climb out through."

He was giving her the gift of exits. A thief would know these things. Her panic receded, and she looked at the doors they were passing, mostly entrances to tiny linen closets and other storage areas.

They were here for a reason. She tried to focus on that. "What am I supposed to be looking for?"

"A way to get past the wards upstairs," he whispered back. "You'll know what I'm talking about when you see it."

Lisette stared at him. "I don't know anything about magic."

"Of course not. I can take care of that part. But you have a devious mind and you look at things differently. That's what I need." He moved forward to follow the tour, leaving her gaping at his back in astonishment.

A devious mind? Part of her knew she ought to be offended, but in reality, he had offered her the one piece of flattery that sailed past all her defenses. Rebuilding watches and other mechanicals often felt like a battle against the forces keeping them from working. Understanding their weak points and finding ways to fix them was a delicate game, with rules that constantly shifted. Lisette lived for those moments.

The fact that this thief understood that, and wielded that knowledge so easily, made him dangerous in ways she hadn't considered.

But right now they were in the depths of Lord Hanley's residence, and she needed to keep her wits about her and learn what she could. She moved forward with the group and shielded her eyes when they turned a corner and came upon the brilliance of the receiving room.

This was the first area actually intended for visitors. If Lisette hadn't seen the duke's ballroom earlier in the week, she would have been even more amazed. The room radiated light, as if it were midday. It took her a few seconds to pick out the spots of magic illuminating the room.

So. Either the city's magic wasn't low enough to warrant conservation everywhere, or the magic powering Lord Hanley's estate had a source other than Aarat. That was interesting.

Even without the magic, the room would still be impressive. Marble floors gleamed beneath her feet, velvet draperies muffled the echoes, and a waterfall built into the corner provided a pleasant source of noise. Padded benches set up in clusters for three or four people were scattered around the room. Crowds of murmuring people provided their own privacy, but in this room, two people speaking quietly wouldn't be overheard. At least not by mundane means.

A warmth in her chest warned her the dragon's magic was reacting to something more subtle than the illusion that had lured Tiffany away. She caught up to the Black Fox and took his elbow, trying to make it look like they were just another couple spending the evening touring fabulous estates. "Can you tell what the spell in this room does?"

"Two parts." He had a pleasant smile on the part of his face she could see below the mask, but his words were flat. "One to inspire trust and affection toward the person control-ling it, and the other to decrease critical thinking." He put his free hand over hers. "Had your suitor convinced you to come here, he would have talked you into more than you intended." He cocked his head. "Or maybe not. The magic does seem to be having a very hard time getting its hooks into you."

When Lord Hanley had been bothering her, she hadn't had the dragon's magic for protection. Lisette again thanked the stubbornness that had kept her from agreeing to go anywhere with Lord Hanley, not even just to keep the peace between them.

Lord Hanley's family had made their reputation as diplomats, setting up treaties and convincing warring parties to come to agreements. When he had been both-ering her in her shop, she had assumed the current Lord Hanley just hadn't inherited the family skill. Now she reconsidered. Maybe the problem hadn't been the person. Maybe it had been the place.

The tour moved along to the formal dining area, with seven large tables and seats for at least one hundred. Servants rushed about, unfolding freshly laundered table-cloths, and placing gold-rimmed dishes in front of each chair. The parties of the Festival of Secrets continued, even after the blow to the duke's magic.

As they passed through one public area after another, the warmth in Lisette's chest remained. Magic bombarded them. The other people on the tour looked about, wide-eyed, their comments reflecting their awe. She wondered if the servants noticed their feelings change as they went back and forth between the public and private areas of the house. Maybe the ones who did found posts somewhere else.

The tour group ascended the grand staircase, moving toward the more intimate rooms of the house. Their guide pointed out the carvings by artisans brought from the Island of Light. Lisette stopped listening as they got closer to the top.

The Black Fox had said she would know what he needed her help with when they went upstairs. Now she saw what he meant.

The landing at the top of the staircase opened into three hallways. The middle hallway had something magical moving around in it. At first Lisette thought it was some kind of animal, perhaps a large dog, prowling in the confined space of the hall. But the longer she looked, trusting the fox to guide them forward while her attention was elsewhere, the more she recognized the movement as mechanical — a slight unbalancing of one limb, a sense of a ratchet slipping. An automaton, even one that large, could be powered by magic. But the artistry required to make such a thing...

Their guide drew them into the left passage. Still thinking about the mechanical creature in the middle hallway, Lisette absently peeked into the family bedrooms, noting the heavy furniture from a different era.

Would a mistress from a freehold background be kept in these rooms? Or was there some other suite in the floors above them, more suitable for hiding a lover not of noble mien? Both options made her skin crawl.

Lord Hanley was the only remaining member of the direct line — the family's fortunes had been in decline for the past few generations until the current lord inherited. Now, at least their finances had rebounded. But not even knowing the fate she had escaped could distract Lisette from thinking about the automaton.

Their group reached the termination of the hallway and the end of their guide's speech about the previous lords whose portraits they had passed, all of them with familiar features and smile of the current title holder. Heading back toward the stairwell, he began talking about the rugs they were walking upon, which had been brought at great cost from across the Grey Desert. Lisette tuned him out again.

Nobody living in Harbor Crag could create such a thing. Possibly nobody currently living anywhere in the world could do so. How long had it been prowling in that corridor? More importantly, how long had it been since any kind of maintenance had been performed?

Lisette's fingers itched to take the thing apart, to study its inner workings and learn how it produced a stride so smooth without living flesh. Of course, the Black Fox would want some way to destroy it, but if she could just disable the thing and spirit it away...

The thief pulled her to a halt, and she came back to herself. She had nearly run into the person in front of her while lost in thought. They had all stopped just before the landing, their guide clearly waiting for something.

Or someone.

Her heart raced. Even before she could see who it was, Lisette knew. Lord Hanley approached.

CHAPTER 33
BRALINOST

L isette's hands and feet went numb as she saw the artfully tousled curls of Lord Hanley appear before them. The rest of him was hidden by the traditional masquerade headdress of the woman in front of her. Lisette had never been so happy about such a ridiculous and inconvenient fashion. If she couldn't see Lord Hanley, he couldn't see her either.

But if Lord Hanley went into the middle hall, remaining at the back of the group would lose Lisette her only chance to see how the automaton reacted to him.

"I need to get closer," she whispered. She couldn't tell how much pressure she used in gripping the thief's arm, couldn't feel the fingers he laid over hers. He guided them through a gap, murmuring apologies.

And there was Lord Hanley, his attention on someone coming up the stairs. Even for a noble, he was attractive, with none of the signs attributable to excessive drinking or other forms of dissipation. His hair and dress might have indicated a lack of seriousness in another man, but everyone in the city knew he had the duke's ear and used that influence regularly.

The fox gave a low hum, as if he were fascinated by something unexpected. "Do you know," he murmured into her ear, "how much power it takes to change a child's features as they are growing?"

Startled, Lisette glanced up at him. He nodded. "They did a very good job, but there are still signs. He's no more related to the people in those portraits than I am."

Lisette looked back at Lord Hanley, forcing herself to really look at him instead of letting her thoughts run in circles about finding new places to hide. In his own home, with the evening guests not yet arrived, he hadn't felt the need to wear a mask, so she didn't even need to rely on her memory. His features looked exactly like all the other portraits in the hall. She shook her head. "I'll have to take your word for it."

Another man, a young noble Lisette didn't recognize, made his way to the landing, breathing heavily from exertion. His gaze traveled over the waiting tour group as if they weren't there. "I don't see why you had to drag me upstairs for this."

Lord Hanley smiled easily and took his arm. "Because I found something I know you will want to see, and I'm not about to show the rest of the house."

As the two men came closer, the automaton paced along the edge of the hallway, reminding Lisette of a guard dog at the end of its chain. She couldn't see what kept it from moving beyond that spot. Both men offered their hand to the thing. Something extended from its back and it *bit* them.

The bite was quick and small, but the unknown man clamped his finger with his other hand, then checked it

before rubbing at it. Remembering the catastrophic consequences of smearing fresh blood on the dagger, Lisette
thought someone would have to be naïve or in great need
to allow blood to be taken like that.

The automaton moved to the side, and the men passed
it. Lord Hanley led the way to a room near the middle of the
hall and opened the door.

The ember of dragon fire in Lisette's chest warmed. But
after a moment she realized this wasn't a reaction to magic
being used on her — this was the feeling of kinship she'd
felt when she'd been in the duke's chambers, trying to
figure out which item on the shelves was the Dagger of
Aarat. Except this was somehow different.

Then the two men went into the room, and Lord Hanley
firmly shut the door behind them.

Lisette breathed a sigh of relief.

The tour group erupted into exclamations and
murmurs, as if the lord of the house had put a spell of
silence on them that had fallen away with his departure.
Maybe he had.

The woman with the big headdress moved across the
landing. "What *is* that thing?" She stared at the automaton
which had ceased its renewed prowling and moved to the
edge of the hallway as she had moved closer.

Panic cut through their guide's bored expression. He
reached out to grab the woman, stopped with his hands an
inch away, and closed his fingers into fists. "If you could
just move away..." The instant she had retreated toward the
group, he interposed his body between the group and the
automaton. "This area is guarded by the creature, Bralinost.
Brought to the house by the fifth Lord Hanley over three
hundred years ago, it has faithfully served the lords of the
house. Anyone entering the hallway uninvited is killed

immediately." His words had taken on the singsong tone of a recited script again, and now he gave a half smile. "I'm sure you all understand why we won't be going into that part of the house."

The other people in the group chuckled. Lisette was torn. The watchmaker within wanted to see Bralinost in action, to observe all the different protections its creators had designed. The more rational part of her pointed out that if she ever did see Bralinost in that mode, its most likely target would be Lisette herself.

The third wing was full of smaller bedrooms for visitors, and Lisette followed along behind the no-longer-rattled tour guide as he listed the names of famous people who had stayed there. These bedrooms showed signs of having been redecorated recently, evidence of the upturn in the fortunes of Lord Hanley.

That was the last part of the house included in the tour. Lisette assumed there was at least one floor above them for the servants who lived in. She'd counted at least five floors from the outside. The others had either been designed for storage, or the house had originally held more people. Lisette didn't particularly care. She just wanted to leave.

After one last look at Bralinost, now back to pacing the hallway, Lisette followed the others down the stairs. When they moved into the servants' hallway, where the magic fell away, she saw a few people make restless gestures, repinning shawls on shoulders or pulling at perfectly straight cuffs. One woman whispered to her companion that the hallway felt haunted.

Then they were whisked through the kitchen, down the garden path, and deposited outside the gate where their guide immediately collected coins from a new group of waiting tour-goers.

Still in the group of people they'd just toured the house with, the Black Fox pulled out his pocket watch. "If we hurry, we still have time to get the last showing at Lady Merou's house." Lisette noted absently that the watch was brass, in good condition, and was a style that had been popular fifty years earlier. A father or grandfather's time-piece? Or deliberately purchased to appear so? She had no idea.

Nobody in the group seemed interested in following them, so she assumed Lady Merou's house wasn't a great favorite. Matching her stride to his, Lisette waited until they were away from the rest.

"You're planning on breaking into that room." The one Lord Hanley and his companion had gone into, she meant, but the thief would know that.

He nodded as he walked. "There's a book I suspect is in there. I'm hoping you might have some ideas on how I can get by the guardian."

Lisette had no idea how to get past Bralinost, but some-thing would come to her. "I'll think about it." She consid-ered Lord Hanley and the magic he was using to sway opinions, and the likely source of that magic.

Before she could change her mind, she added, "And I need to go with you."

CHAPTER 34
TERRIBLE ART

A startled laugh was the thief's only response to Lisette's declaration that she needed to go along during the break-in. They continued to walk at a brisk clip toward Lady Merou's house.

Lisette waited three steps. "If you don't take me with you, I'll have to break in on my own. It just seems like it would be easier if we weren't tripping over each other this time."

The corner of his mouth lifted. "Why? Before we went inside, I got the feeling there was nothing that could induce you to go back. What changed?"

Lisette took a breath, then paused. This man had no need for coins, but she suspected information was a different lure. "I'll tell you, but only if you come with me to look at something this evening." She glanced over at him, trying to see what effect her words had. "I have a problem I think is caused by magic, and I need some advice."

He raised one eyebrow. "And you think I'm the best person for the job."

Lisette grimaced. "You're the only person I could think of who wouldn't immediately run back to the duke."

His laughter added to the noise on the street. "A finely crafted blow to my ego. Very well. I accept. You tell me what changed during the tour, and I promise to give you advice on your problem." He guided them around the corner onto a narrower street with increased foot traffic but no carriages.

Lisette considered how to convey her information. She wished she knew more about magic. Would just saying the word *dragon* attract listeners? She'd already used the word once this evening. Better not to chance it. "You know the area you helped me enter the other night?" Had that really been last night? So much had happened, it seemed like longer.

"I do indeed. And I want you to note I've been the perfect gentleman in not trying to worm the details from you."

If information really was his currency, it probably *had* taken a fair amount of willpower not to pepper her with questions. "I only know one of the..." She searched for the right word for Aarat. "... denizens who lives within."

From the stillness of his face, she knew he understood her meaning.

Lisette continued. "In Lord Hanley's house, when the door was opened during the tour... I think there is something inside that belongs to... Not the one I know, but another one."

"A different denizen."

Lisette nodded. "Yes. And I think it's possible that whatever is there is being used to power Lord Hanley's spells." That part was a leap in logic, but she thought it made sense. Where else would Lord Hanley be getting the power he needed to light his rooms and impress people touring the house? "I'd like to take that away from him."

What Lord Hanley was doing to people, affecting their free will with his spells of charm and recklessness, was a wrong that needed to be stopped. That was a good enough reason to cut any bonds he had formed with a dragon.

But truthfully, Lisette wanted to *destroy* the man, to get some revenge for the way he had tried to steal her life. He had endangered everyone she knew, had forced her to close her business and flee the city for half a year. All because he'd seen her one day and decided he needed to own her.

The Black Fox didn't alter his stride. "I see. Attaining such an item is one thing, but repurposing it..." He gave a wondering laugh. "You already know this. So that *was* you that... But..." He groaned. "I would *really* like to talk more about this, but for now..." He pulled them to a stop at the end of a line. "Right now we have a tour of a not quite as impressive estate to attend."

Lisette smiled at his uncharacteristically jumbled words. "And is there anything in particular you wanted my opinion on here? Or is this another case where I'll know it when I see it?"

"Ah, that will be a surprise to me as well. I haven't been here before."

"So, just a little window shopping?"

He grinned. "Indeed. I have my doubts that I'll see anything here, but you never know. Besides, I wanted to make sure we did something suitably boring after the previous tour. In case anyone followed."

Lisette slowly turned to scan the street around them. "And did someone follow?"

"Not that I noticed, but..." He made a broad gesture

with his free hand. "It would be hard to lose someone without it looking like we were *trying* to lose them."

Which would be suspicious, Lisette understood. They both turned to face forward in the line. "But why would anyone be following in the first place?"

"Because I've stayed in one place rather longer than I really should. They may not know exactly what I look like, but they would be fools not to be watching for someone of my approximate height and build." He placed coins in the palm of the guide who was ushering them through the gate and leaned over to speak in her ear. "And thus we tour the estate of a woman who, by all accounts, has nothing to steal. So this is purely for enjoyment."

NEARLY AN HOUR LATER, they were back on the street, which had grown more crowded and noisy in their absence.

"That was..." Lisette tried to think of the right words to describe it, but came up blank.

"Indeed, it was." He took her arm, and they began walking toward the main thoroughfare.

Lady Merou's house itself might have been lovely had it not been crammed full of furniture and objects acquired on travels. The furniture, threadbare and damaged from long use, hadn't been particularly notable when new. Now it was unlikely to be useful for anything other than a bonfire.

As far as the art and other items taking up every available space, it looked like the sort of thing Lisette had seen being sold on the wharfs to travelers just off ships — they were the only ones gullible enough to buy it. She'd even seen an identical replica of the amphora Barlow had found.

"Do you suppose an affinity for terrible art is inherited?" Lisette didn't see how that much junk could be accumulated during one lifetime. It had to be a family project, carried out over generations.

"Until today, I hadn't thought so, but I admit — I'm revisiting my assumptions now. I might view it as a professional challenge to find anything worth stealing in that house." He shook his head. "Where to now? You said there was something you wanted my opinion on?"

"Yes." As they strolled uphill, Lisette explained what had happened to the children overnight, and then what had happened when she and Tiffany had gone into the tunnels together.

A trio of musicians had staked out a corner and drawn enough of an audience to block traffic. The fiddler had difficulty keeping in tune, though Lisette didn't know if that was due to lack of talent or some problem in the instrument caused by the damp night air. That didn't matter, though, as the chief attraction seemed to be the lyrics. A masked woman threaded through the crowd, shaking a tambourine in time and holding out a hat for people to throw coins into.

The listeners who stayed were laughing and singing along. Other people passing by listened for a bit, then sped up and hurried away.

Lisette and the thief paused on the edge of the crowd.

The singer, a handsome man with flaxen hair, waved his hands to encourage people to sing along as he reached the chorus. "Oh, the taxes are risin'/and the wine barrels dryin'/There's no stew left to thicken/but the duke paints a chicken."

At the last word of the chorus, Lisette grabbed the thief's arm. "We need to get away from here." They hastened up the hill, skirting around the people who had stopped to listen, while the singer clucked a bridge to the next verse. From the size of the crowd, the musicians had been there long enough for the guard to have heard about it. Lisette and her thief needed to get as far away as they could.

The thief kept pace with her. "The other night you said nobody in the city knew..."

"They didn't." Seeing guards running down the hill toward them, Lisette dragged her companion into a smaller connecting street and increased her pace to a run.

She could still hear laughter and the fiddle, which meant they weren't far enough away for safety. If they could make it across to the next road going uphill before the guard extended that far, they could get away.

"Well, *I* certainly didn't tell anyone." He steadied her when she tripped on the edge of a pothole.

"Neither did I. But..." Lisette skidded to a halt, seeing a line of guards advancing down the connecting street ahead of them. "But I think I may be responsible anyhow."

The guards had made a cordon around the area. Lisette and the Black Fox were trapped.

CHAPTER 35
NAMES

L isette stood in the alley and worked on catching her breath. "It would be good if we didn't get caught up in this." Just being in the same area where people were singing a song arguably critical of the duke would be a problem. A song poking fun at his obsession with painting chickens would guarantee years of hard labor at sea.

The Black Fox stood next to her, turning his head to look at both entrances to the smaller street they were on. "I agree." He looked up at the buildings, then drew her toward the entrance of a dark bakery. When he touched the handle, magic sparked. He opened the door and waved her through.

Inside, tables and chairs had been stacked near the front window. Beyond them, a counter and now-empty loaf racks were just visible in the gloom. Lisette inhaled air with the slightly sour tang of fermenting yeast. "The bakers will be here in a few hours."

"The guards will be done arresting everyone or whatever they're going to do long before then. Most of the crowd will run downhill, not up." The thief pulled two chairs off the stack and put them down where they could sit and watch the street through the front window. "And this should give you enough time to tell me why the city is suddenly awash in chickens." He waved her into a chair, but moved behind the counter instead of sitting.

Lisette watched him checking the loaf racks. "If you're looking for yesterday's bread, it's probably in a sack under the counter." At least, that was where Tiffany's baker kept his. Most customers wouldn't be looking for stale bread. But poorer clients, or those who needed it for another recipe, would come in search of a discount.

The thief pivoted and rummaged under the counter. "Aha, here we are." He withdrew a long, thin loaf. Metal clinked against the counter. He had left payment for what he had taken.

How much did she trust this man? He wasn't from Harbor Crag. If someone had paid him to steal magical items, would he inform his masters the city could no longer protect itself?

He sat down next to her, handed her half the loaf, then slipped off his mask and settled back to look out the window.

Lisette looked at him, seeing his face clearly for the first time. Without the mask, she could see the little lines at the corners of his eyes. He looked... vulnerable. And weary. But also like someone who smiled often. He glanced over and caught her looking.

Lisette felt her face heating. "What should I call you?"

"My mother calls me Remy when she isn't angry at me. You might use that."

The way he put it made her smile. "And is she angry at you often?"

"Not so much these days. And what shall I call you?"

"Lisette." There was no point in lying. He already knew

she was a freeholder. If he asked around in the quarter about who Lord Hanley had bothered, it would take him twenty seconds to find out who she was.

Only after she had spoken did she remember what had happened when she'd given her name to Aarat. "Is it safe to give a name to a mage?"

"As safe as telling anything else." He bit off a hunk of bread and chewed while he looked out on the street.

Lisette looked at him for a moment more, then slipped off her own mask. "When I took..." She stopped. "What is it safe to say? The... denizen I spoke about earlier said the duke might be listening, and I assumed that was by magic."

The Black Fox... no, his name was Remy, she told herself. Remy reached under his tunic and pulled out a leather cord threaded through a group of silver charms. He held up one of them. "This should keep anyone from overhearing by magical means. And there aren't any people around to worry about someone listening in person." He dropped the cord back under his tunic.

Lisette nodded and started again. "When I took the dagger to the dragon, he said the bonds with the duke would take many years to fade. But then I touched the blade. And I had blood on my hand." When he looked over in alarm, she gestured at the cut on her face. "It was an accident." An accident, but also ignorance on her part — she hadn't known there was a link between blood and magic.

He almost touched her cheek, but let his hand drop. When he spoke, his voice was little more than a whisper. "You're not... How did you survive?"

Lisette remembered the power of the broken bonds tearing through her, remembered hoping for the release of death. "I nearly didn't. But the dragon..." She rubbed her sternum. "There's a bit of the dragon inside me, from when I agreed to get the dagger. And I had given him my name."

Remy's eyes widened. "You gave a *dragon* your name."

Lisette shrugged, suddenly feeling the unfairness of it all. "Yes. He told me what a stupid thing I had done right afterward, but how was I supposed to know? It's not like I ever set out to meet a dragon." An intense longing to be in the familiar, logical order of her workspace gripped her, and then passed.

Remy nodded his head, but from the look on his face, he was putting all the pieces together. "So you bled on the dagger and that moved the bonds to you. And suddenly the duke didn't have enough power to keep his hobby a secret anymore." He took another bite of bread.

Lisette nodded. "Except the bonds didn't come to me. Or... I don't know. Maybe they did for a bit, but then the dragon took all the power back." She thought of how his color had changed. "He looked different, afterward. I thought maybe he would be free, but the chain was still there."

Remy froze, mid-chew. "Chain?"

Lisette nodded. She described the chain and shackle, and the blistered flesh where it touched the dragon. "I didn't know dragons were chained. I thought they just stayed and protected the city because it was where they lived."

"They're *all* chained?" Remy still sat next to her, bread held in one hand, but she could feel the tenseness in his muscles.

"I don't know. I haven't seen any of the others." She'd been avoiding them, unwilling to chance being turned into a torch before she could get a word out. "I've never seen any of the dragons outside the warrens, though, so I think they probably are."

"That's *monstrous*."

Lisette didn't disagree. "That's partly why I need to get whatever it is I felt out of Lord Hanley's house. I think my dragon will free himself eventually, now that his power is no longer being siphoned." She almost laughed at the idea of calling Aarat *her dragon*, but Remy would know what she meant. "But the other dragons..."

Remy sat in silence for a moment. Lisette wanted to ask him questions, but he was clearly thinking about something, so she took a bite of the bread instead. Seasoned with rosemary and salt, it was a little stale but still flavorful. Outside, the yelling had died down. Two women walked quickly by the bakery, glancing over their shoulders.

Remy turned to look at her. "Your dragon must like you."

A startled laugh escaped her. "I sit here pretending I'm not dying for answers, and *that's* your great thought?"

He grinned. "I'm not really one for great thoughts."

"I see that. And I'm not sure my dragon likes me as much as he is very bored and I'm a new toy."

"You keep surprising *me*, so I can see why your dragon might find you intriguing as well."

Incorrigible flirt, Lisette reminded herself. He likely complimented every person he met. "He probably just wasn't very hungry when I met him. And then we had a bargain." She paused. "Have you ever talked to a dragon?"

Remy shook his head. "There weren't any dragons in the city where I grew up. And then later, when I began traveling, I knew how dangerous they were." He glanced at her with a smile. "I am occasionally a little reckless, but not usually suicidal."

Lisette thought about how she'd first met Aarat. "You just need to be desperate and unlucky. I ran through the dragon warrens to get away from the guard and more or less fell on top of him."

"Inspired, but not nearly as romantic as meeting another thief in the tower."

Lisette blew out a breath. "And I can't seem to get rid of either of you."

He laughed softly. "I'm just flattered to be in the same category as a dragon." He sobered. "But I'm not like that miscreant whose house we visited today. If you want me to go, you only have to say the word."

Lisette *didn't* want him to go. That was a problem all on its own. How could it ever work out? Lord Hanley would target him if she showed interest; on the other side, if she invited him into her life and he was unmasked as the Black Fox, that would put her friends in danger.

But tonight she had a reason for not sending him away. That would have to be enough for now. "You're not getting away that easily. I need you to look at the tunnels, and then we have some things to steal."

Remy replaced his mask, stood, and put his chair back on the stack. "Then, by all means, let us go look at the tunnels."

CHAPTER 36
AIM FOR THE KNEES

They arrived at the entrance to the tunnels without any difficulty. As Remy had suspected, most of the music lovers had fled downhill, not up, so the path to the freeholder quarter remained clear. A crowd of people blocked the street closer to the water, but other than that, it seemed to be a fairly normal festival night.

Lisette lit the lamps she and Tiffany had left behind and led the way. "I might make a few wrong turns," she warned Remy as she came to a fork in the tunnel, "but there's not really any way to get lost down here."

"Understood. I promise not to cry out for someone to save us." Remy seemed fascinated by the walls, running his fingers along the irregular stone. "These tunnels were *made*, not formed naturally. It's entirely the wrong type of rock."

Lisette had started to suspect that. "They were already here by the time the freeholders began building." The light coming from behind her dimmed. She stopped and turned to find him crouched, hand splayed against indentations in the wall.

He glanced up. "Sorry. I just..." He shook his head and

stood up. "You let your children play in dragon tunnels. I don't know whether that's amazing or foolish."

Lisette waited for him to catch up with her. "If dragons *were* here, they've been gone a long time. And the tunnels are safer than the roads." She turned down a branch and found the candle stub Turtle had dropped. "At least, they were until last night. It started at about the same time I broke the bonds on the dagger, so I think it must somehow be related."

They moved into the long tunnel with the striations in the walls, and Lisette led him to the large domed cavern, where the broken chairs waited.

Once again, Lisette saw a flash of purple light and the ember in her chest warmed briefly. She watched Remy. Would his ability with magic protect him from the thing trying to lure them away?

His eyes tracked the thing Lisette could no longer see, and he took two steps forward. Then he stopped, and did a full body shake, as if he were a cat who had been doused with water. "That's a nice bit of work."

"You're not going to run after it, are you? Because I thought I was going to have to knock down my friend to stop her, and I'm not sure how far I'd get if I tried to do that to you."

"Aim for the knees," he said absently as he looked at the other entrance to the cavern. "That works on everyone." Then he turned back to her. "No, I should be fine now. I let it grab me a little more than I normally would, just to get a feel for it. It's definitely a spell, not a ghost. "

The confirmation didn't come as a surprise, but it still made her feel better. Lisette gestured to the niches carved into the walls. "I spent who knows how many hours down here growing up, and I never saw those before this morning. But they don't look new."

Remy turned in a full circle as he looked at the cavern. "I think there are two sets of spells here. Maybe three? One is meant to lead people away, just like it did with the children and your friend. It's a rather benign spell of protection, only triggered when someone looks at that book." At her questioning look, he elaborated. "It could just as easily have killed anyone who walked past the threshold. It has enough power."

Lisette considered a world without Turtle and Pot, and swallowed. "I guess I should be thankful."

He tipped his head in acknowledgement. "I think the second is a spell of hiding. There are just a few wisps of it left. I assume that's why you never noticed what was in here until yesterday."

"And the third?" Lisette needed to know what else the children might be threatened by.

Remy took a breath and closed his eyes. Lisette waited and watched him, letting herself note his delicate fingers, and the way one lock of hair refused to lie in the same direction as its neighbors. They had put their masks back on before they left the bakery, but now she knew the lines in his brow that showed up when he concentrated.

In the distance, she could hear the faint sound of a heavy cart on cobblestones. These tunnels had so many entrances. It would be impossible to keep everyone out. Lisette had to find some way to make it safe.

Finally, Remy shook his head and opened his eyes. "I think there must be another spell of hiding, but it's so subtle I'm not even sure of that. And I don't think it's in this chamber."

Lisette forced her thoughts back to practicality. "So the

second spell hiding everything made it so the first spell leading people away was never set off?" At his nod, she continued. "If the spell hiding everything disappeared when I broke the bonds, that means the duke was the one who created it, right? But why would he do that?" She gestured above them. "This is the freeholder quarter. It's the last place the duke would leave something."

"It wasn't this duke." Remy walked over and started examining the wall under the book as he talked. "That spell was at least one hundred years old, possibly a lot more than that." He curled his fingers and tested a handhold. "How much does the current duke do in public?" He boosted himself up. Another handhold, and then he was splayed on the wall, reaching for the next protuberance.

Lisette watched the muscles in his arms and imagined how he might look without the tunic. "In public? He rides in a few parades every year. I assume he does more than that, but we don't have the same circle of friends, so I wouldn't know. Why do you ask?"

Remy leapt for another handhold, missed, and landed on his feet on the floor. He shook out his hands and started climbing from another spot a few feet away. "Let me try a different question. When you were in the private wing of the palace, did that strike you as the home of the most powerful political figure in the city?"

Thinking of all the chicken paintings, Lisette failed to prevent her laugh from escaping.

Remy blew out a breath of laughter in reply. "That's the problem with hereditary rule. There's always someone who looks at the next generation and thinks '*Now* what do we do?' So you protect what you can and hope they have good advisors." He paused in his climbing. "They almost never have good advisors."

Lisette thought about that for a moment while she watched him work his way up the wall. "So some duke in the past knew this was here, but decided to hide it from his son?"

"Or his son's advisor, or maybe even an advisor of his own that he didn't trust and couldn't get rid of. I'm assuming someone else knew, and the plan was to recover it when conditions were better, but either conditions didn't get better or the message was lost." The last word cut off as he missed a handhold and slid to the floor again.

Lisette stopped him before he could start over. "As much as I'm enjoying watching this, if I stand on the chair and you stand on my shoulders, I think you'll be at the height you need."

Hands on the wall, Remy looked at her over his shoulder. "That might work." He turned and helped her drag the sturdier of the two chairs over to the wall. "I'd offer to switch positions, but I need to get up there to see if I can disarm this spell."

Lisette climbed onto the seat of the chair. "A few more bruises won't kill me."

Remy stepped up behind her. The chair wobbled. "I fear the same can't be said of this chair." His breath was warm against her ear. Then he was standing on the back of the chair, hands on the stone wall above her.

The chair creaked.

"Tell me if this is too much." He stepped onto her shoulders.

For a moment Lisette thought her legs might buckle, but she locked her knees and that fear disappeared. Then it was just a matter of the pain in her shoulders. "Next time I want better padding."

"Next time we should find a ladder," he replied, far

above her head. "I'm going to attempt to disarm this. Give me a moment."

Lisette gritted her teeth and stood still.

Above her, she heard Remy talking to himself. "There. And then... No, I guess not. But you there... Aha! And then..."

Despite the pain in her shoulders, Lisette found the whole thing charming. Listening to him tease out the spell reminded her of being in her workshop, figuring out why something wasn't moving properly. She leaned her forehead against the wall and resigned herself to a long wait.

Except the wall was shifting. Or rather...

"Remy."

"Just a second. I've almost got it."

"Remy, the chair —"

One side of the chair collapsed. Lisette's feet went one way and her head the other. Remy yelped.

Purple light burst through the cavern.

CHAPTER 37
HIGHLIGHTED
WITH GOLD

The cavern glittered with reflected purple light.

As the magic flared, Lisette fell onto the ruins of the chair, with Remy landing half on top of her. The spot of dragon fire in her chest woke again. Or maybe she'd broken a rib in the fall. Lisette struggled to get up. Something froze her muscles.

Then the purple light disappeared, and they were left with the glow from just the two small lanterns. Lisette found she could move again, though she was almost afraid to do so. "Remy?"

"Oof."

"You should consider poetry if this thing you do doesn't work out." Lisette decided she hadn't broken anything in the fall. The squashed chair dug into her hip. "Are you hurt?"

"Just a little singed. You?"

"I did say that a few bruises wouldn't kill me."

Remy groaned and rolled off her and the wreckage of the chair, flopping onto his back on the stone floor. "In hindsight, a ladder might have been a better idea. But the good news is that it's done."

Lisette levered herself off the floor and stood up. The weakness caused by the spell dissipated as she moved around.

The book that had been in the niche lay on the floor, undamaged. The spell of hiding might be gone, but the book still radiated magic. Holding her hands behind her, Lisette leaned over to look at the cover. An image of a dragon in mid-flight had been stamped into the leather and highlighted with gold, but there was nothing else to indicate the contents.

She stood up straight again. "If someone went to all this trouble to hide this, it's probably dangerous." Then she looked at the other things still in their niches. "All of this."

Remy climbed to his feet, staggered two steps, then stood, swaying a little. "If this is your polite way of saying we can't just leave this all here, I agree."

"I could take it to the dragon warrens..." Surely Aarat wouldn't leverage another favor to store these things. Unlike the duke's ring, these looked like curiosities he would want.

"Except you can't get past the guard at the moment." Remy shook out his arms and then stretched. "I'd offer to provide a distraction, but I'm not going to be able to help for a while." He looked at the book and huffed a laugh. "This is why my masters always told me to center myself before attempting anything tricky. But I would wager none of them ever had to perform acrobatics at the same time."

He dragged the remaining chair to the area under the delicate metal vane. It still spun, even faster than it had when they had first entered the cavern. "At least everything else isn't quite so high up. I think I can reach them all without abusing your shoulders again." The chair wobbled when he stepped on it. "I *am* a little disappointed in the freeholder chair building talents."

Lisette held the back of the chair to stabilize it. "This is probably the only furniture the kids could take without someone noticing. And they're a lot lighter than we are."

Remy lifted the vane out of its niche and jumped to the floor. He offered it to her. "Don't think I haven't seen you looking at this."

Lisette took it, surprised by how weightless it seemed. She held it closer to her face. Dials set in the base moved back and forth, their archaic numbering difficult to read. "What is it?"

"No idea." Remy grinned at her. "That just makes it more exciting, doesn't it?" He pulled the chair under the next niche.

Lisette carefully put the vane down on the floor, far enough away that nobody could fall on it, and went to stabilize the chair again. This time, he brought down a silver tiara, delicate vines twisting around to hold a raised claw in the front. Magic pulsed from this piece as well.

She followed him to the next alcove. "Do you have a plan on what to do with these? I mean, this evening. I can't get them to the dragon, and you can't very well carry these across the city to... wherever you're staying." Remy hadn't even brought his satchel with him. Someone walking around with magic this strong would be noticed.

"Well, no, but I figure you must know someplace in the freeholder quarter we could stash them for a bit. Just not here. Your story of ghosts and bright lights luring children away will eventually reach the wrong ears. It's just a matter of time."

Lisette watched him lift down a set of bracers that

looked a lot like what she'd used to climb the tower. There was only one place in the quarter she could be sure nobody else would disturb. "I can keep them in my shop, but anyone looking for magic is going to be able to feel them."

At the next niche, Remy took down a dagger. Lisette expected to feel a tug from the dragon fire within her, but it was quiet. Either this dagger wasn't connected to a dragon, or that dragon was no longer alive.

Remy moved the chair under the final niche. "I think I can convince them all to be... less enthusiastic. At least for the next few days. That will give us a chance to look them over and decide what to do with them."

Lisette froze as he climbed up again. Had he just implied he would be spending the next few days in her shop?

The chair wobbled dangerously. She grabbed the back to steady it.

Angry male voices carried into the chamber from the tunnels. The sound was too garbled for Lisette to distinguish the words. She didn't recognize the speakers.

Remy jumped down from the chair with a metal ball in his hand. He began quickly collecting the items from the floor, holding the hem of his tunic to make a pouch. Catching her eye, he nodded at the lanterns.

Lisette blew out one lantern and hooded the other, letting only a thin crack of light escape. After picking up both lanterns and the vane, she stopped. In the near darkness, Remy grabbed the final item, the book with the dragon on the cover.

If they exited the chamber in the wrong direction, they might run straight into the men. Losing pursuit would be nearly impossible — even if she could remember all the different passages, she wouldn't be able to move through them without any light at all. That would be a beacon for anyone following.

No, they would have to wait until the light from the approaching men made it clear where they were coming from. And then hope the strangers were all in one group and hadn't split up to search the tunnels more efficiently.

Lisette waited in the dark, heart pounding. The voices were getting clearer. She caught a few words, but not the rest of the sentence. Something about *cursed freeholders* and someone who had *waited all day before telling* him. Given the venom in the words, Lisette was glad she wasn't the one who had disappointed him.

Then a new voice spoke, and this one she *did* recognize. The cavern ate most of his words, but she picked out *before the duke* and *looking for this.*

Sweat prickled along her spine. Lisette took a carefully controlled breath. *Lord Hanley*, she mouthed to Remy. He nodded acknowledgement.

Surely the men were coming from the same direction Lisette and Remy had traveled. If she led Remy out the other cavern entrance now, they could get away. She moved closer to that opening and froze. The voices were clearer from here.

She and Remy crept across the cavern to the other entrance. Everything in Lisette strained to run now, but she waited until she saw reflected light bouncing around in the opposite tunnel.

With Remy close behind, Lisette fled into the darkness.

CHAPTER 38
GOOD CONNECTIONS

The tunnels closed around Lisette as she and Remy moved silently through the darkness. Behind her, she could hear the echoes change as Lord Hanley and his men arrived in the big cavern.

Lisette ducked into the side tunnel that would take them closer to the community room entrance. At her back, she heard Remy hit his head and stagger. The items collected in his shirt clanked at the jolt. But he stayed on his feet, so Lisette kept going. The tunnels interconnected, though she couldn't remember exactly how; if Lord Hanley had split his group, Lisette still might run into them.

They needed to get back up to the surface.

Two more tunnels brought them to the wall of names. Lisette slipped through the crack into the empty basement of the community room. The magic in the tiara and book made her fingers tingle as Remy passed everything through to her. Then he squeezed through the gap and they picked everything up again.

Lisette took both lanterns with them. The basement had windows just above street level, and there was enough light seeping into the room to see where they were going. But she didn't want to take the chance of Lord Hanley finding the lanterns before they cooled off. The less this looked like the freeholders were involved, the better.

Out on the street, Lisette kept to the shadows next to the buildings, Remy following closely behind. Not many people were on the streets this late — the festival parties down by the water would last all night, but this high on the hill, there would just be a few small gatherings, and those would end early. After all, it was hard to really celebrate the spirit of the Festival of Secrets when you knew every person around you.

Two cats howled on the roof, three stories above them. As Lisette let them across an intersection, the wind brought the smell of brine from the ocean, and a hint of wood-smoke. Remy moved next to her and threw an arm around her shoulders.

"I've found," he said quietly, slowing their progress, "that people hurrying away from the crime are remembered far more than two people out for an evening stroll after staying late at a party."

Lisette took a deep breath and matched her steps to his. "I don't think I was cut out for this sort of thing." She felt the warmth from his body all along her side, and smelled the vanilla and pepper she associated with him.

"Nonsense." He lengthened his stride to accommodate a particularly large pothole. "I can't think of anyone else I'd rather be doing this with. Smart, able to improvise, and useful as a ladder in a pinch." He was silent for a few steps. "And good connections. You really *might* be the perfect woman."

Lisette turned her head to look at him. "Connections?"

True, some people looked favorably upon the freeholders, but she'd never heard them referred to as connections.

"Of course. Forget your dukes and other nobility. You know a dragon, *and* he likes you. There's no connection better than that."

Lisette scrunched her nose. "I think you might be over-estimating Aarat's regard for me. I'm pretty sure he thinks I'm a minor annoyance who might occasionally be useful."

Remy made a slight choking noise. "I'm sorry. Did you say your dragon's name was *Aarat*?"

"Yes." Lisette considered the truth of that statement as they walked. "Or rather, he told me 'the dagger of Aarat controls the dragon called Aarat'. And then I accidentally broke a bunch of bonds connected to the dagger that were draining his magic. So I'm assuming that's one of his names."

"Wait, are you telling me I had the *dagger of Aarat* in my possession for a day?" Remy's voice, still low, sounded incredulous. "If I'd known... No, it's probably better for everyone that I didn't know. I'd have been sorely tempted to try something, and it would have ended badly." He looked at her with respect. "I'm even more impressed with you now."

Lisette guided them onto the street where her shop waited. "I'm not sure my ignorance is something to be impressed by. I take it you've heard of Aarat."

"He's something of a legend." Remy laughed under his breath. "Nobody has seen him for so long he was presumed dead, or living away from humanity. He shows up in a number of older texts. He's famously short tempered. Most of the illustrations show him breathing fire at someone." He thought about it for a few steps. "But being able to talk to Aarat might almost make it worth it."

Lisette eyed him dubiously. "I've seen him roast a few people. They didn't get a chance to talk first."

"Fair point." Remy switched his gaze to the buildings around them. "So this is you. Very respectable." He huffed a laugh. "A little less ostentatious than I would have expected from someone who is a *friend of Aarat*." That last part was said under his breath. "Sorry. It's going to take me a bit of time to get over that."

"Maybe he has mellowed over the years."

"If he has, he's the exception. Most dragons get larger, more powerful, and even less patient as they get older. I think that's why most of them leave the cities and find their own island as they age."

Lisette thought of the chain holding Aarat in the cavern. Even if the dragon wanted to leave, he couldn't.

At the door to her shop, Lisette set down the lanterns and dug the key out of her belt.

"Ah, a watchmaker. I should have known." Remy read the script on the window. "Allinde. Your family name?"

"Yes." She put the key in the lock and opened the door. Remy followed her inside.

Lisette brushed past him and twisted the lock closed.

Finally. Safe in her home. She breathed in the familiar odors of oil and the cleaning fluid she used to dislodge rust and grime.

Without the noise of the street, it was quiet enough that she could hear her own heart beating. In the dim light, the shop suddenly seemed smaller. More intimate. She kept her voice low. "We should find someplace to put all this stuff."

"We should." He didn't move.

She needed to walk across the room. Make some space

in her workshop. Instead, she stayed where she was. "They'll be done searching the tunnels soon."

"Yes." He swayed toward her.

Lisette leaned forward, breathing in the scent of him. Surely they could afford to take a few minutes to...

Light flooded the room. Lisette jumped back and squinted as Uncle Rye came through the opening connecting their two shops, his lantern held high.

"Who's there?" Rye's face softened as he recognized her. His eyes flicked to Remy. Then he looked almost apologetic — until he caught sight of the items still held in Remy's tunic. "Lisette Allinde, *what* have you got yourself mixed up in?"

CHAPTER 39

TALKING ABOUT DRAGONS

L isette blinked as her eyes adjusted to the light, caught between frustration and laughter. Uncle Rye, in a robe and bare feet, hair rumpled from sleep, still stared at the items held in Remy's tunic.

Remy glanced from Lisette to Rye, apparently decided the other man was not a threat, and went with the practical. "We should, perhaps, move this conversation somewhere that can't be seen from the street. Lord Hanley and his men might be looking for us."

Lisette had shutters lining her bedroom, but not on the display windows below. Rye held back the wall hanging connecting the two shops. "Come along." He raised his voice. "Barlow, we have company."

Lisette followed him through the uncles' shop, past the screen shielding the stock from the customer showcase, and through the maze of crates to the work area. She put the lanterns and spinning vane down on the table and pulled off her mask. "Remy, this is my Uncle Rye."

Remy carefully placed the other items from the cavern down on the table, placing the silver ball inside the curve of

195

the tiara so it wouldn't roll off. He turned to the older man. "Nice to meet you." He gestured at the table. "Give me a moment to shield this all? I don't *think* anyone following us will be looking for excess magic, but I'd hate to be wrong."

Rye's worried face hadn't softened. "Go ahead. There's no point in starting explanations until Barlow and Tiffany get here."

Lisette opened her mouth to protest that Tiffany would be asleep, then stopped. Even if Tiffany had been sleeping, Barlow would be upstairs pitching pebbles across the street at her window to wake her. And there was a strong possibility she'd watched Lisette and Remy go into the shop together. Once Rye had walked in with his lantern, Tiffany would have started getting dressed to come over.

Remy knelt in front of the table. He passed one hand back and forth over the objects, tapping the table on either side. As he worked, Lisette could see a faint strand of magic spooling from his finger, almost like a spider web. With each pass, she could feel less of the magic from the book and tiara.

The bell on the front door clanged. Just as Remy got to his feet, Barlow and Tiffany appeared.

Barlow cocked his head, then looked at Lisette. "So this is your mystery man." Tiffany just looked him over from head to toe.

Lisette cleared her throat, hoping social niceties would derail them. "Remy, this is my Uncle Barlow and my best friend, Tiffany."

Barlow wasn't about to be turned away. "Our Lisette is usually not the secretive sort, so it's a little worrying when she keeps quiet."

"Especially after that business with Lord Hanley," Tiffany added.

Rye gestured at the table. "I just want to know what all this is."

Barlow's eyes widened as he took in the table. "Creatures of the deep, Lisette, what are you doing with *those*?"

Lisette sighed. "If you all would stop talking for a few seconds, I might be able to explain." She glanced at Remy, then stopped and really looked at him. "Do you need to sit down?" He looked pale, and she remembered him saying that he wasn't going to be good for anything after disarming the spell around the book. She took his arm and pushed him into the only chair in the space, then perched on a crate next to him. Glancing up at the others, she added, "It's been a long night." Then she glared at Barlow until he abandoned the joke he'd been about to make and closed his mouth.

"The good news is that the tunnels should be safe for the kids to go in again." Lisette glanced at Remy for confirmation and relaxed when he nodded. "Or they will be as soon as Lord Hanley and his men aren't in them anymore."

Barlow grimaced. Rye let out a long breath. "I thought we'd finally gotten rid of him. But now he's been in the quarter twice this week."

Tiffany caught Lisette's eye. "Are you alright?"

Lisette nodded. Her life had been turned upside-down in the last week, but on the Lord Hanley front she was feeling relatively stable. She nudged Remy's arm with her elbow. "Will your charm protect a conversation from being overheard between this many people?"

"As long as everyone stays in this area, you can talk about dragons to your heart's content."

Rye dropped onto a crate opposite them. "Dragons?" His voice held dread.

Barlow and Tiffany pulled a crate closer and sat down.

The wood creaked. Barlow patted the corner, as if the crate were a protesting horse. "Out with it. Now."

Where to start? With the tunnels this evening? Giving the dagger to Aarat? "I broke into the duke's tower to steal money for the taxes," she finally said. "And when I was running away from the guard, I went through the dragon warrens and fell into a dragon's den."

She'd been expecting to be peppered with questions, but Rye, Barlow, and Tiffany just stared at her in shock. That made things easier.

She told them about the agreement she had made with the dragon to bring the dagger to him, then the second bargain she'd made when she'd brought the duke's ring. That brought a sound suspiciously close to a whimper from Remy.

She continued. "Then I... we... stole the dagger from the duke during the ball, and the next night I took it back to the dragon. And that took back a lot of his magic from the duke. And *that* was when Turtle and Pot were almost trapped in the tunnels. So Remy and I went there tonight, and he got rid of the spell, and then we heard Lord Hanley coming, so we grabbed everything and ran." She looked at Remy. "Does that cover everything?"

He nodded. "A remarkably succinct summary." He huffed a laugh. "Especially the part where I almost killed us both in disarming the spell."

The rest of the group still stared.

Rye recovered first. "What I don't understand," he said, looking at Remy, "is how *you* got involved with all this."

"Ah." Remy rubbed his forehead and seemed to notice for the first time that he still had his mask on. He slipped it off and put it down on the workbench. The move transformed him from a figure of mystery to... Remy. "I ran into

Lisette when we were both trying to steal things from the tower."

"You brought the guards down on me!"

"I apologized for that, didn't I? And I saved you hours of breaking into strongboxes that just held sand."

Rye shook his head. "So you're a thief?"

"Not exactly." Remy looked over at Lisette, as if worried about her reaction. "To be completely truthful, I'm a spy."

CHAPTER 40
A LONGSTANDING TRADITION

The familiar shabbiness of the uncles' stock area suddenly seemed less cozy to Lisette. "A spy?"

It was bad enough that she had accidentally knocked out half the duke's power — the power protecting the city. But she had done it along with an enemy of Harbor Crag? She was an idiot. And a fool.

She'd been falling for this man, and he had been playing with her.

Remy reached for her, then dropped his hand when she stiffened. He cast a wary eye at Rye, Barlow, and Tiffany, who all looked like they were about to improvise weapons from the articles around them. "Can I explain?"

Lisette waited, keeping her eyes dry by force of will.

"Two generations ago, the cities on the coast were roughly equal, and were living in... well, we won't call it peace, but at least the squabbles were small and quickly settled. Then things changed. It started so gradually that nobody really noticed at first, but Harbor Crag seemed to have outstanding luck. Ships didn't fall to creatures in the depths, contracts were more favorable, things like that."

Rye frowned. "But that's just the way of the sea. And good negotiating."

Remy nodded. "It is, yes. But the inequality has only gotten worse. One cargo ship flying the Harbor Crag flag goes down in a big storm about every three years. But unallied firms lose one in five ships in the open waters every summer. It's not the ships themselves. And it's not the crews — the sailors move from ship to ship. It's as if something is luring the sea creatures to the vessels that aren't from this city."

Barlow shook his head. "That's not possible. Nobody could control the creatures of the deep."

Remy shrugged. "Everyone agrees on that. And that's why it took so long to notice. But there were other things. Do you know how much magic this city squanders?" He paused. "Or it *did*. Lisette seems to have cut that down a bit. Though it's still outrageous. Lighting up ballrooms. Creating costumes. Hiding the signs of aging. No other city would dream of using magic for these things. Yet Harbor Crag wastes it on all that and more." He looked over at Lisette again. "So I was sent to find out how it was being done."

Lisette thought about the items he had been stealing. Books, mostly, from what she could tell. That made sense if what he was telling them was true.

Rye was more suspicious. "Sent to find out how, or to stop it?"

"I was sent for knowledge." Remy turned to Rye and lifted his shoulders. "Perhaps Harbor Crag had learned a way to turn the monsters of the deeps away from their ships. One might think they would share such a thing to protect others, but perhaps not. I'm not entirely sure *my* employers would. It provides such a large advantage." He smiled. "Spying on each other is a longstanding tradition for the cities on the coast. We all do it." Then he sobered. "But what I found is more concerning."

Lisette met his eyes. "The dragons are chained."

"Yes. The dragons are chained. Your duke is a puppet manipulated by men with power of their own. This man claiming to be Lord Hanley is no relation to the man who had the title before him." He sat back. "It was clear to me something was wrong the moment I stepped foot in the city. But it never would have occurred to me to just go talk to the dragons."

Lisette wanted to protest that she hadn't exactly planned to do that either, but Barlow cut in first. "What's this about that gorro, Lord Hanley? His father died when he was young, but I remember him. They could have been twins."

"Yes. Someone molded the current lord's features as he grew. The signs are subtle, but they're there."

Tiffany frowned. "But why? Who would do that to a child?"

Remy sat back. "I can think of a dozen reasons, but my best guess is that someone wanted a backup plan." He looked around at his audience. "The current duke is unreliable, at best. I'm guessing the duke's father was similar. A constant flow of magic can cause a certain type of madness and..." He looked around the room, apparently trying to pick suitable words. "And quenching of desire."

Because she knew them, Lisette was watching for it when Barlow elbowed Tiffany. He spoke in a low voice. "Three children with your baker — definitely no magic around here." Tiffany covered her mouth to keep her giggles in.

Remy had turned his attention to Rye. "Whoever was

running the city through the previous duke must have worried they wouldn't be able to keep up pretenses at some point. Or maybe they knew the line would die out despite every effort. I've seen your duke around women — he's of an age to be producing an heir, and things don't seem to be going well."

Lisette thought about the duke's bedchamber. He likely could have any partner in the city, but there had been a disuse that suggested a second person had never been in the room. And the current holder of the title had been the only issue of the previous duke, a late-in-life child when the city had despaired of there ever being an heir.

Remy continued. "Whoever was in charge needed an alternate candidate, and one who could handle magic."

Lisette nodded slowly. "And not many of the nobles are mages."

"Hardly any, in fact. So why not put a mage's child in a perfectly respectable noble family that has lost what magic it had and fallen on hard times? After the child has grown, he can start restoring the family's fortunes. And by the time it's obvious the duke isn't fit to rule, there's a suitable replacement waiting."

The room was silent as everyone thought about it. From the street came the sound of two men laughing.

Lisette finally shook her head. "But why not just swap the baby in for the duke's child? That seems like it would be easier."

"Because a duke's heir has to be seen at events, and this type of spell might make that... difficult at certain times."

Rye let out a long breath. "Or they didn't want to put all their eggs in one basket. If Lord Hanley isn't who he seems, who's to say they haven't done that in other families as well? Then they'd have a few to choose from."

Remy inclined his head toward Rye. "Yes. I wouldn't be surprised if that were the case." He cocked his head. "Do you perhaps play scribecounter?"

Barlow moaned. "Oh, gods, don't get him started."

Lisette and Tiffany shared a look. Rye's obsession with teaching others the strategy game had led to rainy afternoons devoted to learning the offensive capabilities of different pieces. Tiffany wasn't a bad player. Lisette understood just enough of the game to appreciate watching others play.

Rye refused to get sidetracked. "The real question is what we do now. If you go back to..." He waited for Remy to fill in the city, but Remy merely smiled. "Fine. If you go back to whoever sent you here and tell them what's happening, are they going to invade Harbor Crag? We can't let that happen."

Lisette tensed at the implicit threat in Rye's words, but Remy didn't move. "Harbor Crag still has more than enough magic to defend itself. Even if it didn't, none of the other cities are in any position to attack."

Rye looked at the items shimmering under the ward on the table. "Then we get rid of all this stuff and keep our heads down. If the duke or Lord Hanley or any of those people find out we're involved, they'll burn the quarter."

Barlow clicked his tongue. "Be reasonable, Rye. We can't just ignore this."

Lisette caught Rye's attention. "I still owe the dragon a favor. And Lord Hanley is using magic on everyone who goes into his house. Maybe on people outside as well. I can't let that stand."

Rye drew his shoulders back. "I promised your mother I'd keep you safe."

Barlow laughed. "And everyone in that room knew you were making promises you had no chance of keeping. You can't keep someone safe without keeping them caged, Rye, and her mother wouldn't have wanted that." He looked over at Lisette. "Not that you could cage Lisette, even if you tried."

A pounding on the door to Lisette's shop startled them. The shouted words, still audible despite the closed door and the distance, made her skin crawl. "Lisette! Lisette! I know you're in there! Come out and talk to me!" Lisette curled her hands into fists and dug her fingernails into her palms.

Barlow swore. Nobody moved.

Remy turned to Lisette. "Lord Hanley?"

Lisette nodded. Her mouth was dry. "How did he know to come here? I was sure they hadn't followed us."

Rye shook his head. "I don't think that's why he's here. This is the sort of thing he used to do."

Tiffany took a breath. "Especially when you were gone. He'd stand in the street and yell up at your window for hours."

Barlow sighed. "We started paying one of the fish market vendors to keep a cart with rotting fish parts in the street in front of your shop overnight. I couldn't open our windows for weeks."

The yells continued. "Lisette! You can't hide from me anymore! I know you're up there."

Lisette smoothed her hands on her leggings. "We don't have a cart of fish guts now. And I can't even go talk to him to make him go away. He would see that I wasn't coming down from my room. Even if we didn't have all this to hide, I don't want him over here." Rye and Barlow had almost died helping her fight back against Lord Hanley last time.

She wouldn't let that happen again. "He'll give up eventually, right?"

Rye, Barlow, and Tiffany exchanged glum looks.

"That won't do. Simi has strong opinions about people who show up late with her breakfast." Remy stood up. "Is there a way to get up to a window overlooking the street without being seen? I think I can help."

CHAPTER 41

NOTHING PERMANENT

As Lord Hanley continued to yell for Lisette to come down to talk to him, Rye escorted Remy through the maze of crates up to the uncles' bedroom above.

Tiffany took the opportunity to move over to the vacant seat next to Lisette. "You always did have weird taste, but I approve."

Lisette stared at her friend. "He's a thief. And a mage. And a *spy*."

"That's bad, but at least his horrible mother doesn't live two streets away."

"True." Lisette suspected both Tiffany and her baker's mother enjoyed the adversarial nature of their relationship. They worked together easily enough during an actual crisis.

"And by your own account, he's gone out of his way to keep you safe more than once. Plus, the way he looks at you when he thinks nobody else is watching..." Tiffany fanned her face. "Back me up here, uncle."

Barlow came over to look at the items on the table.

"With Lord Hanley scaring everyone off, I'm not sure how many other choices you're going to have."

Lisette breathed out a laugh, and Tiffany rolled her eyes.

On the street, Lord Hanley's yelling halted. Lisette tensed. Then she heard his voice again, sharp and dismissive. "Go back and keep searching the tunnels, you idiot. We know it must be down there somewhere." A pause. "Lisette! Come down and talk to me. I just want to talk."

Tiffany made a rude gesture toward the street. "I had really started to hope *that* one had given up on you."

"I went to his house today," Lisette said. "Lord Hanley's estate, I mean. Not Remy's."

"Really?" Tiffany looked up at her.

"Did you know the nobles let people tour their houses for a bit of coin?"

"What?"

Barlow broke off his examination of the tiara to look over at them. "Have I never taken either of you with me on one of those tours?" He sat back down on the packing crate. "It's a good way to scope out who has what tastes, and know which pieces might be available if a new spouse moves in and redecorates."

Tiffany's look of disbelief didn't wane. "But... They just let total strangers wander through their houses?"

Barlow shrugged. "Through part of the house anyhow. And they have someone watching, to make sure nobody nicks the silver. But yes."

Tiffany shuddered. "I could never have strangers in my place."

Lisette put a hand over her mouth to muffle her laughter at the thought of someone paying to tour Tiffany's rooms across the street. "There'd be no room for a stranger to *stand* in your place." Tiffany had more space than Lisette, but with Tiffany, her mother, the baker, and the three children all living there, it was a tight squeeze.

"That's the truth. Ooh, did I tell you Bosco is thinking about moving in with his daughter? If we moved to his spot, we'd have an extra room. Come with me to look at it tomorrow." Tiffany shook her head once and settled back in the chair. "So what was it like, his estate?"

"Ordinary, for the most part, I guess. Other than all the magic to make people trust him."

Tiffany made a face of disgust. "I might have known. How else would he had fooled so many people in the quarter, even after he started making trouble for you?"

"And he has some sort of mechanical creature guarding one part of the house." Lisette went silent as she pondered how it worked and how to disable it.

Tiffany and Barlow exchanged a look.

Barlow raised his brows. "It's a good thing Lord Hanley really never understood you, or he would have lured you to his house with the promise of taking the thing apart."

Tiffany nodded. "And you would have gone."

Lisette acknowledged the underlying truth in their words. Then she thought about why she'd gone to the house that evening and smiled.

Tiffany elbowed her. "What?"

"Nothing."

"Come on. You were thinking about Remy, I can tell."

Lisette felt her face heating. "I was just thinking that he asked me to come along with him today because he wanted my opinion on the creature."

"See! He understands more about you in a few days than that idiot outside did after a year."

Lisette's chest tightened — not the dragon fire this

time, but something simpler. She kept her voice low, for Tiffany's ears only. "It scares me how much he sees through me."

Tiffany's smile was encouraging. "That's as it should be."

"But this can't work out. He's..." Remy was a lot of things, but his being a spy for another city should really have ended her interest once and for all.

Tiffany nodded. "I agree. A baker is definitely easier to plan a life with, though you have to accept that you're never going to sleep past dawn. Ever. But you find who you find. And the two of you seem suited for each other. Even if it doesn't work out, he's far better than..." She jerked her head toward the front of the shop.

The yelling in the street cut off with a yelp in the middle of Lisette's name. After a pause, Lord Hanley started again. "Lisette! Come down —" His words cut off with another cry of pain. "Ow! What is — Ow!"

Lord Hanley yelled again, but this time to one of his own men. "Get the carriage! Now!" He ended on another yell of pain.

Remy came back into the room and took the free seat next to Barlow. "That seems to have worked, at least."

Rye followed. "I may need to get a few of those for next time."

Lisette winced at the thought of a *next time*. "What did you do?"

"A tiny dart of something that will make his doctors think he's passing a kidney stone for the next twelve hours or so. Nothing permanent. The dart feels like a bug and gets brushed off." He held up a little tube. "Hitting your target takes some practice."

Barlow took the tube and examined it. "Probably better

if he doesn't realize it only ever shows up when he's on this street."

"Or," Tiffany said, a malicious edge in her voice, "we could follow him around and dart him once a day until he's so miserable he can't do anything else."

Lisette shook her head. "If he's getting his power from a dragon and we can stop it, hopefully that will take care of him for good."

"Do we really need to choose just one or the other?" Tiffany sighed. "How come *I* never get to talk to a dragon?"

"Because you were never stupid enough to run through the dragon warrens." Lisette rubbed her sternum. "Trust me. That's a good thing."

"Bah." Tiffany stood up and yawned. "I need to get some sleep or I'm going to be stabbing needles into my fingers all day tomorrow." She kissed Lisette on the cheek. "Be careful. But not *too* careful, if you know what I mean." She turned to Remy. "It was nice to meet you. Hurt my best friend and I'll hunt you down and remove your innards." She nodded to Rye and Barlow. "Uncles."

Barlow went with her to let her out the front of the shop.

Remy stood again. "I need to get back to my lodgings before I fall down." He gestured at the table. "Is it possible to leave this all here for now? I'd originally intended to put them somewhere not quite so out in the open, but if we move them now, I'll have to create a new ward, and I'm not sure I have it in me at the moment."

Rye nodded. "I'll keep Barlow from touching it. Somehow." He raised an eyebrow at Lisette when she stood. "*You* should probably not go anywhere near the front of the shop until we're positive Lord Hanley has left the area."

Lisette wondered if he was worried on that account, or

if he wanted to keep space between Lisette and this man who was a spy. Remy's lips quirked, as if he'd had the same thought. He said, "Perhaps we could talk about Bralinost and some way to get past it tomorrow evening?"

Lisette nodded. "It hasn't had any maintenance in a long time. That's obvious from the way it was moving. There must be some way to take advantage of that..." She broke off when the two men shared an amused glance. "I'll think about it."

Rye got to his feet. "I'll see you out." He eyed Lisette. "Don't go anywhere. I have something that you should see."

Lisette watched Remy go. Then she got distracted by the dials moving on the base of the vane. What did they indicate? Would Aarat know? If this thing had been a dragon treasure before it was hidden, perhaps she could give it to Aarat to replace the zoetrope she'd broken when she'd first fallen into the cavern.

She heard a crate bang against another and got up to investigate. Halfway through the maze to get to the front of the shop, a new pile blocked her way. Barlow stood on the stack, handing small crates down to Rye. "It's either in this one or the one below it."

Lisette leaned over the crate in front of her and watched Rye open the clasps on the one Barlow had just taken down. "What are we looking for?"

"A painting." Rye flipped through a stack of canvases. "You said that thing's name was Bralinost, didn't you?" He let the canvases fall and fastened the lid. "It must be in the other one."

"Yes. That's what the guide leading the tour called it."

Rye grunted as he handed the closed crate back to Barlow. "I've heard that name before, but it took me a bit to remember where." He opened the other crate and then sneezed. "Where does all the dust come from? I spend half my days..." Pushing packing straw out of the way, he pulled out another stack of smaller canvases and looked through them. "Aha! There it is. *The Creation of Bralinost*. It's an older piece. The brush work is a bit sloppy, and the composition isn't great, but every once in a while we have a client who likes art showing magic, so I thought I'd clean it up someday..." His voice trailed off.

Barlow reached down to touch his shoulder. "Rye?"

Rye looked across the crates at Lisette. "Why are you in a three-hundred-year-old painting?"

CHAPTER 42
THE PAINTING

Lisette looked at the canvas in the light of the lantern while the uncles re-stacked crates and replaced everything. As Rye had said, the painting was old and discolored, but the brass nameplate attached to the frame was still legible: *The Creation of Bralinost.*

A man in mage's robes stood in front of a reasonable facsimile of the automaton Lisette had seen in Lord Hanley's house. White swirls filled the space between the two, which she supposed symbolized some sort of magical spell being cast.

In the background, a workbench very similar to Lisette's held a variety of tools. The artist hadn't tried to fill in the details, but knowing how she laid her own tools out made it obvious that *there* was the movement holder, and *there* was the caliper. It was a watchmaker's space, no doubt about that.

Seated at the bench, seen only in profile, as if she had been added just to fill space, sat Lisette. Or, if not Lisette, someone who could have been her twin — curly hair pulled back in the tangled mess that happened after working too long without a break, dark brows pulled down into a slight frown, and the same nose Lisette had seen in her mother's profile. This woman had to be a relative. If Lisette put on a historical costume, she could pose for a newer version of this same painting.

The connection to her ancestor made it harder to give the painting back to Rye, but that was just silliness. "She must be a great-something grandmother or aunt." The guide had said Bralinost had been brought to the house over three hundred years ago. If she believed that, the woman in the painting had been in the first few generations of freeholders. Unless the painting had been done later and the artist had used whatever models were handy. "How old do you think this is?"

Rye held the painting closer to the lantern. "I'll have to clean it up to be sure, but I think the highlights of the water are done in azurian. That hasn't been used by amateurs since the mines of Laktor were lost, so at least two hundred fifty years. Possibly longer. As I said, it might be more obvious after it's cleaned."

Barlow climbed down and peered over Rye's shoulder. "Did your people come from the Island of Light?"

"Maybe?" Lisette had a vague idea that her mother had said something like that once. "Why?"

Barlow pointed to the high windows in the painting's background, and then to three spots where metal instruments gleamed, even through the coating of grime. "This motif, with one path of outside light illuminating more than anything else. It's a sign the location is the Island of Light." He leaned against Rye more closely, squinting to see more details. "An expert in the time period might be able to determine the exact place and time. The painters in that period were very clever about encoding information." He stood up straight and looked doubtful. "Though, as Rye said, this was done by an amateur. The other information might not be there."

Rye picked up the lantern and headed back through the maze of crates. "I'll clean it in the morning. But right now I'm going to pile some things in front of the workbench, so I don't have to explain all *that* in case someone comes in." He waved his hand at the back of the shop, where the book, tiara, and other magical items waited under Remy's ward. He turned to Lisette. "And *you* should head to bed. Even you young people need *some* sleep."

Lisette kissed him and Barlow on the cheek. "Good night, uncles. Sleep well."

She headed for the passage to her own shop. Sleep would be nice, but she had something more important to do first.

In the dark, she climbed the narrow staircase and closed the shutters over her windows before lighting the lantern and placing it on a shelf. If Remy's darts had worked, Lord Hanley wouldn't be back during the night, but there was no point in being careless.

The frame of her bed allowed storage within. Lisette suspected it had been meant for things like extra blankets only needed during winter or spare linens, but in the tiny bedroom it was one of the few places to keep anything that didn't need to be easily accessed. And for as long as the bed had been in the tiny room, that meant one thing: the Allinde logbooks.

Lisette rolled up the thin mattress and removed three of the slats it rested upon. Underneath lay dozens of journals, tied together in bundles of four or five with leather cords to protect them and make shifting them around easier. The bundles were organized roughly by date, which made finding the right books easier. She pulled out the two oldest bundles, replaced the slats and mattress, and sat down to examine them.

The leather bindings were worn and patched, though Lisette suspected most of the damage had been caused by hard use rather than age. Her current logbook sitting on her workbench downstairs had seen its share of trouble, between cleaning fluid spills, ink blots, and numerous falls to the floor when she'd shoved it out of the way while concentrating too hard on what she was doing. Earlier members of the Allinde family hadn't been any easier on their logbooks.

She untied one bundle and carefully separated the books. When she'd been younger, she'd read through her mother's and then her grandmother's. She'd started on the previous generation, but her great-grandfather's writing had been nearly illegible, and she'd had trouble deciphering the older style of lettering. She had meant to go through them someday.

As she opened the first book, the smell of old paper and oil wafted up, making her sneeze. She turned pages until she found a date. Two hundred sixty years. Unless her assumptions were wrong, this book was too recent. She set it aside and opened the next.

Book after book, she looked to see how old each was, and then closed it again. A diagram of the workings of a clock with a light source distracted her briefly. She rubbed her eyes and puzzled out the construction. Ah, a clock meant to light up a dark bedroom instead of ring an alarm. She closed the book and put it on the stack.

When all the books had been checked, her eyes were burning and the air smelled faintly musty, but she had seen nothing old enough to be from the time Bralinost had been created. Perhaps there hadn't been a logbook. Or if her ancestor had been on the Island of Light, maybe the book had gone with another branch of the family. All she knew was the logbook wasn't here.

Lisette paused in retying the bundles. Had she looked at that one? The brown leather had saltwater stains, as if it had been misted by ocean spray. She didn't remember seeing it before.

But this was a fool's errand. The logbook wasn't here, and she needed to get to sleep. Remy would be back to talk to her tomorrow. She would need a clear head for that.

Lisette finished tying the books together and stopped again. She still hadn't looked at that journal yet. Biting her lip to wake herself up, she undid the cords and reached for the book.

This time, she noticed the twinge of magic and kept her hand in place, even when she was overwhelmed with the feeling there was no point in bothering.

Forcing herself to concentrate, Lisette grabbed the salt-stained leather and lifted the journal. Someone had spelled this logbook to prevent it from being read.

Lisette opened the cover.

CHAPTER 43
THE JOURNAL

In her quiet bedroom, Lisette settled in to read the logbook.

Though the leather cover was salt-stained and worn, the interior of the journal had been protected from the elements and age. Lisette wondered if that was a side-effect of the spell convincing people not to open it. Remy might know.

Once she had flipped open the cover, the insistent voice telling her to abandon the journal ceased. Inside, she found pages of archaic script in neat rows, interspersed with diagrams and cramped comments by the same hand in the margins.

Scanning from the beginning, she found entries similar to her own logbook downstairs: records of commissions, addresses where fixed items should be sent, quirks in pieces that came back on a regular basis, notes about owner preferences. There wasn't any payment information; that would be in a separate ledger.

Lisette didn't recognize any of the addresses or family

names. Perhaps this journal really was from the Island of Light.

Halfway through the book, she saw notes that a certain M. Xavier had discussed a commission for a magically animated creature intended to carry messages throughout the city. A spell would bar her from communicating with anyone else about it. Accustomed to her unnamed ancestor's notes by this time, Lisette decided the writer didn't trust M. Xavier and really didn't like the secrecy involved, but... the lure of creating such a complicated automaton, powered by magic, overrode her good sense.

Lisette sighed. That was a trait she had inherited. She and the writer of this journal were definitely related.

The next few months of entries were full of diagrams of individual parts of the creation, with iterations after the writer made prototypes and tested them. The lower leg joints alone took four pages, and the writer still hadn't been satisfied when she had moved on to the next part.

M. Xavier appeared at intervals to power the tests. Was the M an honorific indicating Xavier was a mage? Lisette would ask Barlow in the morning. In later entries, M. Xavier pushed harder for quicker results, claiming the client was pressuring them to finish.

Even as the entries about M. Xavier grew more tense, the writer's pride in what she was building shone through. The first time the writer assembled the complete body of Bralinost — for this was indeed Bralinost — and saw it animated, Lisette could feel the joy in her script across hundreds of years.

It was at that point that M. Xavier had changed the requirements. First, he had added a special limb to sample the blood of the message recipient. Then there were weapons. To allow the automaton to protect itself and its message, M. Xavier claimed. Reading between the lines, Lisette could tell the writer was uneasy, but the spell preventing her from speaking about the commission meant she couldn't talk it over with anyone she trusted. Increasingly isolated and unhappy, the writer began surreptitiously following M. Xavier when he left her studio, trying to determine the identity of his unknown patron.

By this time, Bralinost was nearly finished. A junior artist from the local painting school had been brought in to commemorate the event. Lisette's ancestor had written scathing notes about being forced to sit in one spot for hours as the boy dabbed at the canvas, paint smearing his face and clothes.

And then Bralinost was complete. M. Xavier took the automaton away in a crate for a demonstration with his secret patron. If all went well, he would return in the morning with the final payment. The writer tried to follow M. Xavier, recognizing this as her last opportunity to find out who was behind this, but she had been on foot. She lost M. Xavier's carriage when the traffic cleared. On her way back to her shop, the writer had seen a knot of people at the wharf, pulling something from the water.

The face of the junior artist was still smeared with the same colors as it had been when she finished sitting for him. Someone had slit his throat and dumped the body in the water.

Taking only her tools, her coins, and the journal, the writer sneaked onto a cargo ship and hid in the hold. Nuts and watered ale comprised her diet until they arrived at the next port three weeks later.

Lisette's many times great-grandmother had arrived in Harbor Crag.

Once there, she had taken a new name, and rented a

desk in the back room of a seamstress' shop — with constant complaints about the dust from the textiles — until she had enough money to purchase her own tiny space in the freeholder quarter. From that point, the book continued with entries similar to the first pages, listing customer dislikes and addresses Lisette recognized from the estates near the water.

Lisette paged back to the diagrams of Bralinost. The writer had made a note that M. Xavier required a space of certain dimensions inside the body that could be accessed easily by the owner. At the time, the writer had assumed the cavity would be used to store the messages the automaton would carry, but in a more rushed hand had scribbled *Internal power?* and then a symbol Lisette didn't recognize. And then in a third ink, *Dragon magic!*

Puzzling over that notation and wishing her ancestor had been a little less cryptic, Lisette closed the book. Knowing how Bralinost had been built, she had a few ideas for disabling it, but all of them required getting close enough to touch the automaton without it tearing her apart.

Lisette put the water-stained journal aside and replaced the other logbooks in their storage spot beneath her mattress. The magical side of the process eluded her. She would show the diagrams to Remy tomorrow, but she had a bad feeling they were going to need Aarat's help with this.

Dragons. Mages. The journal reaffirmed the wisdom of a sensible watchmaker having nothing to do with either one. Lisette brought a hand to her heart and sighed.

CHAPTER 44
COOKING OIL

L isette woke in the morning with a clear head and fresh resolve. Remy was attractive, yes. In more ways than just the physical. Lisette could be honest enough with herself to admit that.

As a spy, Remy was like a tantalizing treat that a child might steal off a table, despite the consequences. But Lisette was an adult. She would use his skills to help her steal the dagger in Lord Henley's possession. Then she would send him on his way.

She dressed and combed her hair back. It was good to have that settled.

Two hours later, she gritted her teeth and repeated that resolution, forcing herself to remember why she had made the decision. If the entirety of Harbor Crag would quit bothering her, she would be happy.

Rye entered the shop with a mug of tea after she sent the third customer on his way. "Lisette, my dear, it worries me when you quote prices you really should be charging." He put the mug down on the counter separating her work space from the rest of the shop and backed away.

Lisette gritted her teeth. "He tried to fix his pocket watch with *cooking oil*." The object in her hands stank of fish and potatoes.

"Yes, but even so, suggesting that he might as well drop it in an oven and be done with it lacked a certain..." Rye stopped and shook his head. "Never mind. You've built up a reputation for this sort of thing. I suppose it's a form of advertising. Would you like to tell me what's really bothering you?"

"*Cooking oil!*" Lisette sat at her bench and began the process of disassembling the pocket watch so she could clean it. Seeing it like this caused her pain that was almost physical.

"Mm hmm. So this is about your friend."

Lisette's fingers continued their work even as her jaw tightened. "Remy's not my friend. He's a —" She stopped long enough to look up and make sure nobody else had entered the shop. "He's a *spy*."

"I see. So a thief was one thing, but a spy is a step too far."

"Isn't it?" Long practice kept Lisette's actions steady as she clamped the watch's movement into the holder. "Maybe you're right. Being a thief was already bad enough."

Rye stayed silent for a few minutes as she worked. Then he leaned his upper body on the counter. "When I was old enough to leave home, I joined the army."

Lisette looked up, her thoughts completely derailed. "You? In the army?" She couldn't imagine her Uncle Rye getting dirty or going without his comforts.

Rye waved a hand. "I was younger then. And it turned out to be more a band of soldiers paid to extort the lord's enemies than a proper army." He shifted his weight. "The group attracted two types: wide-eyed innocents and those who enjoyed hurting people. Only one type stayed long."

Lisette went back to stripping the movement as she tried to imagine Uncle Rye sleeping on the ground. Or obeying someone else's orders. Uncle Rye didn't back down in an argument. The whole idea was so odd, it cut through her dour mood. "Wait, did you have to ride on a *horse*?" The corners of her mouth lifted.

Rye sighed. "I'm glad to see my life lessons are so funny to you. And no, I wasn't high enough rank to ride a horse. I just had to clean up after them."

Lisette bit her lip to stop laughing at that image, which caused her to snort. "Sorry."

"As I said, I was younger then. But my *point* is I've known people who were not safe to be around. And I don't think your Remy is one of those people."

Lisette sighed. "But..."

"Has he asked you to do anything that would harm the city?"

Lisette thought about it. *She* had been the one who had brought down the city's defenses, albeit accidentally. From what she could tell, Remy had just been trying to steal a book or two. And he'd been ready to leave her out of it entirely. "No."

"It's something to think about. From what the two of you said last night, there are things going on that *need* to be looked into. And if that requires a spy and a thief and a mage, well... Life is often strange."

"But..." Lisette put the mesh basket holding the watch pieces into the cleaner and started its cycle. She wiped cooking oil off her bench with another rag. The shop would never lose the odor of fried fish.

"Just think about it." He stood up. "I'll deal with your

customers while you go look at Bosco's rooms with Tiffany." He sniffed. "Though after that last client, I suspect word will have gotten out."

Lisette sipped the tea Rye had brought with him, now lukewarm but still spicy. "Cooking oil." The idea still boggled her mind, but no longer made her angry. "The man thought he could save money by dousing it in cooking oil."

"Yes, and I thought the best way to get away from home was to learn how to use a sword and join the army. We all make mistakes. At least his didn't kill anyone." He glanced through the shop windows where two girls were running toward the door, one limping slightly. He waited until they had run inside. "Speaking of mistakes..."

"Uncle Rye!" Turtle and Pot swarmed up him, and by the time Tiffany came through the door with Ziggy, Rye had one child in each arm and was pretending to collapse under the weight.

Rye edged past Tiffany. "She's all yours. It has nothing to do with the cooking oil."

Tiffany watched him head into the other shop with her two oldest children giggling in his arms. "Cooking oil?" She inhaled deeply. "Is that why it smells of fish in here?"

Ziggy tilted her head to look up near the ceiling. "Kitty?"

Tiffany smoothed her daughter's hair back. "No kitty today, love. Maybe someday soon." She raised her eyebrows and looked at Lisette.

Lisette rolled her eyes. "Very subtle. I don't know. I got up this morning all ready to keep him at arm's length. Now I'm not so sure." She shook her head. "Did you know Uncle Rye was in the army when he was younger?"

Looking at the passage to the shop next door, Tiffany huffed a laugh. "Uncle Rye? *Our* Uncle Rye? A soldier?" She let Ziggy slide down to the ground. "Remember, no touching Auntie Lisette's things." Ziggy charged off through the wall hangings to follow her sisters. "She's getting so big. I miss having a cuddly baby."

Lisette opened the pass-through and went out into the customer area. "Time for number four?"

"Bite your tongue. We're bursting at the seams as it is."

"Which is why we're going to look at Bosco's rooms. If you move there... four, five, and six won't be far behind."

Tiffany blew out a breath. "Creatures of the deep, can you imagine the chaos?" But she sounded more intrigued than horrified by the prospect.

Lisette had been her mother's only child. "How much worse could it be?" As Lisette had intended, Tiffany laughed. Lisette lowered her voice. "I found a journal last night. Before my great-something grandmother came to Harbor Crag, she helped create that creature guarding Lord Hanley. Then she ran, because she thought they were going to kill her."

Lisette hadn't found it difficult to open the book this morning, but she wasn't sure if that was because the spell protecting it was gone or if she had just passed some test. Now she had a way to find out. "Stay here for a second."

"Don't take too long," Tiffany called after her as Lisette ran up the stairs. "The latest fashion is fox tails. I've sold fifteen of them today already, and I think I can sell at least another ten if I make them fast enough."

Lisette grabbed the journal from her bed and trotted back down to the shop. She handed the book to Tiffany. "Have a look."

Tiffany glanced at the salt-stained leather cover and then let it hang by her side. "We should get going."

Lisette drew her attention back to the book she was holding. "Can you open it?"

Tiffany lifted it again. "This? Why would I want to look at this?"

That answered the question of whether the spell still protected the book. Lisette took it back and opened it. "She must have paid a mage to keep anyone from reading it."

Tiffany looked from her empty hand to the book in confusion. "That was weird. It just..." She wiped her hand off on her tunic. "If she didn't want anyone to look at it, I wonder why she didn't just destroy it."

"I don't know, but I'm glad she didn't." A figure passing in front of the shop window alerted her, and she had already closed the book by the time the door opened. The woman who entered had the fine clothes of the nobility — and unless Lisette was seeing things, she was using magic to enhance her features.

Rye came through the passage between the two shops before Lisette could say anything. "How may I help you?" He glanced over at Tiffany and Lisette. "Barlow is off gossiping, and the hoodlums are currently unmonitored over there."

Tiffany bolted for the other shop. Lisette was only a few steps behind. She brought the journal with her, unwilling to leave it, especially with that particular visitor in the space. The nobles didn't run their own errands. Most likely, the woman had heard about Lord Hanley's renewed interest and was here to satisfy her curiosity. But Lisette didn't trust anyone she didn't know. Any hint of magic made her question a person's motives these days. Rye would deal with the woman and send her on her way.

Tiffany handed her youngest daughter to Lisette. "Hang

on to her. She gets distracted and chases after kitties and doesn't look to see what might be coming in the road." She raised her voice. "Come on, you two."

As a noisy, giggling pack, they went out of the shop and into the quarter.

CHAPTER 45

THE WATCHER

osco's rooms faced the same direction as Lisette's shop, but were further up the hill at the end of the street. They covered the area above three stores, with an entrance through the one in the middle. Tiffany told her the specifics as they walked. The current configuration, after hundreds of years of freeholder modifications, had four bedrooms, a bathroom, a large family room, and even an area meant for cooking. Individual kitchens were something of a rarity in the quarter — most families had arrangements with a restaurant or two.

The noisy group went up the stairs together and fell quiet when Tiffany opened the door. She put a hand over her mouth. "His daughter said he'd been collecting, but *this...*"

Lisette imagined the family room would appear much larger when it was cleared out, but it was currently filled with plants. The kids spread out, taking advantage of the different paths they could fit through. Tall, short, upright, cascading — there were more plants in this one room than Lisette had ever seen in her life. Most of them were dead and dried out. She ducked under a leaning palm and threaded through the pots taking up the floor space. "Has it always been like this?" Bosco's children were older than she was, and his wife had died two decades ago. Lisette had never had a reason to come in here.

"His daughter says not. The plants have accumulated in the last year or so." Tiffany's voice came from the other side of a forest of brown leaves. All three children had disappeared somewhere in that section. "There isn't enough light in here to grow things like this."

"Especially not with the shutters closed." Lisette picked her way to the window, nudging pots out of the way to create room for her feet. Leaves had fallen onto the tiled floor and had begun decomposing. "Cleaning this out is going to take some effort."

Tiffany's voice was stronger now. "But worth it, if the floor is sound."

The latch holding the shutters closed was stuck. Lisette put her great-grandmother's journal in her waistband to free up her other hand; if she put anything down in this mess, she'd never find it again. When she finally opened the shutters, a gust of fresh air blew dust into her face. In the street below, a pony clopped by, pulling an empty dray behind it. "You won't be able to watch me come home at night from here."

Tiffany laughed. "That's definitely a drawback. You'll have to get better at telling me everything." She opened the other shutters further down the wall and coughed. "But I'll be able to see who Jonno's keeping company with at the moment. That will provide some entertainment." The tailor's ever-changing relationships kept the whole quarter talking.

A man idled in the street closer to Lisette's shop,

leaning against the wall as if he were waiting for someone. She wondered why he didn't go to one of the street cafes meant for that sort of thing. Turning her back on the street, Lisette sighed. With the extra light, the extent of the dead vegetation seemed to have multiplied. A rustling of branches between her spot and the stairs was accompanied by whispers and giggles. "You might lose the kids in here if you aren't careful."

Tiffany laughed and wended her way across the space. "It's never worked before."

They went into the bedrooms. Because they were at the end of the street, the two rooms on the east side had windows. Both were filled with plants. Lisette climbed over a stack of pots to open the shutters in the second room. "How did we never notice Bosco bringing this many plants here?"

"I have three children. The only other person I can keep track of is you." Tiffany peered at the ceiling. "That's leaked at some point. We'll have to check the roof before the rainy season."

Lisette noticed the possible move had turned into a sure thing, at least as far as Tiffany was concerned. "Barlow's not going to be able to throw pebbles at your window to wake you up anymore."

"Maybe we can rig some sort of system across the rooftop."

They threaded their way back through the open area to the rooms on the other side. The third bedroom had one window to the street, and the fourth, a dim interior cave, held Bosco's bed and personal things. They looked inside, checked the ceiling and floor for obvious damage, and then closed the door again.

Lisette and Tiffany adjourned next to the window overlooking the street. Tiffany gestured at the interior. "What do you think?"

"I think we should hire a big cart, park it in the street, and toss all the plants through the window." Lisette looked down, calculating how much of the street would be blocked if they did that. "Might have to do it at night when there's not much traffic." The man down the street still stood in the same spot. As she watched, the noblewoman who had come into Lisette's shop crossed the road, spoke to him briefly, then walked away. She didn't look pleased. The man stayed where he was.

"You could take our old rooms, you know." Tiffany bumped Lisette with her elbow. "You'd have space for more than one person there."

Lisette glanced at her with a smile. "And you'd be able to see me coming home at night from here."

"The thought never crossed my mind." Tiffany paused. "What are you looking at?"

"I think there might be someone watching my shop. Or maybe the uncles' shop." Lisette moved to let Tiffany stand in front of her. "That man there. The one who looks like he's waiting for someone. The woman who came into the shop as we were leaving just talked to him and left."

"You think it's this business with your man?"

Lisette opened her mouth to protest that Remy wasn't her man, and then closed it again. She had learned one thing while watching Tiffany's children grow. Anything said within earshot might be repeated, generally at the worst possible time. "I don't know. It could also be Lord Hanley trying to keep track of me." The thought made her stomach hurt. She really didn't want to have to leave the city again.

Tiffany patted her shoulder. "We'll figure something

out. If I'd known Uncle Rye had been a soldier the last time..."

Lisette rolled her eyes and pointed to the dead vegetation. "You worry about how to clean all this up and let me deal with my own problems." Somehow she needed to warn Remy off, so he didn't come to her shop to talk about Bralinost as they had planned.

"In case you hadn't noticed, your problems have a habit of becoming everyone's problems." Tiffany pulled the shutters closed. "I have to get back to work. Come with us. We'll send the uncles a message so they know where you are in case *someone* comes by."

They finished refastening the shutters and tracked down the children hiding in the foliage, then bustled down the stairs and back out to the street. With Ziggy on her hip again, Lisette glanced toward the man watching her shop. His attention was focussed on what was in front of him. If he was supposed to be watching for her, he'd missed her when she'd exited from the uncles' shop with Tiffany and her children, and he wasn't going to miss his chance to catch her coming back.

"Extra coin, miss?" The barefoot street girl with a scar through one eyebrow stood in front of Tiffany. She was shorter than Turtle, but seeing the children side by side made Lisette realize her initial estimate of the girl's age had been too low. She had to be at least eight or nine.

Tiffany put a hand on Pot's shoulder. "No, but if you need something to eat, you can come with us to the soup vendor."

For just a moment, the girl appeared nonplussed. Then she sidestepped Tiffany and approached Lisette, peering at Ziggy suspiciously. "You have watchers at your place. Cat man wants me to bring you to him again." She twirled away, darting behind the tea vendor on the corner.

Lisette handed Ziggy off to Tiffany. "Looks like I need to go."

"Be careful."

"I will." With one last glance to make sure the man watching her shop hadn't noticed, Lisette followed the street girl around the corner.

CHAPTER 46
NOT THAT TWISTY

The girl with the scarred eyebrow twirled ahead of Lisette, dancing to music only she could hear, her ragged dress hinting at bird wings when she leaped. Occasionally, she bumped into people on the street and spun away. Lisette wondered how many of those people were missing valuables afterward. Unable to fit through the same gaps in traffic as a small child, Lisette struggled to keep up.

They left the freeholder quarter, heading uphill, through the dockworker housing. Then the girl turned a corner and was gone. Lisette stopped at the side of the street to look for her. A familiar vanilla and pepper scent tickled her nose. She was already turning when he spoke.

"Your shop is being watched." Today, Remy wasn't wearing a mask, and she could see all the lines from laughter and worry on his face. His satchel dangled from one shoulder. Simi's head was visible under the flap. The calico purred when Lisette reached forward to rub her cheek.

"I was trying to figure out how to warn you." Lisette felt

suddenly foolish. This man was a spy. Of *course,* he would notice any watcher that she had seen. "I found something I need to show you."

"Tea?" At her assent, he led the way downhill. The smell of bruised onions overwhelmed everything. He gestured at the changing style of the buildings and pedestrians they passed. "I find Harbor Crag's insistence on sharply delineating neighborhoods very helpful in finding out if someone is following me." Remy guided them around a collapsed vegetable cart blocking the street.

"*Is* someone following us?" Lisette wanted to turn around and look, but forced herself not to.

"If they are, they're better at their job than I am at mine." He laughed softly. "Though I should admit, it's not as comforting a statement as one might expect. Since you can't teach mage craft to a spy, if you want a spy who is also a mage..."

Lisette understood. "You have to start with a mage and teach him to be a spy."

"Yes. They did their best, but they were given poor material to work with. My instructors despaired of me ever understanding ciphers." He sighed. "My mind just isn't that twisty."

Lisette thought about that as they walked. "They must have chosen you for a reason." She looked over at his face. "Out of all the mages, I mean."

Remy guided her to the entrance of a tea garden on the edge of butcher's lane and held the door for her. "I was one of the few who could pass for anything other than a mage."

They made their way through the dark building — full of plants, Lisette noticed, and wondered how the tea shop kept them alive in this light — and followed the proprietor outdoors to a private alcove in the courtyard. Lisette sat on one low bench while Remy took the opposite one. Once tea and pastries had been settled on the table and they were alone again, Remy continued. "Imagine it. Galfigon College for Magecraft is filled with respectable students, almost all from famous families, with perfect manners and the power to match their status. But none of them could walk into a bar without everyone noticing."

He poured out tea for both of them. "And then there was me. Not quite bad enough to be thrown out of the college, but more often mistaken for a cleaner than for a student. *Not* from a famous family. Known more for my ability to climb things than any spell craft." He settled back, wrapping long fingers around the porcelain cup. "I suspect they kept me around at the college because they were worried about what I might do otherwise."

"It does seem like you'd have the makings of a very good thief." Lisette inhaled the steam coming from her cup, enjoying the earthy smell of expensive tea.

"If I didn't know better, I'd say you've been talking to my mother." Remy smiled and sipped from his cup. "In any case, when the bureau of external affairs decided they needed someone with different skills, the college leapt at the chance to get rid of me."

At her quizzical gaze, he elaborated. "Once a student is accepted, the college is responsible for housing them until they are employed elsewhere. It's a safeguard — *nobody* wants a bunch of shiftless mages wandering the city with nothing to do. The college thought they might have to build me my own hut behind the kitchens so they could forget about me." He spread his hands. "Anyhow, here I am."

Lisette thought there might be a grain of truth somewhere under the self-deprecating story, but possibly not a very big grain. She pulled her great-grandmother's journal from her waistband and pushed it across the table. "After you left last night, Rye and Barlow found a painting of Bralinost with someone who looked a lot like me. So I searched my family's logbooks and found this."

Remy absently pulled the book toward him. Then his gaze sharpened. "That's a clever piece of work there." He glanced up. "You got past it, of course."

"I'm stubborn."

His smile warmed her more than the tea did. "I'll take stubborn over well-trained any day." He opened the cover and puzzled over the entries on the first page. "I take it most of this is shop talk for your profession."

"It's nearly identical to the logbook I keep, though my handwriting is more legible." Lisette scooted around the table to sit next to him. She reached over to pull the book closer. "Things get interesting about halfway through." Even after being handled for a day, the book still gave off the smell of old paper and leather as she turned pages. She found the entry with the final diagram of Bralinost's body. "Here."

Remy concentrated on the diagram, and then looked over at her, wonder on his face. "Someone in your family *made* it."

"And nearly got murdered for her reward." Lisette pointed to the cavity in the automaton's body, where her many times great-grandmother had written her other notes. "I *think* this must hold something that animates Bralinost. If we could get close enough to remove it..."

Remy considered that for a moment. "I think the problem may not be getting close enough, but staying alive long enough to do anything once we're in range." His shoulder rubbed against hers companionably as he peered at the book. "Does that say *dragon magic*?"

"Yes. But I didn't see anything else in the journal about dragons, so it might just be a guess." Lisette flipped back a few pages. "The other thing I was looking at are the joints here." She pointed at the final design of the legs. "She was worried about whether they would be damaged too easily... Well, that was back when she still believed Bralinost's purpose was to carry messages around the city. But I think she was right to be worried. That joint wasn't working properly on one leg when we saw it. There might be a way to take advantage of that."

Remy flipped back to the first drawings her great-grandmother had made after she had accepted the commission, and started reading. Lisette forced herself to relax and let him look over the pages at his own pace. She wanted to explain the diagrams, to make him understand how incredible the images were. But he needed time to absorb the other information first.

And maybe the beauty of well-designed machinery would be lost on him. Most people weren't awe-struck by those sorts of things.

She poured herself another cup of tea. Remy's satchel moved, and then Simi walked across his legs toward Lisette. He petted the cat absently as she went by and turned another page. Simi moved onto Lisette's lap, circled twice, and lay down, purring loudly enough to be heard over the nearby fountain.

Remy reached the page on which the writer had come to Harbor Crag. Then he turned back to look at the final diagram of Bralinost.

Having the cat gave Lisette something to do with her hands. It also gave her a valid reason not to move back to her original seat on the other side of the table. She recalled her earlier intention of keeping Remy at arm's length. Simi butted her hand when her fingers stilled. "Sorry." Lisette went back to scratching the calico's cheeks.

Remy glanced over at her words, saw the cat, and smiled. "Ah, she's got you under her spell now. One might think she would tire of it at some point, but she'll sit there forever if you keep petting her."

"Is it common for spies to carry cats with them?"

That got another smile from him. "Simi was my key to passing the class on coercion. I'd been putting it off, and I either had to pass the test or leave the college. The students had to make some creature traverse an obstacle course." A look of distaste flashed over his features. "The idea..." He shrugged. "Most students used something like a cockroach. Easy to overpower, and even easier to replace if the spell went wrong. Which they often did. Meanwhile, I looked at the assignment and realized it didn't actually say we had to use coercion to accomplish the goal."

Lisette raised her eyebrows and waited.

"So I raised a kitten and taught her tricks." He gave a rueful smile. "It turns out I'm *much* better at training cats than I am at coercion magic."

"And you passed."

"Not without some controversy, you understand. It certainly wasn't what they had intended. But the college teaches over and over that the contract is everything, so when I pointed out the test said nothing about requiring magic, well... They changed the test after that. But I still passed."

"And then you had a cat."

He nodded. "It wasn't as if I would put her back on the streets after all that. They tried to get me to leave her behind when I came here. Something about her making me too noticeable. But she's better at this than I am. And she's a good disguise. I mean, really, what kind of spy would bring his pet cat along with him?"

"So she's just a regular cat?" Ever since she had realized Remy was a mage, she had assumed there was some magical connection between him and Simi.

He looked a little uncertain. "She definitely started out as a regular kitten." He held his cupped hands in front of him and smiled at the memory. "She was so tiny when I first saw her. But I raised her in the dormitory where all the students live. I never intentionally spelled her, but..." He made a face. "There was a lot of stray magic flying around, most of it mine. I have no idea what that does to a cat."

Simi purred and rolled on her back.

Remy gazed fondly down on her. "Then again, maybe she is just a normal cat who is excessively spoiled. I'm not sure how I would tell the difference." He turned back to the book. "I think you're right. There must be something powering Bralinost that goes in this spot. And I think I even understand why it was made that way, as opposed to just setting up some outside spell."

Lisette worked her way through his words. "You mean like the spells that light up rooms."

"Exactly. If you wanted to create a creature to defend something, having the spell powered externally leaves it vulnerable. Anyone could get by if they could interrupt that spell first. Like if, say, someone disrupted the bonds tied to the Dagger of Aarat." He stopped and closed his eyes. "It was in my *hand* and I didn't realize it."

He opened his eyes again. "But never mind. This design fixes that weakness. Nobody can disrupt the spell without gaining physical access to Bralinost."

Looking up at a point in the sky, Remy frowned for a few seconds before continuing. "Though presumably it would need to be given more power on a regular basis. The owner must take the source out, recharge it, and put it back. Maybe if we could figure out when..."

He lapsed into silence. "No, I don't see a way to make that work. It can't need fresh power very often or the owner would be tied to the house in order to keep it working."

"Maybe there's some way to overwhelm it from a distance." Lisette exhaled softly. She'd known it would likely come to this when she'd seen those words scribbled on the page the night before. "We need to talk to a dragon."

Remy's eyes lit up. "Yes! And there's no time like the present."

Lisette hoped she could keep them safe from a grumpy dragon long enough to make their case. "I need to go back home to pick up a few things first."

CHAPTER 47

CHEATING

B ack in the freeholder quarter, a different man loitered on the street across from Lisette's shop.

"We *could* remove him," Remy said, "but I'd rather not." The excitement about meeting his first dragon hadn't worn off yet, and he kept smiling at the slightest provocation. "That might give whoever hired him more information than they already have."

"You create great distractions, but I need you to come with me." Lisette looked up at the building. "I think we'll have to go over the roof."

Lisette hadn't brought the tools she would need to open Bosco's door, but Remy used the same trick he had employed on the bakery lock a few nights earlier. Once inside the room packed full of dead and dying plants, he cocked his head. "The owner is..."

"Going to live with his daughter so she can watch out for him," Lisette finished. "Tiffany's going to move in here. After a lot of cleaning."

She made her way to the bedroom without windows. "I think Bosco won't be back until the evening." She really *hoped* that was the case. Otherwise, she was going to have to explain why she was taking a stranger through his bedroom. That would be awkward.

In a similar manner to the roof access in the uncles' bedroom, a ladder had been created here by planks set in the wall. Lisette climbed up first, opened the hatch, and moved onto the roof.

Remy hoisted himself out a few seconds later. "I must say, it feels like cheating to do this sort of thing during the day. Where's the excitement of not being able to see anything in front of you?" Simi, still in his satchel, poked her head out and looked around.

"Replaced by the excitement of roof tiles that sometimes slide around. Be careful." Lisette moved over the peak of the roof to the other side, where they could only be seen by someone watching from the parallel street. They made their way toward the uncles' shop.

"Forgive me if this is an indelicate question." Remy's voice betrayed no sign of tension as he walked on loose tiles high enough off the ground for a fall to kill him. "You seem to have a lot of experience with this. Are you *sure* you're a watchmaker?"

Lisette laughed. "I grew up in the quarter. Children here explore everything they can. And someone has to come up here to fix the roof when it leaks." She stopped when they were near the hatch she wanted. This would be the tricky part. If the man on the street looked up at the wrong time, he would see them.

After going back over the roof peak, she crouched by the hatch, lifted it a bit, and felt around for the connector. Rye and Barlow weren't lax enough to leave a hatch going straight into their bedroom unlocked, but there was a way to unseat the hinge if you just... There. She flipped the hatch open and scrambled down the stairs, Remy close behind her.

Lisette jumped to the floor and turned to the doorway.

Barlow stood just outside, a stout club resting on his shoulder. "Been a while since I've caught you coming down this way."

Lisette moved forward, ignoring the club, and kissed his cheek. "Someone's watching the front of the shop."

"So Rye told me." He looked past her. "Hello, Remy."

"Good afternoon. Sorry to intrude like this."

Lisette tapped Barlow's chest until he moved to the side. "We just need to pick up a couple things and then we'll go away again." She headed down the stairs to the main shop and heard both men follow.

Down on the ground floor, someone had shifted around the stock at the front of the shop. Now there was a path to get from the stairs to the maze at the back of the display area without ever being visible to the street. Lisette waited until they were among the packing crates and kept her voice low. "You were expecting us to come down from the roof, weren't you?"

"Certainly not so soon. But Rye thought it might be a good idea to redecorate the front. It gave the men across the street something to look at, anyhow. *I* wanted to go out and invite them into the shop to help us move the heavier furniture, but Rye wouldn't let me." Barlow gave a theatrical sigh. "He also wouldn't let me wait on the customers over in your shop, though I can't see how I would make any bigger hash of it than you do."

They had reached the area with the workbench, now hidden behind piles of other stock. Barlow rolled a clothes rack to the side and glanced at Remy. "You should have heard her this morning. One might have thought the customer had defaced a precious painting from the way she carried on. *Cooking oil!*" The last sentence was given in a falsetto that sounded nothing like Lisette.

The insult to the pocket watch hit her again. "You don't just dump used frying oil on delicate machinery and expect it to work better."

Next to her, Barlow laughed softly and placed a hand on her arm. "I'm sorry. I know what he did was unforgivable. But listening to you from over here was the highlight of my week." He moved another crate to give them access to the workbench and continued in a more sober tone. "Quite a few people have been coming into your shop today, Lisette. About like it was the first time."

The first time Lord Hanley had fixated on her, he meant. Lisette's stomach dropped. She'd been halfway to convincing herself his appearance the night before had been an aberration. But if the nobles were queuing up to get another look at her... "You and Uncle Rye have to promise you'll be careful. Remember what happened last time."

"We'll be fine." Barlow patted the club he'd set on top of a crate.

Remy placed his hands on the dome of magic obscuring the items on the workbench. "What happened last time?"

Lisette answered before Barlow could downplay it. "Someone tried to burn their shop down because they were helping me. They would have died if Rye hadn't woken up and put out the fire before it really caught."

Freeholder buildings were difficult to burn, but the building didn't need to catch on fire to kill everyone inside. Generating enough smoke from burning the contents would do the trick.

The magic under Remy's hands flickered and then disappeared. "Might be worth keeping a few extra buckets of sand around until we deal with this Lord Hanley problem." He opened his satchel and handed Simi to Lisette. "Though he seems like the type to try something different if the first approach fails." He loaded up his satchel with everything they had brought back from the tunnels the night before. "Anything else?"

"The concentrator." It was the only other thing in the building that might get them into trouble if it was found. She looked at Barlow. "Can you get it from my shop? It's in the second drawer on the right, under my workspace." She thought about what else was there. "It's the only thing in the drawer that doesn't have a chain on it."

The bells on the front door jingled. Barlow picked up his club. "Rye's probably still busy next door. Let me deal with my customers first, then I'll grab it for you." He caught Lisette's look at the weapon and smiled. "Not with this. I just want to keep it handy in case we have trouble."

Lisette watched him leave. Simi draped herself over Lisette's shoulders and purred.

Next to her in the gloom, Remy spoke quietly. "May I offer a bit of advice?"

Lisette turned her face to him and waited.

"You can't take responsibility for the risks others choose to take. It's not fair to either of you."

Lisette knew what he was saying, even agreed to some extent, but this was different. "If I had just stayed away, they wouldn't be in danger from Lord Hanley right now."

He took her face in both hands. "You are not responsible for what Lord Hanley does."

The sincerity in his voice made her want to believe. "But —"

Simi rubbed her head against Remy's hand and Lisette's cheek.

"Not responsible." He let his hands fall. Lisette missed the warmth. "If it helps any, I think you were an extra attraction for him, but not the main pull." He patted the satchel. "My guess is he was planning to clear out the freeholder quarter completely so he could tear it apart looking for these. Having the duke raise your taxes would have accomplished it if you hadn't ruined that plan for him."

"Then why is he still here?" Lisette let her frustration bleed into her voice. "It sounded like he figured out all those things had been taken away."

"Ah, well. Just because you weren't his primary goal doesn't mean he has forgotten about you." His mouth quirked up. "You're a hard person to forget, Lisette Allinde, watchmaker, thief, dragon-touched, and friend of Simi."

Lisette smiled at the appellations. "Oh, well, if the cat likes me..."

Before she could think about what she was doing, Lisette leaned forward and touched her lips to his. She'd meant it to be a brief peck, nothing more, but he followed her when she rocked back, deepening the kiss.

Lisette forgot about where they were, forgot about the other people in the shop, even forgot the man in front of her was a spy. Heat shot through her body as she explored his lips with hers.

Then Remy sprang back. "Simi!" He touched the scratch next to his eye and looked at his finger. "See if I get you the expensive fish snacks next time." His voice held laughter, but Lisette noticed his breathing wasn't any steadier than her own.

Simi shook her outstretched paw, then groomed it, settling down on Lisette's shoulders again.

Lisette reached up to touch the skin near Remy's eye. It

hadn't started bleeding — Simi had just left four lines that were turning red. "Maybe she doesn't like me after all."

"Oh no, she just wants you to herself." He touched her hand with his. "Maybe we could revisit this later when Simi is someplace else. *After* we talk to the dragon."

"And defeat Bralinost."

"And take care of Lord Hanley once and for all." Remy moved her fingers to his lips, then let her hand drop at the sound of footsteps.

Barlow was practically stomping as he came into view, a change from his normally light step. "Oh good, I'm not walking in on anything." He handed Lisette the concentrator, then caught sight of Remy's face. "What did you... Oh, hang on, those are cat scratches." He looked at Simi, still grooming herself on Lisette's shoulders, and then to Remy's face. Barlow grinned. "I see."

Lisette sighed. "We're leaving now. Tell Tiffany I said hello and that she should be careful, too." There was no way Barlow wouldn't be analyzing this scene with Tiffany within the hour.

Barlow looked between them. "Try to stay safe. At least as safe as you can."

"We will." Lisette kissed him on the cheek and led Remy back through the maze, to the stairs, then up onto the roof again.

Time to introduce Remy to Aarat.

CHAPTER 48

DRAGONS LIKE CATS

The guards no longer surrounded the dragon warrens, but traffic remained light, as if the city occupants worried the explosions might return.

When nobody was around to see, Lisette guided Remy through the crack in the wall, and then down into the main tunnel.

She whispered, "Maybe we should have left Simi with Uncle Barlow." The calico had been content to stay on Lisette's shoulders as they walked through town. But Aarat had shown himself to be mercurial in the past, and if Lisette had to jump out of the way to avoid a blast of dragon fire, she didn't want the cat to get hurt. "Is there any way you can convince her to stay right here?"

Remy glanced wryly at the cat. "Unfortunately, her ability to stand still disappears the second I'm out of sight." He stopped and leaned to look into a side tunnel they were walking past. "Somehow, I think she's more likely to find trouble if she's on her own than if she comes with us." He rocked back, and they continued walking. "Besides, if you believe the old stories, dragons like cats." After a few more steps, he looked over. "Though maybe it would be best if she stays with you, at least in the beginning."

They had arrived at the entrance to Aarat's chamber. Lisette put one hand on Remy's chest to stop his progress, then ducked through the opening. On the other side of the room, the dragon crouched, watching her. His scales glowed, amber to the tips, with a dark edge where they connected to his black skin. The magic Lisette had released by bleeding on the dagger remained.

"*Lisette.*"

With one word, Aarat made her heartbeat stutter. As her pulse fell back into a regular rhythm, Lisette acknowledged the truth: Aarat was not happy with her.

Her carefully planned introduction flew out of her head. "There's another dragon," she blurted. "I mean, I'm pretty sure there's another dragon, and Lord Hanley is using them to power his spells. I want to stop that, but we need your help."

"We." The word was snorted in anger, a blast of steam hitting the ceiling.

So that was the problem. Well. No use apologizing now. She stepped to the side. "This is my friend..." She'd almost said Remy's name. Could she do that without giving Aarat power over him? "He helped me get your dagger. I never could have done it without him."

"I see." Suddenly, Aarat sounded amused.

"You can tell him my name," Remy said. "As long as I don't do so, it won't be binding."

Aarat's eyelids lowered. "So they *do* still teach the way of dragons." Now he sounded pleased.

Since the dragon wasn't breathing fire at them both, Lisette decided she hadn't made as much of a mess of things as it seemed. "This is my friend, Remy."

Remy bowed. "It is an honor to meet you." He stood and entered the chamber. "Am I correct in thinking you are the dragon known as Aarat? The one who once laired near the mage college on the Island of Light?"

Another puff of steam hit the ceiling, but this one seemed to be more an expression of surprise. "Long before you were born." A ripple of magic flowed down his body to the tip of his tail.

Lisette gestured at Remy to open his satchel. The sooner they finished this, the better. "I brought a... thing for you." She took the vane Remy handed her. "I'm not actually sure what it does," she admitted as she held it out in both hands. The top spun even faster than it had in the caverns beneath the freeholder quarter. "But it seemed like something you would like." She owed him a curiosity to replace the zoetrope she had destroyed during their first meeting.

Aarat stepped forward until he was crouched in the middle of the cave. With the bulk of his body away from the wall, Lisette could see the chain, though the shackle on his leg remained hidden. The dragon reached forward with one arm and plucked the vane from her hands with the tips of two claws.

From her perch on Lisette's shoulders, Simi batted at the claws as they withdrew.

Aarat put the vane on the ground and stared at the cat. "Oh ho! The little hunter wishes to take on bigger prey."

Lisette placed a hand over Simi's paw. Aarat hadn't *sounded* offended, but how could she be sure? "Sorry about that. This is Simi. She lives with Remy."

Aarat tapped one claw on the ground, an enticement. "Your little hunter is safe with me."

Lisette glanced at Remy, but Simi made the decision on her own. She leaped from Lisette's shoulder and ran across the cavern, wrapping her front legs around the dragon's luring digit and kicking at the skin with her back feet. Lisette halted her involuntary impulse to grab the cat when she noticed Aarat hadn't moved.

Simi scrambled up the dragon's leg, over his shoulder and up his neck. Once on top of his head, she rolled onto her back, rubbing her forehead against his.

Lisette looked over at Remy again. He shrugged. "Simi picks her own friends."

Aarat kept his head still. "I have missed cats." He blew out a breath, though Lisette noticed the movement of the air didn't touch Simi's fur. His attention went back to the vane. "This *thing*, as you called it, tracks the currents of magic around us. A skilled user could estimate the location of a fleet if a mage traveled with it. Or predict the arrival of a dragon." His eyes focussed on Remy. "Perhaps even track you throughout the city, mage."

Remy nodded at the appellation. "Perhaps, though my strengths lie mostly in using what little magic I have. My instructors were never particularly impressed with my raw power."

"Bah." Another gout of steam, which also didn't ruffle Simi's fur. "Your instructors have been hiding away to hoard their power for centuries, not even noticing the magic building up in this city. If your skill brought you here, it is stronger than their force."

Lisette wanted to point out that *she* had ended up in Aarat's chamber by nearly falling on top of him. Perhaps bad luck or idiocy had its own power.

Remy put his satchel against the wall of the cavern and dug out the journal Lisette had found. "We need to get past a mechanical creature that guards Lord Hanley's study." He flipped to the page with the final diagram and held it up.

Lisette wondered how a dragon that big could read writing that small, but Aarat appeared to be concentrating on the page. "If I understand this correctly, the source of its magic is carried within, so I won't be able to disrupt it from a distance."

The tip of Aarat's tail twitched. Simi stopped lolling about on his head and crouched. "I have seen such a thing before. Sheer power will overcome it." The dragon's voice became dry. "This would appear to be an exception to skill being stronger than force."

Simi sprang, scrambling across the scales on Aarat's body and grabbing the tip of his tail.

"*I* could overpower it if I were not rooted to the earth." Aarat shifted his head so he could see the cat, but his eyes were on Lisette. "If the concentrator you had before still worked, you might take enough dragon magic with you to accomplish the task."

Lisette dug it out of her pocket. The metal gleamed even in the dim light of the cavern. "I repaired it as much as I could. But without knowing exactly how it runs normally... Some pieces had rusted away and I had to fashion replacements." She clamped her lips shut, overcoming the urge to give more excuses. She had done the best she could, and she *was* the most skilled watchmaker in Harbor Crag.

Next to her, Remy leaned forward to look at what she held, but Aarat plucked it from her grip before Lisette could tilt the concentrator to show it to the man. Magic rippled over the dragon again. Simi sneezed.

The concentrator hummed, but there was a grinding edge that hurt Lisette's ears. Something in the mechanism wasn't right. Perhaps if she opened it while it was working, she'd be able to see...

Aarat blew out a breath. "It holds some, but it will lose

that quickly." He flipped the concentrator toward Remy, who plucked it out of the air.

Remy looked at what he held. "Now, how does this..." His words seemed directed at himself. Then he found the slider on the side. "Oh. I see." He nudged it upward. Holding out his other hand, he snapped his fingers and a ball of flame drifted up. The ball grew in size as he edged the slider up. The flames were the size of his head when they abruptly fizzled out. In Remy's other hand, the concentrator made one last grinding sound and fell silent.

Lisette threaded her fingers together so she wouldn't give in to the urge to take the concentrator apart and start poking at it right there. "I might be able to make it work better if you're at my shop to test it."

Remy looked up. "With Lord Hanley watching? It might be safer to work here."

Lisette tried to imagine moving enough of her tools here. That could be done, but then she wouldn't have her workbench, and her lights, and the cleaner. She'd be running back and forth between her shop and the dragon warrens multiple times per day. Someone would surely notice.

But perhaps there was another way.

Lisette held out a hand. "Can I see the journal again?" She turned to the page with the diagram. "If we can't have it hold magic long enough to overpower Bralinost, would it be possible to do the opposite? Take it there and drain Bralinost's magic into the concentrator?"

Silence greeted her words. Lisette suddenly realized she, who knew nothing about magic, had just made this suggestion to a mage and a dragon. "Never mind. I'll shut up and let the two of you figure it out." Maybe she could play with Aarat's tail while they worked, like the cat.

Remy frowned. "That could work. I think." He stared up at the ceiling of the cavern as he thought. "If we set up a calling spell and..." He lapsed back into silence.

Aarat harrumphed. "It might indeed work."

Suddenly, the dragon flattened his scales against his body. He lowered his head and charged straight toward them.

CHAPTER 49

THE DRAGON-BORN

A t the sight of an enormous dragon charging across the chamber, Lisette's brain deserted her. She stared, mouth agape. Luckily, Remy's reflexes were more useful. He lunged to the side and knocked them both out of the dragon's path.

But Aarat's progress stopped abruptly as he reached the end of his chain. He drew in a breath. Lisette knew the fire would come out when he exhaled. Aarat was still focused on the entryway to the cavern. Had the guards followed them?

The street girl with a scar across one eyebrow danced forward and patted Aarat on the nose.

Lisette's hand flew up to cover her mouth. The girl was going to be incinerated, and there was nothing Lisette could do. Next to her, Remy choked out, "No!"

Aarat blinked. He didn't exhale.

The girl twirled past his face and threw her arms around the dragon's neck.

Lisette pulled her scrambled thoughts together. "Please don't hurt her. She's not a threat." She stopped when she noticed the dragon's stillness. Somehow, it reminded her of the way Aarat had reacted to the cat. Simi was still over on the other side of the cavern, pouncing on a bug next to the wall, unconcerned that his giant playmate had just sprinted away.

The girl leaned against Aarat, humming and twirling as she moved down his body, somehow avoiding the razor-sharp edges of the dragon's scales. Aarat was holding himself still to *protect* her.

Lisette kept her eyes on the dragon and the girl, but spoke to Remy. "Do you understand what's happening here?"

"Not a clue." Then he must have noticed the shackle around Aarat's leg, and the blistered and weeping skin around it. "That's horrible!"

To Lisette's eye, Aarat's leg looked marginally better than it had the first time she'd seen it. Any human who had sustained such a wound would have had healers at their bedside every day until the skin healed — or until they died. How long had the dragon been imprisoned? How had he not gone mad?

The girl stopped spinning when she reached the shackle. She grasped the chain and then let go and flapped her hand, as if she had held something hot. Frowning, she placed her palms on the intact skin higher on Aarat's leg.

"Bad magic." Her outline wavered as a ripple of power went over her. "Wash it clean."

Remy's voice was full of awe. "That's... That's impossible. She's too young. There aren't any..."

Under the girl's hands, the blistered dragon skin sparkled and healed, leaving no trace of the scars such a wound would cause. Flakes of dried blood dropped to the cavern floor. And the shackle itself glistened, as if covered in oil. Protection from further harm, Lisette realized.

When the glow around the girl faded, Aarat's skin looked as if it had never been damaged. She patted his flank. "All better."

Then she walked to the edge of the cavern, lay down with her head on a mound of gold coins, and fell asleep.

Silence echoed.

Lisette looked between Remy and Aarat. Both of them stared at the sleeping girl. "What just happened?"

Remy blinked, as if he had forgotten where he was. "She's dragon-born."

Lisette looked back at the girl. "She looks pretty human to me."

That brought a little smile to Remy's face. "No. Or rather, yes, she's human. But..." He took a ragged breath. "Let me try again. While a human child is in the womb, if the mother is near dragon eggs that are close to hatching, it *changes* the child. At least that's what the texts say. I've never met one."

Aarat spoke for the first time since the girl had come into the chamber. "That is true."

Remy nodded, though Lisette thought it was a sign that he was trying to pull his thoughts together. "They have... an *affinity* for dragon magic. Not to use as a mage would. But it gives them the ability to heal dragons." He nodded again. "I can see that part is true as well."

Lisette looked at Aarat's leg, the shackle glistening on unbroken skin. "I'm surprised more women don't make that happen for their children." Surely a child who could heal dragons could support an entire family. In a place where children were set to work as soon as they could hold a needle or a knife, it would be a gain for everyone, including the child.

Remy rocked one hand back and forth. "Leaving aside the logistical difficulties of finding a dragon egg, there's also the concern about other changes. It isn't just the child's ability to wield magic that is different. They... In some ways, they pick up traits of the dragon in their personality."

Both Remy and Lisette looked at Aarat. Lisette tried to imagine the girl breathing fire.

The dragon sounded amused. "The dragon-born are independent and drawn to gold and curiosities. They are clever in some ways, but rarely live among other humans."

Remy nodded. "The texts speak of them almost as if they are feral children. As adults, they often withdraw and live with their favorite dragon."

Aarat puffed out a breath. "But that is *not* the reason they have become rare. Mages began stealing the dragon-born and using their blood in spells to tame the dragon magic. Such was used to forge the Dagger of Aarat. When dragonkind realized what was happening, we stopped allowing new dragon-born to be created."

Remy's jaw dropped. "The mages did *what*?"

Lisette's thoughts finally caught up with what Remy had said before. "Wait. Are you saying a dragon hatched in Harbor Crag a few years ago and nobody noticed?" She looked up at his face. "Or could she have come here later?" That would make more sense. If all the dragons in Harbor Crag were chained, they would hardly be producing baby dragons. Or would they?

Remy shook his head. "If I understand correctly, a dragon egg can be close to hatching for years. And that's after pausing its development for centuries." He shrugged, glancing at Aarat. "They have a different timescale than humans."

"Indeed." The dragon walked back to his regular resting spot and lay down again, with the tip of his tail curled around the girl. Simi abandoned her bug chase and climbed back to her spot on Aarat's forehead. "But dragon-born who are no longer near the egg as infants lose their abilities. And dragon-born who are old enough to travel won't leave."

Keeping a handful of people from talking about the duke's love of chickens was one thing. Lisette didn't believe news of a dragon hatching in Harbor Crag could be hidden. That left one alternative.

"There's a dragon egg somewhere in the city."

Aarat's voice brooked no argument. "You must find it and bring it here before it hatches."

Lisette sighed. So much for getting her life back again.

CHAPTER 50

IMPROVISE

The easiest way to find the dragon egg in Harbor Crag would be to ask the girl currently asleep with the dragon's tail wrapped protectively around her. But Lisette wasn't about to risk her own life by shaking the girl awake while the dragon loomed over them both.

"She looks like she's going to sleep for a while." Lisette shook her head. "We really need to find a name for her. I can't just see calling her 'that girl'." And they definitely couldn't refer to her as *that dragon-born girl* outside this chamber.

Remy sat down with his back against the rough stone wall, examining the concentrator. "I heard one of the other children call her Sunny." His tone said he didn't believe it was her real name.

"That will work until she can tell me what she wants me to call her." Lisette sat down next to him. "How much preparation do you need to do before we try to get past Bralinost?"

"Beside convincing Simi to come with me instead of staying with her new friend?" He glanced over at his cat,

263

who was now curled up, sleeping in the hollow between Aarat's shoulder blades. "I think the sooner we do this, the better. Especially now we know there's a dragon egg close to hatching somewhere." He turned his head to look at Lisette. "I bet Lord Hanley's going to return as soon as his kidney stone problem disappears. If he thinks the egg is there, that would explain why he's been trying to drive out all the freeholders."

The last thing Lisette wanted was for another dragon to be chained. "So, how do we get in?"

Remy grinned. "The same way we did last time. But this time the tour will be interrupted. Having one person responsible for the tour only works if everyone sticks together."

Lisette tried to imagine the placid leader of the tour handling people darting every which way. No. He wouldn't be able to contain them.

"Then we hide for a bit until everyone assumes we've gone. Once the coast is clear..." He gestured to the concentrator.

"You like to improvise."

He raised one eyebrow and gave her an arch look. "I'd love to plan quite a bit more, but getting the information I need increases our risk of getting caught before we start." Then his face relaxed, and he grinned at her. "Of course I love to improvise. That's how I keep people from noticing half my magic is just sleight of hand."

Lisette didn't believe someone who had graduated from a mage's college would be as ineffectual as he claimed to be, but it didn't matter. Compared to hers, his magic was infinite. "We'll need festival masks. As long as nobody is watching Tiffany's work area, she'll set us up with something." Not having masks would make them stand out during the Festival of Secrets. But more importantly, Lisette wanted to be unrecognizable, just in case Lord Hanley was still there when they arrived.

Remy's smile faded. He reached over and took her hand, his strong fingers warm against hers. "Maybe it would be better if I did this one alone. If I get caught..." He shrugged. "Thieves get caught all the time. The owner of the residence isn't fixated on me." He paused. "I don't know what would happen to you."

Lisette suspected she wouldn't be allowed to leave, but she refused to think about how that would play out. "I have to be there. You didn't feel the tie to the other dragon. What if you can't tell what holds the bonds? You won't be able to take everything." They wouldn't have a horse cart waiting outside. But the real reason Lisette wanted to be there had little to do with the dagger, or whatever held the bonds to the other dragon.

She wanted to be there to keep Remy safe.

The thought made no sense — Remy had the training and experience for this and she was just a watchmaker who had blundered into this mess — but her heart didn't care. If she sent him off alone and he didn't come back, she would never forgive herself.

"You just want to take Bralinost apart to see how it works." He squeezed her hand. "It's probably too heavy to bring back with us, you know."

Lisette followed his lead to lighten the conversation. "It's worse than that. I want to take Bralinost apart and do all the maintenance nobody has thought about for hundreds of years. I think I could fix that leg if I had a few minutes."

Remy laughed and got to his feet, using his hold on her hand to bring her up with him. "Remind me to never get between you and something mechanical." He turned to look across the chamber. "Simi, love, it's time to go to work." He clicked his tongue. The cat hopped down from her dragon perch and trotted across the room.

Remy bowed to the dragon. "It has been an honor to meet you."

Steam rose from the dragon's nostrils. "Perhaps not all mages are as useless as I had thought."

From the look on Remy's face, he'd received the biggest compliment of his life. Lisette shook her head. She gestured to the girl they were calling Sunny, still asleep on her pillow of gold coins. "Will she...?" She stopped, suddenly realizing how inane her question had been. If something could harm the girl while Aarat was there to protect her, Lisette would be of no use in stopping it.

Aarat's nostrils twitched. "The dragon-born will rest safely here." He turned his head to look squarely at her. "Take care. I would not have our bargain broken through your death."

While Lisette was trying to figure out whether that had been a threat or a blessing — or both — Remy crouched and unloaded the rest of the items they had taken from the tunnels beneath the freeholder quarter. "May we leave these here with you? It would be better if Lord Hanley did not have access to them." Simi jumped into the satchel when he was done.

The dragon silently assented.

Remy straightened up and took Lisette's hand again. "Let's go steal from Lord Hanley."

CHAPTER 51
FIREBIRD AND APPLE TREE

As Lisette stood next to Remy outside Lord Hanley's estate, she tugged at her headpiece, trying to get it to quit poking into the corner of her eye. "Why did I let you talk me into this monstrosity?"

Tiffany had been delighted to provide them with costumes for the evening, and had the perfect ones waiting, a firebird for Remy and an apple tree for Lisette. The leatherworker had laughed at the look on Lisette's face when she had brought them out. "I made these for a client, and then he broke up with his lover and couldn't face taking them with him. Still paid me, though. So you might as well get some use out of them."

Lisette had stared at her headpiece, which had a gnarled rattan trunk rising from the crown, with five branches, each bedecked with green silk leaves and dried berries for apples. It added a foot to her height. The framework to keep it from falling over wrapped around the skull and was covered by a mossy hood made of more silk. She would have a simple green domino mask under it all.

Remy's mask took up less space, but was equally eye-catching. White leather with red and gold stitching hid his upper face, and a spray of gilded feathers extended up from the back and cascaded to his shoulders.

Both masks came with matching cloaks.

Now, in the queue outside Lord Hanley's estate, Lisette wished she had held her ground and insisted on just the plain domino mask, perhaps with a bit of glitter as a nod to the holiday. Her cloak hid her plain clothes, but she was aware of all the attention they attracted.

Remy put one arm around her shoulders and murmured in her ear. "These costumes are perfect. Nobody will remember us at all. Besides, I needed someplace to store a few things." He brushed the tip of one finger along the line of her jaw. "And as an added bonus, I am *forced* to act the part of a lover, as such a costume demands."

Lisette's mouth went dry as heat pooled in her body. "Such a sacrifice." The legend spoke of two lovers who remained true, even after they were cruelly transformed by a wealthy man's mage into a firebird and an apple tree.

"Of course. It might buy a few extra minutes before discovery if searchers assume a couple has just found a quiet place to... converse." His fingers trailing along her skin belied the businesslike words.

Two could play at that game. Lisette tilted her head toward his ear as much as her headdress would allow. "Perhaps we should have started with another tour of Lady Merou's house. I might have found such a place." Who was she kidding? If they hadn't been on a mission to save a dragon and heading into the home of a man who terrified her, Lisette would have dragged Remy into the nearest corner and worried about propriety later. Much, much later.

Remy's low laugh did more things to her body.

The voice of the guide cut through the air. "This way, please. Those who are taking the tour of the famous Hanley estate, this way, please."

Lisette felt Remy's groan down to her soul. They moved forward with the rest of the queue, passed over the necessary coin, and went through the small trade gate into the stunted garden.

The same two women in the kitchen ignored the tour group again. Lisette wondered what it would be like to have people wandering through, treating your work as if it were part of a performance put on for their benefit.

She answered her own question: probably similar to the way she had felt when all of Lord Hanley's acquaintances had stopped by to evaluate her. Lisette silently apologized to the kitchen women for her part in this scene.

They went through the dark hallway with its linen closets and memories of Remy explaining where the exits were, and then out into the public area. The magic hit her again, and was easily brushed off. But this time she was waiting for it, and saw the exact moment when her fellow tour-goers fell under its sway. Their eyes widened, and one woman licked her lower lip.

The last time they had been on the tour, the house had been active, with servants bustling about to prepare for a large festival dinner; Lord Hanley had been finishing his daytime business and getting prepared for the parties of the night. This time, the large dining hall was empty. All the activity seemed to be happening on the second floor, with messengers running up and down the stairs.

As the tour moved from room to room, following the same script, Lisette was aware of Remy reaching up to her headpiece when nobody else was in sight. He'd done something to the apples back in Tiffany's workshop, with Tiffany's enthusiastic participation. Lisette couldn't imagine sending one of her creations off to be destroyed, but her friend had been unconcerned. "By next year, something will have squashed it, or bugs will have eaten the fabric or the stuffing. And masks like these usually get knocked into doorways." She had raised an eyebrow with a sly grin. "Or crushed under people."

The guide recited his facts about the staircase being built by artisans from the Island of Light as the group climbed. An adolescent boy in messenger's livery pushed through the group without apology, on his way to deliver another note.

Lisette wished she could stop time for a moment so she could read the message the boy carried. Who was Lord Hanley sending messages to? Were her friends in the freeholder quarter safe?

When the group reached the landing, Bralinost crouched just behind the invisible line that defined its domain. Now that she had seen the diagrams of its design, Lisette wanted to see it in motion again. She and Remy would disable it, perhaps for good. That seemed an even bigger waste than destroying her headpiece, though even more necessary. Still, to create something that lasted for hundreds of years... Lisette might have been envious of her ancestor if the task hadn't cost the woman her home and all the family she'd ever known.

Remy drew her along. "You'll have more time to examine it later," he whispered.

In the wing with the family bedrooms, the door to the main suite was closed. As they passed, another messenger slipped out and Lisette glimpsed Lord Hanley lying in bed, face drawn and pale. Then the door closed again. Whatever Remy had done to him the night before hadn't worn off yet.

Joyous spite coursed through Lisette. She grabbed Remy's hand and threaded her fingers through his.

The tour continued, past Bralinost, who was now pacing back and forth at the end of its hallway, and through the wing with the guest bedrooms. Finally, they headed down the stairs.

A quick squeeze of her hand was all the warning Lisette got before smoke billowed from the receiving room. The guide sprinted ahead of them and yelled, "Fire!"

People in the tour reacted in two different ways. Three people ran toward the fire, yelling suggestions about smothering it with drapery and closing doors. Everyone else fled, most heading on the familiar path through the kitchen, and a few passing closer to the smoke to run out the main doors at the front of the house.

For just a moment, Lisette wanted to follow them. Being trapped in this particular home and burning to death were two of her top fears. Combining them didn't make either better. But Remy tugged her back toward the dining rooms, and she sprinted with him. They passed two servants running in the other direction, drawn by the sounds of the chaos behind them.

Her headpiece got caught on the second doorway, pulling away to fall on the ground. But when she would have stopped to retrieve it, Remy pulled her forward. "Leave it. They might remember that nobody went through the gate with an apple tree on her head, but this will make them believe they just missed you going by." He doffed his feathery headpiece, looping a piece around a door handle as they ran, and pulled on a plain black domino mask.

At the back of the house, he flung open the door, looked around both inside and out, and then drew Lisette back along the corridor they'd just traveled. "Excellent! Now we find a place to wait."

CHAPTER 52
AND THEN THERE'S... THIS

Their hiding place, while they waited to take down
Bralinost, turned out to be a small room off the
large dining hall, where freshly washed table-
cloths hung from racks mounted under the ceiling. Lisette
and Remy brushed past the fabric to find an alcove not
visible from the door. A tiny window near the ceiling, far
too small for a person to get through, provided just enough
light to see their surroundings and a bit of fresh air. Remy
nodded. "This will do nicely."

Lisette glanced around. "You knew this was here?"

"I saw the window from the outside. I was *hoping* this
would be here." He shrugged. "I had another three places
picked out if this didn't work." He sat down with his back
against the wall and opened his satchel. Simi popped her
head out and looked around.

Lisette sat down next to him and let Simi settle in her
lap. "What if they search the house?"

Digging around in his satchel, Remy sniffed. "Effec-
tively searching a house this size without extra help is
nearly impossible. And they don't really have a reason to

think they should. As far as anyone knows, a spark from the fireplace landed on a cushion and caught. Bad luck, really. Aha! Here it is." He pulled out the concentrator and looked up. "But if they do search, and they actually look back here, I can keep us hidden."

Then he sighed. "As long as nobody actually steps on us. That's the problem with spells of hiding. People don't see you and then they trip over you and it gets awkward."

Lisette ran her fingers through Simi's fur as the calico purred and gently stropped her leg. "That seems unlikely to happen back here."

He grinned and sat up straighter. "See how good at this I am? Remember this when you become convinced I don't have any redeeming qualities." He patted her knee. "Now stop distracting me so I can work out how to get this thing spelled properly."

Lisette looked at him. "You... didn't do that before? I mean, there's improvising and then there's... this."

"I knew we would have some time to wait." His lips twitched. "You see why I wanted you to remember the part I did right?" Then he lapsed into silence, staring at the concentrator.

Lisette went back to petting Simi so he could work in peace.

Half an hour later, her worries about being caught had fallen away and she was wishing she'd brought a book along. Her ancestor's journal or the book they'd found in the tunnels under the freeholder quarter would have been nice, but they'd left both in Aarat's chamber. Not that she'd have been able to read for much longer anyhow; the sunlight coming through the window had faded quickly, and now they were just getting reflected light from the lanterns illuminating the streets. Simi had fallen asleep in her lap, and Lisette was considering joining the cat in that occupation.

Next to her, Remy stiffened. "Do you hear that?"

Lisette hadn't noticed anything. "Hear what?"

"Carriages stopping in front of the house. I think Lord Hanley is heading out."

"Or they've sent for another doctor."

Remy huffed a laugh. "That *would* be rather ironic, wouldn't it, if our plans to rob the man were foiled by the dart I put into him last night." He shook his head. "But doctors don't usually travel in packs. I think he's leaving with his men." He buffed the metal of the concentrator on the sleeve covering his forearm. "I think this should work."

"I just hope it doesn't fail completely. I had to make some guesses about how the parts worked." Lisette shoved down the fear telling her they should have waited until she'd made it better. Lord Hanley's renewed attention meant she was in danger every time she stepped into her workshop.

And now they had a dragon egg to find before it hatched. *That* reminded her of a different problem. "How much do you know about dragon eggs?"

"I think I've told you everything I know." Remy slipped the concentrator into his shirt pocket and raised one hand, ticking points off on his fingers. "They can wait hundreds of years before hatching. They're responsible for the dragon-born. And... little dragons come out from them."

He paused. "Oh, and one book mentioned the shell is mauve, not white. I suppose that will be helpful if we're trying to make sure what we've found is a dragon egg and not some sea creature." He laughed quietly. "Can you imagine? Triumphantly bringing the egg to Aarat and having some tentacled monstrosity break out?"

Lisette smiled. "Aarat might consider it a delicacy." She forced herself to return to her original question. "But what I really wanted to know is how big they are. I mean... is this something we're going to be able to shove into a belt pouch and carry back to the dragon warrens? Or are we going to need to rent a horse and cart? That could be difficult to sneak through the wall."

"Ah, I understand the question now." Remy stared up at the ceiling for a few breaths. "I don't know that I've ever read anything that gives dimensions, but there's a lithograph in the early editions of Falstoy's *Dragons of the Outer Islands* that shows a man standing in a cave next to two eggs. The eggs were about mid-shin height."

He looked back at her. "So, assuming the artist was given accurate information — which might be a large assumption — the egg should be something a person could carry in one arm."

Lisette nodded slowly. "At least that's one worry laid to rest."

Remy slapped his hands down on his thighs. "Excellent." He stood up and reached a hand down to her. "The carriages have left. Let's go deal with Bralinost."

CHAPTER 53
SNEAKING UPSTAIRS

.

L isette crept after Remy, trying not to bump into anything. It helped that all the windows had been left open, probably to rid the house of the lingering stench of burning wool and horsehair. Traffic noise from the street camouflaged their footsteps.

It felt wrong to be heading toward the grand staircase; the tours hadn't shown the servants' stairs, but they would surely be less exposed. After a moment, Lisette realized the defect in that plan. With Lord Hanley and his confidants out of the house, only the servants remained.

Scraps of conversation from the receiving room floated back as they headed toward the front of the house.

"... never get this clean ..."

"... order a new one. He'll have to replace them all."

Remy peeked around the corner. With his lips next to Lisette's ear, he whispered, "Two people, looking the other way. Just keep walking."

She nodded.

Remy took her hand. They walked around the corner, in plain sight of two women cleaning up the mess in the receiving room. Soot stained the walls and floor. One woman was on her hands and knees, scrubbing at the tiles, and another woman, younger than the first, wiped the wall.

Remy and Lisette were halfway to the staircase when the woman cleaning the wall took a step back and lowered her rag. "It's going to have to be repainted, I think."

"Still has to be washed down," the other woman grunted as she scrubbed.

Lisette followed Remy up the staircase, placing her feet carefully so the footsteps wouldn't make a sound.

"Yeah, I know. I was just saying. Maybe himself could just wave his hand and it would be good as new."

"Stop talking nonsense and get back to work, or we'll be at this until dawn and get no sleep at all."

By that point Lisette was far enough up the stairs that the women were no longer visible through the doors of the receiving room. She relaxed.

And then she tripped, lurching forward

The sound of her boot sole hitting the marble of the stairs echoed throughout the room. Lisette froze.

"What was that?" The younger woman's voice was louder, as if she had turned away from the wall to face the door. "I heard someone moving around upstairs."

The sound of bristles on tile paused. "It's probably that *thing* up there. You know how it rattles around when himself is away." The scrubbing sounds resumed. "And he's going to throw you to it if you don't quit skiving off when there's work to be done."

"Ugh. Keep your hair on. I'm working, I'm working." There was a brief pause. "He wouldn't really let that thing have someone, would he?"

Remy and Lisette slowly climbed the rest of the steps.

Lisette breathed a sigh of relief when her boots were safely on the rug covering the landing.

In front of them, Bralinost prowled around the hallway, coming right to the edge and then moving away. Remy took the concentrator from his pocket, placed it on the floor, and sent it past the barrier with one neat kick.

Bralinost ran forward. It examined the metal, seemed to decide it wasn't something to be torn apart, and went back to prowling the area.

Remy drew Lisette to the hallway with guest rooms. "Now we wait," he whispered.

From this vantage point, they couldn't see Bralinost, but they could hear it moving up and down the hallway. More importantly, they were hidden from anyone coming up the staircase. If a servant came upstairs to clean Lord Hanley's room or take care of the other hundred chores to be done in a house this size, Remy and Lisette could duck into the bedroom.

The noises of the house continued. The two women in the receiving room were joined by a man who carried the fire-damaged couch to the basement. Then a bell rang, and an arriving messenger was sent away with instructions on where to find Lord Hanley. Lisette couldn't make out exactly what was said, but she heard "up the hill". So he wasn't at any of the balls held at the fashionable estates near the waterfront. Lisette hoped her friends were safe.

A few minutes later, a new voice spoke downstairs. "Cook says dinner's ready." Then the noises coming from below ceased.

Remy pushed off the wall. "Let's see how things are progressing."

They went back to the landing. The concentrator

remained in the same place Remy kicked it, but the metal had discolored and the top bulged. It was completely silent.

Lisette grimaced. "That doesn't look good. I think it must have overheated." She looked at Bralinost, standing halfway down the hallway. "We might have to leave and figure out something else." Maybe they could use a broom to retrieve the concentrator so Lord Hanley wouldn't know about this attempt.

Remy looked at her and raised one eyebrow. He deliberately moved one foot inside Bralinost's boundary.

The automaton hurried forward. Two extra limbs ending in blades unfolded from its body. But its movements seemed uncoordinated and slow, at least compared to its previous speed.

Remy pulled his foot back. "I think we can take it. I'll distract it, and you pull out the pack that powers it."

"What?" Lisette looked from Remy to Bralinost and then back again. "Are you insane?"

Remy shrugged. "Possibly. But I think this is the best chance we're ever going to get."

Lisette took a breath and blew it out. He was right. This *was* their best chance.

Images of both of them being sliced to pieces ran through her head.

But... If she didn't do this now, Lord Hanley would continue to have the magic he needed to sway people's minds. He would keep coming back to her shop until she left the city again. Her friends would remain in danger.

"Fine." She took another breath and blew it out, rubbing her suddenly freezing fingers together for warmth. "But Aarat's going to be really mad if I die before I perform that favor for him."

"I'll keep that in mind." Remy took her hands in his,

providing the warmth that seemed to have disappeared from Lisette. "Kiss for luck?"

Lisette tried to laugh, but gave up. She leaned forward.

Their lips met and lingered. Sweet, but with a hint of banked need, a promise of things to come.

Lisette pulled back and squared her shoulders. "Let's do this."

They stepped into the hallway to face Bralinost.

CHAPTER 54

SHALL WE?

T he instant Lisette and Remy stepped past the line, the automaton charged forward, blades raised high. Lisette jumped to the side, her back against the wall.

With less magic to power it, the damage to Bralinost's back leg was more obvious. But even so... Lisette's heartbeat thudded in her ears. That thing was going to slice them apart.

Ahead of her, Remy jumped the other direction and kicked the body of the mechanical creature, pushing it toward the damaged limb. It wobbled, then shoved upright again, slashing at his chest. He jumped back, landing further down the hallway.

From the grunt Remy made, Lisette thought at least one blade must have caught him. But now she had a better idea of where the compartment she need to open was.

Bralinost, given the choice between the two of them, decided Remy was the more immediate threat and turned toward him. Lisette still had a path to safety, but Remy couldn't get away without getting past Bralinost again, unless there was an exit in the other direction. She braced herself, ready to push off against the wall.

Bladed arms whirling, the automaton danced closer to Remy. He snatched a painting off the wall and thrust it in front of him. Canvas tore. A solid *thunk* rang through the hall, and then the rectangular frame sagged and twisted. Remy threw the remains over Bralinost's head, halting its advance for a second while it pushed the canvas to the side.

This was Lisette's chance.

She lunged forward, wrapping her arms around the back end of Bralinost's body, adding all her weight to its damaged hind leg. The automaton crashed to the ground, one bladed arm buried beneath it.

Unfortunately, that left one arm with a blade free, and Lisette's face was within easy reach. Her fingers scrabbled to find the catch on the opening. If the design had been changed after her great-grandmother had left... If it required tools to open... If she didn't get the plague-taken thing open in the next second, she was going to lose an eye and probably her life.

Bralinost's body jolted, as if it had been hit with something. She didn't have time to see what had happened. Lisette's fingers found the catch. She ripped the section open and yanked out the chain within.

The automaton collapsed.

Lisette blew out a breath. She pulled her arm from under the thing and pushed herself to her knees. In front of her, Bralinost lay still, legs sprawled at angles no natural animal could replicate.

"Well done!" Remy whispered. "Are you hurt?"

Lisette looked down at herself. "No." She climbed to her feet, ignoring her trembling legs. "You?"

Remy dug through his satchel. "Nothing of consequence." He pulled out a narrow roll of cloth, then wrapped it around his forearm. "It's not deep, but I'd rather not leave my blood here for another mage to find."

Having seen an example of what blood could do, Lisette agreed. She regarded the automaton at her feet. If they left it like this in the hallway, any servant passing by would know it had been damaged. She knelt again. The arms with blades should snap up like so... Yes, and the covering pulled down, clicking as the magnet engaged. She rolled it on the other side and forced the other bladed arm to retract as well. Then she dragged it closer to the hallway entrance. The servants were used to seeing it there.

When she had finished, Remy had tucked in the end of the bandage and picked up the remains of the painting and frame. He swept his hand toward the closed door. "Shall we?"

The room they had seen Lord Hanley enter wasn't locked. But why would it be? Bralinost had guarded the hallway against all intruders for three hundred years. Remy turned the handle and pushed.

As soon as the door was opened just a crack, Lisette could feel the dragon magic. The spark within her chest burned anew. "Can you feel that?"

Remy glanced at her. "Just an overwhelming amount of magic. You?"

"A dragon. Or a link to one anyhow." Lisette stopped before crossing the threshold, remembering how the duke's room had been alarmed. "Is it safe to go in?"

"I think so." Remy suited action to words, stepping inside. He looked up and cocked his head. "Still alive."

Lisette followed him in. Light shone from the ceiling, bright as the mid-day sun. Aside from a table in the center, the room was filled with shelves and cabinets. Maps, books, and scrolls lay scattered on every surface. The skull of some beast, larger than Lisette's torso, grinned down from the ceiling in the corner where it had been strung up with wire. On the higher shelves, crystals, figurines, weapons, and mechanicals Lisette couldn't identify crowded together. Somewhere in all that was a connection to a dragon.

But while she had felt the Dagger of Aarat from across the room in the duke's palace, here she couldn't get a sense of direction. Or rather, the pull came from everywhere. Maybe if she got closer to whatever it was, she'd be able to figure it out.

Remy blew out a breath. "It may take me a bit to find what I'm looking for."

Lisette blinked. She'd nearly forgotten he wasn't here just to find something bound to a dragon. He had been planning to come here even before she got involved. "Should I keep an eye out for anything in particular?"

He gave a wry grin. "This is one of those 'I'll know it when I see it' times, but if you notice something talking about sea monsters..." He glanced up at the skull in the corner. "Anything that looks like our friend over there."

Lisette nodded. She dragged a chair over to the far end and climbed on it to look at the top shelf. A crystal bottle in the shape of a turtle held an oily green liquid. Next to that lay a silver ring shaped like a cobra. As she watched, the metal snake stirred, like it scented her. She pulled her hand back, and it settled again.

Next to the snake ring, a cluster of red and pink crystals winked in the light, casting reflections on the wall behind them. Lisette could see tiny figures moving within. She rolled her shoulders to ease the tension. "You're a mage, right? When you settle down, are you planning on keeping a room of creepy magic stuff?"

"Hm?" Remy looked up from the book he'd been paging through. "No. Don't worry. If I live that long, I'll probably just keep a staff. If you don't have anything to steal, you don't have to deal with thieves." He grinned. "And I would know." He glanced over at Simi, who had left the satchel and was prowling around the room, and then nodded at the shelf in front of Lisette. "Besides, I'd rather not find out what happens when Crystals of Drolaria get knocked off a shelf every day for a month. I know the spirits within are supposed to be permanently trapped, but I'd rather not test that."

"Glad to hear it." Lisette turned back to the shelf before he could see her blush. What did it matter what he did or didn't keep in his house? It wasn't as if... She forced herself to pay attention to the things in front of her. Next to the spirits trapped in crystals was a tarnished spike, curved nearly around on itself in a loop big enough to pass her hand through. She hesitantly brought one finger closer and the ember in her chest flared.

Avoiding the sharpened tip, she lifted the spike and climbed down from the chair. "Got it."

Remy abandoned the book in front of him to come see what she held. "Interesting." He opened his satchel and then loosened the drawstring on the leather bag within.

Lisette dropped the spike inside. The burning in her sternum eased as Remy pulled the drawstring tight. Her sense of urgency returned. They could get out of this house before Lord Hanley came back. "Now I can help you find..." She trailed off as she felt the tug of dragon magic. "Oh, no."

"What's wrong?"

Lisette swallowed. "There's more than one." That was why she hadn't been able to tell where the link to the dragon was — multiple items were calling to her. They couldn't leave yet. She dug her fingernails into her palms.

Remy put a hand on her shoulder. "It will be alright. We have time. I'm not done yet anyhow."

Lisette nodded, forcing back panic. She would find the other links while he searched, and they would leave before Lord Hanley finished whatever he was doing. "Right. Sorry."

"You took down Bralinost. Nothing can stop you."

Lisette took a breath and blew it out. "I did, didn't I?" She dragged the chair over to the next section and climbed up again. "You stayed alive long enough to distract it, of course."

"I'm good at that."

This shelf had a wood carving of the coast, with the islands just visible at the top. A knot in the wood moved. She picked it up by the frame and held it down to Remy. "Is this the sort of thing you're looking for? Something is moving in the water."

Remy took it from her and watched it for a moment. "I'm not sure what that is. Definitely worth further study. Thank you."

As she moved along the shelves, Lisette found more things with links to dragons: a dagger, and a brooch with a sharpened pin on the clasp, and then a knife that could have been used to cut meat on a plate. Each time, she dropped the item into Remy's pouch and hoped it would be the last, and each time she felt a new tug.

After she had added yet another dagger to his bag, Remy looked worried. "Just how many dragons *are* there in Harbor Crag?" He had added two books, a few scrolls, and the wood carving to his satchel and was just waiting for her to finish.

"I don't know. I've only ever seen Aarat." Lisette rubbed her chest, which burned again. She wanted nothing more than to run from the house, but that would mean coming back again.

"Keep going. As long as things still fit in the bag..."

Lisette nodded and moved the chair again. "I think we might be getting close." They were getting easier to find, as if without everything clamoring at once, she could follow the trail. She climbed up and used two fingers to pick up a caltrop, avoiding the spikes sticking in all directions, then dropped to the floor again. "You're going to have to be really careful taking things out."

Lisette was reaching to drop it into the bag when the door flew open.

CHAPTER 55

GOOD BOOTS ARE WORTH THEIR WEIGHT IN GOLD

A guard stood in the entry, crossbow in hand. His grey hair was clipped close to his skull, and the lines and scars on his face showed he had both age and experience. When he saw them, he turned his head to call over his shoulder. "In here!" The crossbow came up to point at Remy's chest. "Hands up."

In raising his hands, Remy caused his bag to shift, and the spiked weapon Lisette had dropped missed the opening and fell on the floor. She bent to pick it up, but the crossbow swung in her direction. She froze.

Remy slowly turned his head in her direction. "Just relax and don't move. Don't give them any reason to panic. We'll figure something out later."

Lisette nodded, hoping he couldn't see her hands trembling.

A second guard, younger than the first, appeared in the corridor. "I didn't find anyone else. It's just these two."

The first guard nodded without moving the crossbow. "Make sure they aren't armed, then put shackles on them. Him first."

Remy bowed his head. "I'm flattered. Though I feel I should point out we're neither of us fighters."

Lisette stopped herself from adding that Simi was the most likely to injure someone. If they hadn't noticed the calico yet, better to leave it that way.

The second guard edged past the first and came around the table toward Remy.

Remy pointed at the floor. "Watch out for the..."

The guard, possibly suspecting a trap, didn't look down. The caltrop embedded itself into the sole of his boot. He took a step back and raised his foot so he could look at what was stuck to the bottom.

Remy winced. "You'll want to be very careful pulling that off. In fact, if it were me, I would just take the boot off and buy another pair. I know, I know, good boots are worth their weight in gold, but that particular weapon embedded right there means it is no longer a good boot. Thought I suppose you could just buy one new one and —"

The guard with the crossbow cut through Remy's words. "Shut up."

"I just want him to —"

"Shut. Up."

Remy subsided.

The younger guard braced his ankle on the opposite knee, grasped the center of the caltrop, and pulled. It popped out of his boot, and he put his foot down. "There." He glanced at the first guard, caltrop on his bare palm. "What should I do with this thing?"

"Put it down someplace you won't step on it again." The first guard sounded exasperated, as if tired of telling the other man what to do. "Then make sure they aren't armed and get the shackles on them."

As Lisette watched, the second guard dropped the caltrop on the table. It landed on a paper shoved into a book and slid toward the edge. He reached out to grab it. "Ow."

A tidal wave of magic swamped the room, centered on the younger guard. He opened his mouth in a silent scream. All his muscles locked.

Both Lisette and Remy took a step away. Even the guard at the door rocked back, though the crossbow remained fixed on Remy's chest.

Lisette remembered the sensation of magic overfilling her body and wishing for death in order to escape. Aarat had drained the magic from her through her name, but this man didn't have a dragon to assist him. She looked at Remy. "Can you do anything?"

He looked dubious. "Probably just die messily right next to him." He met her gaze. "You survived."

"I had help." Aarat had been a part of the bonds she had broken when she'd bled onto his dagger. She had no idea if Aarat could help manage the magic released by bonds with a different dragon. And now seemed like a very bad time to test that.

The guard still stood, holding the caltrop. His body withered under the uniform. Magic swirled around them, making Lisette's skin tingle. She took another step back.

With a crunch, the guard dissolved into ash, bits of charred skull and skin raining down onto the floor along with his untouched clothing. The overwhelming magic disappeared.

The guard at the door swallowed. "What happened?"

Remy left his arms out. "He bled onto something anchoring spells to a dragon, but he wasn't strong enough to hold the magic himself." He glanced over at Lisette. "The bonds would have snapped back to their owner. He had to have noticed."

Lisette gave a small nod of understanding. Even if the guard hadn't called him back earlier, Lord Hanley would return soon. If she couldn't get past this guard now, she would never get away. But he had a crossbow leveled at Remy, and he didn't seem afraid to use it. There wasn't even a window she could throw herself through.

Remy drew his shoulders back. "We're both men of the world. Surely we can come to some understanding here. There are riches in this room that a man could take his whole lifetime spending." He looked at the ash on the floor. "Who's to say that's one person, not two? With another uniform left behind, there wouldn't even be anyone looking for you."

The man looked at the floor, apparently considering Remy's offer. Then he shook his head regretfully. "No. Lord Hanley would know, and I have no desire to die slowly." He gestured to Remy. "Put down the bag. Carefully." When Remy had complied, he jerked his chin at the far wall. "Now both of you turn around, put both hands on the wall, and lean forward."

Lisette turned, took hold of a shelf on the bookcase attached to the wall, and leaned forward. She looked over at Remy. "I'm sorry. We should have left as soon as you found what you needed."

"And have to come back again? Nonsense. I should have been prepared for someone to find us." He looked over his shoulder. "How *did* you find us, anyhow?"

The guard closed one shackle around Remy's wrist. "Bralinost never rests when we do our rounds."

"Ah." Remy nodded. "We couldn't really do anything

about that." He gave a little shrug as the other shackle closed. "Sometimes things just don't go as planned."

As the guard fastened metal around Lisette's wrist, she closed her eyes, fighting off the panic that threatened to steal her breath. They had broken into Lord Hanley's house, and she would never escape.

A high-pitched howl erupted in the space behind her, ending with an extra grunt of effort as metal met flesh and bone.

The guard stumbled into Lisette and collapsed next to her foot.

CHAPTER 56
SEEING DOUBLE

Lisette twisted, and the shackle connected to her wrist swung wide with the movement. A dark-haired woman faced her, eyes wild, holding a bronze statue of a dragon in both hands like a club.

"Where's the other guard? They travel in twos." The woman looked around the room.

Lisette pointed at the uniform and ash next to the table. "He's..." She had planned to explain, but her brain finally caught up to what her eyes were seeing.

The face of this woman was the same one Lisette saw in the mirror. Not exactly, of course. Lisette's chin lacked a dimple, and her cheeks still bore a scattering of freckles not found on the face looking back at her, but still... They could have been sisters, separated at birth. This double was even dressed in clothes that Lisette would wear in her shop.

The other woman seemed to have realized the same thing. Her face twisted into a bitter smile. "You're her, aren't you? The one he really wanted."

Lisette covered her mouth with one hand, her stomach threatening to rebel.

A pulse of magic came from Remy, and his shackles dropped to the floor with a clatter. He reached over to touch Lisette's wrist and the metal fell away. "Might I suggest we have this conversation elsewhere? These two guards may no longer be a problem, but more will be on their way."

The other woman shrugged. "You're on your own. I'm leaving." She turned to go.

"Wait!" Remy tugged on the back of the woman's tunic and then ducked a wild swing of the statue that might have killed him if it had connected. He dropped the fabric and held up a hand. "Just didn't want you to step on that," he said, pointing at the caltrop on the floor. "That's what did in the first guard." He reached past her and carefully grasped the center of the caltrop. "Let me just take care of this before anyone else gets hurt." He dropped it into the leather bag within his satchel.

As soon as the caltrop disappeared, another item on a shelf tugged at Lisette. This time she could tell exactly where the dragon-linked article was, but she couldn't turn away from the woman who bore her own face. "He did that to you. I'm so sorry." Lisette hadn't known Lord Hanley would recreate her features on another woman, but she'd known he would fixate on someone else — had known and had deliberately ignored it, because she couldn't do anything else.

Now she was faced with the results.

The other woman looked at her, the features the same but the expressions different, as if her muscles were used to another arrangement. "I *know* it's not your fault." The smile left, but the bitterness remained. "Yet I wish in my soul it had been you instead." She held up a hand to stop anything Lisette might say. "You'll want to be gone before he returns." She ducked out the door.

Lisette still felt ill, but the other woman was right. They needed to be gone before Lord Hanley arrived. She dragged the chair over to another bookcase and picked up a hatpin.

Remy stood next to her, holding the leather bag open. "How many more do you think there are?"

She could tell now. "Two." She could even tell where they were, but the shelf was out of reach. "They're both up there." She pointed to the shelf mounted on the wall behind the skull of the sea creature. "We may have to leave them."

Remy put his satchel down on the ground and knelt. "Simi, love, time to earn your fishies." When the calico ran to him, he boosted her up to the skull. Using the monster's eye sockets as steps, Simi scrambled up to the shelf. Once there, she daintily knocked down another dagger and a metal finger cuff that extended to a spike.

Remy put both things in the satchel. "Is that all of them?"

The ember in Lisette's chest had gone back to sleep. "I think so."

"Excellent." Remy closed the bag and slung the satchel over his shoulder. "Come on, Simi. Time to go."

Simi knocked the last item off the shelf, a crystal container. It fell on the floor and cracked, releasing a purple liquid with a noxious smell. Remy jumped back, catching the cat as she jumped down. He pushed Lisette into the hall and yanked the door shut behind him.

Remy gulped a breath. "Don't let anyone tell you cats are easy to live with." He squeezed the cat against his chest. "Trying to kill us all." His lips twitched. "Though I can't think of a nicer homecoming gift for Lord Hanley."

The woman with Lisette's face had disappeared. Another open door further down the corridor showed where she had come from. Remy took Lisette's hand, and they ran for the main staircase.

They passed the lifeless automaton at the end of the hall. Two steps down the staircase, the front door burst open. Lord Hanley's voice roared. "Find the thief!"

Remy reversed and pulled Lisette back in the other direction. They sprinted past Bralinost, then beyond the workroom they had just left. Through the other open door, Lisette glimpsed a windowless bedchamber and then they were at the end of the hall where a tiny alcove led to a narrow door. Remy pulled Lisette against him in the small space. She could hear booted feet running up the main stairs. Simi purred and rubbed her cheek against Lisette's nose.

The door had no handle on this side, just a flat metal plate riveted to the solid wood. Remy put his hand against it. He frowned. "They must have closed the servants' stairs in this wing."

With Bralinost guarding the hallway, that probably cut down on staff turnover. Lisette whispered, "Can you get it open?"

In the hallway, someone opened the workroom. The door slammed shut again, and the sounds of retching covered up yells from the staircase.

"It's..." Remy grunted. "Rusted." A stronger pulse of magic hit the door. "If I'd known we'd be leaving this way, I would have oiled everything when we got here."

A male voice called from the bedchamber. "This one's gone." Another voice Lisette didn't recognize snarled back. "Keep looking. If we don't give him a better target, he'll be coming for us."

A second person was sick in the hallway. The odor of

vomit mingled with the noxious purple liquid and drifted through the air.

Lisette leaned closer to Remy's ear. "Now would be a good time for one of your distractions." Her stomach roiled.

He grunted again. "Nearly there."

Lisette pushed further into the alcove.

Booted footsteps came closer.

CHAPTER 57
ABOUT THAT CORNER

The footsteps faltered. A man coughed, then half-retched. The footsteps abruptly receded as the man ran toward cleaner air.

Under Remy's hand, metal rasped against metal. "There we go," he whispered. He pushed on the door. It didn't move.

Lisette threw her shoulder against it, and tumbled through the opening, narrowly missing the stairs heading down. She slammed into the far wall of a dusty landing. Simi dug her claws through Lisette's tunic and hung on.

Remy followed more sedately. "Well done." He pushed the door closed after them, leaving the stairwell in absolute darkness. Lisette heard the scraping of metal as he relocked the door. Then there was a pinpoint of light coming from Remy's index finger. He held out his other hand. "Shall we go?"

Lisette followed him down the stairs. Abandoned tea cups and chipped plates showed the area had once been used by the servants to take their breaks. Everything was covered by a thick layer of dust. Either a new group of people had entered service without learning about the abandoned stairwell, or something had blocked the other door.

When she glanced behind them, she could see clear footprints in the dust. "If they open that door, they're going to know which way we went."

"It would probably be best if we were gone by then." Remy nudged a plate to the side with his foot and stepped down to the landing. An open space to his left held the stairs going to the cellar. "Let's see where we are." He held his glowing fingertip toward the doorway. "Ah."

This doorway not only lacked a handle — the entire door was missing. Instead, a wall of bricks faced them where the opening should have been.

Lisette nodded slowly, forcing down her panic. "That's... not an exit."

"Well, no. But it explains why everyone forgot about this stairwell." He gave the bricks an experimental nudge. "I suspect we *could* get through if we needed to, but it would make enough noise that we'd have people waiting for us when we finished. Let's see what our other options are." He headed down the staircase.

Lisette followed, one hand trailing along the wall for balance. Simi still purred against her neck. "Remy?"

"Yes?"

Something slimy grew on the stones lining the stairwell. Lisette stopped to wipe her hand off on her leggings before hurrying after him. "If we can't get out of here —"

"We're getting out of here."

"Yes, but if we *can't*, do you think I could break the bonds to the other dragons the same way I did with Aarat's dagger?" Then at least Lord Hanley wouldn't have access to all that power.

Remy turned to look at her. "I don't know. We're going to get out of here, so we don't need to find out." He faced forward and started moving again. "I suspect Sunny could learn to do it safely if she talks to the other dragons."

Lisette refrained from pointing out that neither Sunny nor the other dragons were stuck here in Lord Hanley's home. If it turned into a choice between being caught or trying to break those bonds, she'd open a vein and accept turning to ash as the second best of all possible outcomes, right after the top spot of Lord Hanley dissolving into a pile of powerless goo.

They reached the lower landing. At least it had a door, even if the door didn't have a handle. Remy put his hand against the plate. Magic pulsed. He shook his head. "If I ever build a giant house to store all my magical trophies, remind me to make maintenance a priority." Magic pulsed again.

Lisette scratched Simi's chin; it seemed like a better idea than curling up in a ball and screaming. "I thought I just had to make sure you had a spot for a staff."

Remy turned his head and gave her a huge grin.

Only then did she realize what she'd said. "I mean —"

He wagged his finger. "Nope, no taking that back." Magic pulsed through the hand still on the door, and she heard metal scrape. "Now we *have* to get out of here just so I can find out what spot you had planned. Am I to be relegated to a corner under the stairs? Or —" He stopped talking as the door moved. The light went out as Remy dropped his hand.

Compared to the Stygian darkness of the stairwell, the gloomy cellar seemed almost bright. Lisette crept forward to put an eye to the opening, feeling Remy do the same above her head. Warm humid air blew against her face, such an unexpected feeling that she looked around for the source. There. A fire burned under a vat connected to copper pipes going into the walls. The pressure-release valve hissed and sent a jet of steam into the area. Condensation covered the ground-level windows near the ceiling.

From her vantage point, Lisette couldn't see a door to the outside, but at least there wasn't a squadron of guards waiting for them, either. That was the good news.

The bad news was that the cellar had been treated as convenient storage, and the sealed door considered available wall space. A stack of old furniture had been piled in the spot, keeping the door from opening any further.

Lisette eased upright. "Maybe if we both push against the door, I can squeeze through and pull things away from the other side."

"Our other option is to try the roof." Remy kept his head pressed against the door. "My big concern is that someone might remember they need to bank the fire under the boiler. It can't always be hot enough to vent like that or they'd have fungus growing down here."

Lisette leaned forward to look again. "You think someone added fuel to heat some water and then forgot about it."

"Or got told to help search the house instead of whatever they'd planned on doing," Remy said.

Lisette considered the room. "I'd rather walk out the door than try to climb down from the roof."

"Mmm. I have to agree with you there. Especially when there are people with crossbows around." Remy removed the satchel from his shoulder and put it down on the ground. "Don't let me forget to take that when we leave."

He pushed against the door. It opened just wide enough for Lisette to get her arm through. Simi went through the gap and curled up on one of the chairs blocking the door. Remy gave a low laugh. "Thanks for helping, Simi."

Eventually, they shoved hard enough to make a space they could both squeeze through. Lisette climbed out first and took the satchel Remy handed through. After he had slid out, they closed the door and propped an old hatstand against it to hide the signs it had ever been opened.

Water dripped from the ceiling as the steam emitted from the boiler collected on the colder surfaces of the room. Lisette jumped as a drop hit the back of her neck. "I was hoping they would have assumed we'd made it out before they got back," she whispered as they hurried to the other side of the room. "But if the servants aren't moving around, they must still be searching the house."

Remy stuck his head around the corner where stairs led up to the outside, then moved back again. "Definitely still searching. There are two guards posted by the door." He opened his satchel. "If we can lure them down here, I can hide us on the landing until they go by. As long as they don't feel around in the empty space, we should be fine. Then we could go out. But we need a distraction and I haven't had a chance to restock." There was a trace of humor in the exasperated look he gave her. "You're hard on a man's supplies."

"I try." Lisette regarded the boiler. "I can think of something that doesn't require magic, but it might go wrong."

"More wrong than getting caught?"

"Probably not." Lisette pointed to the source of the steam. "If we block the valve, the vat will eventually fail. Possibly catastrophically."

Remy considered the boiler. "So... loud noise, hot water flying around?"

Lisette shrugged. "Or possibly shards of metal, windows blown out, and flooding if the pipes from the cistern are damaged."

Remy nodded. "That sounds distracting."

If they were hiding on the landing when the boiler failed, there would be a wall to protect them from flying debris. But if the guards opened the door too far when they rushed in, would they notice the hidden people standing behind it?

Lisette pulled off the tie holding her hair back. "I'll take care of the boiler while you do your magic thing to make us invisible." She looked around. "Where's Simi?"

Remy leaned over and scooped the cat from a broken cabinet where she'd found refuge from the indoor rain. "I'll take care of her. We'll be on the landing."

Disabling the valve was simple enough; Lisette looped her hair tie around the arm that kept the plug anchored, then tightened the knot until steam stopped escaping. The vat creaked as she was adding an extra hitch. Her mind conjured up an image of what would happen if the boiler exploded while she was standing in front of it. Lisette tugged one last time at the knot and ran for the stairs.

The landing was empty.

Remy would *not* have abandoned her here. Lisette took a breath. That gave her brain time to catch up. Remy and Simi were behind the spell to hide them. She just needed to get up there with them.

Through the window in the door, she could see two guards waiting. They probably couldn't see into the gloomy interior. And if she was still on the stairs when the boiler failed, she'd be caught for sure. Lisette forced herself to keep moving up the stairs to the landing.

Going through the invisibility barrier made her ears pop, but suddenly she could see Remy and Simi. Given the decrease in the street noise, Remy had added sound dampening to his invisibility spell. He pulled her against him. "Well done."

Lisette relaxed against the warmth of his body and let Simi's purr calm her mind. "I hope this works."

"Of course it will." Remy rested his forehead against hers. "In the meantime, I thought maybe I would get a few more details about this corner you're planning to leave clear for my staff."

"Really? You're going to hold me to that now?" Lisette smiled. "I'm not sure I'm responsible for anything said while running from the guards."

"What better moment of truth? Now, would this be a corner in a basement, where your friends would give me pitying glances and talk about that poor besotted man who just won't take a hint, or perhaps something a little closer to home?"

Lisette pretended to think about it. "Well... I don't *have* a basement, which makes that option difficult. So I'll have to study the problem a little more." Her lips found his, a playful kiss.

"And is there anything I can do to help with this decision?"

This time the kiss went a little deeper, and Lisette forced herself to remember there were guards on the other side of the door.

She drew back to leave a hint of space between them. "I suppose the far corner in the shop is a possibility. It's hard to get back there to change the displays, so the space is mostly wasted anyhow."

She felt Remy's low laugh against her chest. This time, his kiss teased, leaving her wanting more.

Lisette took an uneven breath. "Or I guess we could discuss some other places."

He had just lowered his head to hers when the boiler exploded.

CHAPTER 58
OVER THE WALL

Remy's spell protected them from the initial shock wave as steam blasted into the cellar, but the explosion still pushed Lisette harder into Remy. Simi yowled her displeasure.

Steam and dust filled the air, making it hard to breathe. The door flew open, hitting Lisette's shoulder, but the guard who rushed down the steps didn't notice. The other guard stood in the opening, holding the door open and watching him descend. "What is it? Is it him?"

The first guard raised the neckline of his tunic above his nose and went around the corner. There was a clatter of falling stones, and another cloud of heated dust billowed around the corner. The first guard ran up the stairs and pushed the second away from the doorway.

Before the door could swing closed, Remy whisked Lisette and Simi through the opening to stand in the gravel. Lisette was amazed the guards couldn't hear the hammering of her pulse.

The first guard bent over, coughing. "Boiler exploded. If

anyone was down there, they're in pieces by now." He coughed again. "One of the beams came down, and part of the ceiling with it."

The dark night was lit up by torches. Lisette could have reached out a hand to touch the man's shoulder.

Both guards moved back to get a better look at the upper stories of the house, and Remy moved Lisette along the path the guards had been blocking.

The second guard shook his head. "If a beam came down, that's bad. My cousin's a builder, and he says that's the sort of thing that can get expensive. Shifts the foundations and all."

The first guard wiped his face. "Surely himself will just..." He waved an arm. "Magic it all back in place."

Remy held Lisette against his side and kept moving forward.

The second guard made a derisive sound. "Not saying it couldn't be done, but you'd have to know about foundations. My cousin says they can be tricky things. I know *I* wouldn't want to live in a building with that sort of damage without getting a good builder in to check things over."

Remy and Lisette went around the side of the house. He leaned closer to her ear. "Even your *distractions* are better than mine. Perhaps I deserve a spot in the basement, after all." Three men came running along the path toward them and Remy swung her off the path to press up against the building.

The men ran by. Another rumble echoed from the broken window near their feet. Lisette felt the ground shake.

Remy whispered, "If everything hadn't been so wet, you might have burned the place down." He guided Lisette back onto the path and they moved toward the front of the house. She could see the gates that opened onto the street. They were almost out.

Except Lord Hanley stood on the drive leading to the house.

No matter which path Remy took them on, they would have to pass near him.

When the building rumbled again, a drain spout gargoyle fell and shattered on the flagstone in front of Remy and Lisette. Lord Hanley glanced over at the sound. His eyes narrowed.

Lisette stiffened. "Remy..."

"I see him." Remy pulled her off the path into the bushes near the wall surrounding the estate. "Change of plan. Up and over. Ready?" He cupped his hands.

Lisette lifted one foot and let him boost her up. She scrambled onto the top of the wall, lying down to keep a low profile. Simi joined her through far more graceful moves. Reaching a hand down, Lisette helped Remy gain the top of the wall.

Lord Hanley's voice rang out. "Over there! Stop them!"

Lisette grabbed Simi and tumbled to the other side, just in time to evade a swarm of crossbow bolts. She landed on her rear in an ornamental pond, her boots filling with water. At least the muck at the bottom cushioned her fall. Remy splashed down nearby. A crossbow bolt stuck out of his satchel, but he seemed unharmed. Simi climbed to the driest spot on Lisette's shoulder and dug her nails in.

The house on this side of the wall was dark, with just one lamp burning on the top floor, likely a servant left behind while the owners were away at a festival party. If Remy and Lisette made their way around the house, they could easily get out the front gate. But that would put them in the street next to Lord Hanley's estate.

Remy had reached the same conclusion. "Over the back wall," he whispered. He pulled her up the bank of the pond onto dry ground, and they ran across the rocky slope. Behind them, a pursuer splashed into the pond and swore loudly.

Up and over another wall put them in the bushes bordering the patio of an estate where a large party was being held. Going out through the front would put them on a different street, but they would need to pass hundreds of people.

Remy reached up and plucked a leaf from her hair. "Hungry?"

Lisette looked at her wet and muddy clothing. "We're not exactly dressed for it." At least they both still had simple domino masks on.

"No, but we could be." He gestured at the fountain on the other side of the bushes. Its broad base held water that came halfway up her calf. "A little drunken horseplay — I doubt we'd be the first. Maybe not even the first tonight."

Lisette looked out at the party. Most of the guests were inside the house, but a fair number were strolling outside. "Simi's not going to like it." The calico was already furiously cleaning herself.

"Simi can be exempt from this part." He held out a hand. "Ready?"

She looked down at the satchel by his hip, where the crossbow bolt gave evidence of their earlier activities. "You might want to do something about that first."

He raised his eyebrows, then followed her gaze. "Oh, *that*. I thought you meant something else entirely." When she laughed, he leaned forward for a quick kiss. Then he straightened and yanked the bolt out and tossed it to the side. "Much better. Ready now?"

"Ready."

CHAPTER 59
TURNABOUT IS
FAIR PLAY

L eaving their hiding spot in the bushes took effort, but Lisette forced herself to stand up when Remy did.

With a whispered promise of extra treats, Remy picked up Simi and had her balance on the top flap of his satchel, which he held in one hand. Then he pulled Lisette close with his free hand and staggered backward toward the fountain, laughing loudly as if he were drunk. Lisette giggled, hoping the guests wouldn't hear the nervous edge.

Her whoop of surprise when Remy tipped backward into the fountain felt more realistic. Then they were in the water, with Lisette lying on top of him. She took the opportunity to kiss him, forcing his head underwater. He surfaced with a grin. "Turnabout is fair play, you know." With a move that caused a wave to slosh over the edge, he flipped their positions, kissing her thoroughly as the water around her ears muffled the sound of the party.

There. That gave them an excellent excuse for the state of their clothing.

Remy stood up, drawing her with him. Telling herself it

was all for the sake of performance, Lisette wrapped her arms around his neck and found his lips with hers, letting the heat of his body protect her from the chill of the evening air.

He swung her around so her back pressed up against the statue. Water cascaded over her shoulder. She threw back her head and laughed. "You win."

Looking over her shoulder into the darkness, he smiled. "They peeked over the wall and didn't see anything. I'm sure they'll be back, but now might be a good time to go."

The other guests gave them indulgent looks when the pair stepped from the fountain. Lisette made a show of wringing water from her hair as Remy picked up Simi and his satchel from where he'd set them down before falling backward.

Then they were working their way around groups of people. Remy handed her a flute of champagne he took from a tray. She leaned against him to hide the satchel and cat. Anyone looking for intruders would pick them out immediately, but the party filled the house and Lisette knew any event with this many people would have at least one couple acting like fools. Most people who saw their dripping clothes either raised a disapproving eyebrow or hid a smile. Nobody questioned their presence.

As they staggered through the front door, Lisette handed her champagne to a bemused doorman. "Lovely party," she said.

"Yes, miss."

They kept up their uneven pace when they joined the revelers in the street, leaning heavily on each other for the benefit of anyone watching. Remy guided them toward the waterfront.

Simi jumped into her arms, for which Lisette was grateful. Soaking wet in the chill of the night, she shivered. "We need to get back to the warrens. Before Lord Hanley gets the guard to block them off again."

"And we will. But it would be better if they follow a false trail first. And you need something warmer before you freeze to death."

Lisette rested her head against his shoulder as they walked. "You got us out of that house."

He gave a low laugh. "You nearly brought the whole thing down first. You're a frightening woman, Lisette Allinde." He pressed a kiss to her temple without slowing their progress.

Lisette smiled. "I am, aren't I?"

Remy bargained with a street vendor for two cloaks with hoods, which they pulled on as they turned a corner and started walking uphill. Simi snuggled against her under the cheap fabric, just the cat's nose peeking out at the neckline.

"If we can break the bonds for all that stuff," Lisette said, tipping her head toward the satchel now hidden beneath Remy's cloak, "will Lord Hanley have any power left? Magical, I mean." He would still have the power that came with his name and his money, no matter what happened with the dragons.

"He'll still be a mage." Remy abruptly turned and walked over to a vendor selling warm, candied nuts in a cone of sweetened pastry. When he came back, he handed her one. "Someday I shall take you out for a proper meal. One which doesn't involve running from the authorities."

Lisette smiled at that. Whether from the protection of the robe or because they were walking uphill, she was finally warming up. "That would be nice. Though you'll probably be running off to sneak into some other city, won't you?" Surely, the people who sent Remy here would have other targets. No matter how much she wanted to imagine a future with him in the freeholder quarter, it was impossible.

"Ah." He was silent for a moment. Around them, a bustle of people in elaborate costumes laughed and shouted to each other. A horse clopped by, headed down to the waterfront with a cart full of lemons. "I've been rethinking things." His expression went grim. "If the mages truly were responsible for the kidnapping of the dragon-born..."

Lisette stayed silent. She didn't think Aarat had been lying about that.

Remy sighed. "When I started this, it made sense to level the playing field. But I worry the lesson learned has become 'Dragons can be chained' and not 'We need to free the dragons of Harbor Crag'." He moved closer to her to make space for a dog with a whole plucked goose hanging from its mouth and the man running after it. "I suspect I'll be out of a job soon."

"I'm sure the freeholder quarter would be willing to employ you." Lisette tried to keep her face straight. "You wouldn't mind sweeping the streets at night, would you?" She waited for him to finish laughing. "But really, people need a mage who isn't beholden to the duke or the other nobles." She flicked a look at his face. "If you wanted to stay in Harbor Crag, of course."

"It seems like a nice enough place. When nobody is trying to arrest me."

They climbed in silence for a few steps.

Lisette cleared her throat. "So, during the first five minutes you were in the city, then."

"Well, yes."

They reached a level cross street and stopped without a word. Up ahead, the city guard was forming a line around the wall of the dragon warrens. A brewer's cart with another twenty guards passed them, the horses sweating as they trotted uphill.

"That's a problem." Lisette tugged Remy to the west. "I was hoping we would get here before them."

"Too slow," another voice sang by her side. "The old one sent me to tell you to hurry, but you took too long. Now things have changed."

Lisette looked down and wasn't surprised to see Sunny skipping next to her. Presumably, *the old one* was Aarat. "Any idea on how to get through?"

The girl twirled, bouncing off a group of revelers heading the other direction. Gold glinted in the torchlight, then disappeared. Sunny skipped forward again. "You have bigger problems. That lord is at your shop holding that woman's girl with a knife to her throat and he says he wants to talk to you."

CHAPTER 60
MAGES AND PAIN

Ice water flooded Lisette's veins. "Lord Hanley has Tiffany's daughter?"

Sunny nodded as she swayed on the cobblestones to some music only she heard. Her face took on an odd expression. "The old one really doesn't like him."

Lisette didn't care who Aarat did or didn't like. She turned to Remy. "I have to go." Balling her hands into fists to keep from grabbing his satchel, she said, "You need to get all that inside the warrens."

Lord Hanley would certainly want to bargain — the things they'd stolen for the life of the child. For the safety of the dragons and everyone in the city, Lisette knew she *couldn't* give them back.

But if she had them with her, she would hand over anything to keep her niece alive.

Lisette handed Simi to Remy and turned to go, but his hand on her shoulder stopped her. "Wait a moment." He knelt and opened his satchel, pulling out the leather bag stuffed with the dragon-linked weapons they'd stolen. He held it up by the drawstring knots and looked at Sunny.

"Can you take these to Aarat as soon as you can get there safely? Be careful with them."

Sunny took hold of the cord and held the bag up, sniffing at the opening. She made a face. "Stinks of mages and pain." Then she let it down by her side. "You'll owe me a favor."

Remy nodded. "A favor of your choosing, as long as it's within my power to perform."

The girl lifted her chin and twirled away, almost swinging the pouch with its deadly sharp implements into another group of revelers.

As Sunny danced out of sight, Remy stood and took Lisette's hand. "Now we can go."

LANTERNS LIT the street when they arrived in the freeholder quarter, breathless and sweaty from running. Lisette and Remy peeked around the corner and found Lord Hanley's carriage waiting in front of her shop, with ten men in uniform stationed around it. The inhabitants of the quarter filled the street in front of the horses, some still in their festival costumes.

At the front of the group stood Tiffany. Barlow, holding Ziggy in one arm, stood next to her with his other arm around Tiffany's shoulders. Pot peeked out from behind her mother, but Lisette didn't see Turtle anywhere. Rye was missing, as well.

From the darkness in the alcove where they had stopped, Lisette bit her lip. She let go of Remy's hand. "He'll be looking for you, too. Stay hidden. I'm counting on you to get me out when everything dies down." She already missed the warmth of his hand.

Remy pulled her close. Bending his head to touch hers, he said, "Do whatever you need to stay alive. I'll be there." His kiss was fierce, a promise she wouldn't ignore.

Lisette pulled her cloak around her and stepped out, chin held high, walking toward the lights. The guards opened a path to the door of her shop.

Tiffany moved forward to meet her. Her face was pale, but her eyes were dry. "He has Turtle. Says he'll give her up when he has you."

Lisette enveloped her in a hug. "I'll do everything I can."

Tiffany slipped something under her belt. "Gut him like a fish," she whispered savagely. "Rye's in his shop with weapons if you can get over there."

Lisette nodded. She let go of her friend and stepped around her. Through the glass window, she could see Lord Hanley seated on the chair she kept for visitors. A lantern rested on the counter, throwing one side of his face into shadows. He anchored Turtle to him by holding her braid in one hand; the other held the dagger resting on the girl's shoulder. But he was looking through the glass, all his attention focused on Lisette.

Lisette swallowed the lump in her throat and kept walking. The only thing that mattered was the little girl with the stubborn expression on her face that meant she was trying not to cry.

Setting her jaw, Lisette opened the shop door and stepped inside.

CHAPTER 61
LIKE A FISH

Lord Hanley's magic rolled over Lisette, igniting the flame in her sternum. She ignored it. "I'm here. Let her go." She wanted to talk to Turtle, tell her how brave she was, and promise to get her out of there. But if she did that, Lisette was fairly certain she, herself, would lose all rational thought and try to scratch Lord Hanley's eyes out.

The magic flared again, making the dragon fire burn so bright she was amazed her skin didn't catch fire. Lord Hanley cocked his head. "Why doesn't it work? It *always* works."

Gut him like a fish, Tiffany had said. Lisette couldn't do anything until Turtle was safe. She worked to make her tone bored. "You wanted to talk to me? Then talk. I have other work I could be doing."

His hand clutched harder at the knife on Turtle's shoulder. "You broke into my house, you destroyed Bralinost, you *stole* from me, and then you damaged my ancestral home. I should have you killed."

Lisette shrugged. "You've been trying to kill me since

the day you met me." This wasn't working. She needed him to let go of Turtle long enough for the girl to get outside. Lisette took a step forward and used the cover of her cloak to pull the knife Tiffany had given her from her belt. From the weight of the hilt, she could tell it was the knife Tiffany used to cut leather. Tiffany kept her knifes well-honed.

Lord Hanley's eyes widened. "I've *loved* you since the day I met you."

"If you call that love, you don't know the meaning." Lisette reversed the knife, so the blade was flat against her forearm. She couldn't stab Lord Hanley without leaning past his dagger, but maybe she didn't need to. "Whoever raised you and made you look like all those Hanley portraits probably didn't give you a good example."

Hilt of the knife hidden in her palm, Lisette stepped forward and pulled Turtle's head against her side. She put her other hand on top of Lord Hanley's wrist. The touch of his flesh made her skin crawl, but it drew his eyes as she'd intended.

His breath quickened. "You don't know what you're saying."

"But I do." Lisette ran her hand over Turtle's head until she came to the base of the braid. With one quick jerk of her arm, she severed the hair.

Lisette turned, scooped up Turtle, and got two steps toward the door when she was yanked back by the hem of her tunic. She thrust Turtle toward the door and shouted, "Run!"

Turtle pelted out the door. For a moment, Lisette thought the guards around the carriage would stop the girl. Uncle Rye ran forward and scooped her up in one arm. With the flat of his long-sword blade, he deftly batted aside the reaching arm of the nearest guard. Then he backed toward the crowd where Tiffany waited. The guards glanced toward the shop, the crowd, and the carriage, and let him go.

Lisette felt a blade at her neck. Now Lord Hanley was close enough for her to stab, but she'd lost the knife when she grabbed Turtle.

At least her niece was safe. That was all that mattered. Turtle's short brown braid lay on the floor next to her foot, the hair already unraveling.

"You *stole* from me," Lord Hanley grated out next to her ear. "But I have *you*. And that thief you were with will bring back my possessions or your friends will never see you again."

Lord Hanley had no intention of ever letting her get away, whether the dragon-bound weapons were returned or not. Anger and fear made Lisette's hands shake. That one person could cause so much misery was so *unfair*. She wanted to argue with him, to let everyone waiting outside see what he was *really* like.

But she had promised Remy she would do whatever was necessary to stay alive. Lisette forced herself to keep quiet.

"Now we're going to go outside and get in my carriage and go home."

Magic rolled over Lisette again, making her breath catch from the pain in her sternum. She wouldn't give him the satisfaction of knowing how much it hurt.

Lord Hanley grunted behind her and tightened his grip on the collar of her tunic. "Are you the child of a mage? I can't feel it, but you shouldn't be able to fight me."

"Maybe you aren't as strong as you thought you were," Lisette offered lightly. She didn't resist when he pushed her forward. With a knife at her throat, the only thing she could do was obey and wait for her opportunity to get away.

They walked to the door. Through the glass, Lisette could see the crowd, Tiffany near the front with her arms around Pot and an unevenly shorn Turtle. Barlow still held Ziggy, but now Rye stood in front of them all, sword raised. Near him stood the tea vendor, leaning on a thick branch as if it were a cane — but Lisette had seen him use it before and knew any guard who came near would be sorry. Other people held window-opening rods and ladles and long-handled pans.

The guards surrounding the carriage would prevail, but the freeholders of the quarter would make them pay dearly.

Lisette lifted her chin, squared her shoulders, and opened the door. She walked outside as if the man behind her was of no consequence. One wrong move would start a battle that would kill all of her friends. The only thing she could do to stop it was get in the carriage with Lord Hanley. If she couldn't get out on her own, Remy would come for her.

Two steps from the carriage, Lord Hanley stumbled, holding himself up by pulling on her tunic. "It's not possible," he muttered. He pulled Lisette to a halt, and she felt the icy blade press against her skin. "What have you done?"

An enormous figure glided over the rooftops, blotting out the stars.

CHAPTER 62
UNBOUND

A wave of murmurs went along the street as one person after another looked toward the sky. Even the guards stared, their swords drooping as they took in the sight.

An amber and black dragon circled the quarter, magic rippling over his scales as he slid along the currents of air.

Aarat, unbound.

"What have you done?" Lord Hanley repeated, his knife still at Lisette's throat. "That dragon maintains the defenses of Harbor Crag."

Lisette wondered what all the *other* dragons in the warrens were being forced to give up their magic for. "A city that depends on chains deserves to fall," she gritted out, momentarily forgetting her plan to go along with him until she could escape.

"If the dragon is loose..." A wordless snarl erupted next to her ear. "We'll have to leave. The Island of Light. We'll go there. For now." Lord Hanley raised his voice to speak to the guards. "To the harbor! We'll board the *Winds of Vauron*." Then he spoke to Lisette again. "Get in the coach."

Going to a residence within the city, one she had already gone into with Remy by her side, was bad enough. But there was absolutely no way Lisette was getting on a ship with the mage behind her. She planted her feet and leaned back. "No."

"Move!"

"No." Lisette reached up and grabbed his hand, trying to pull the knife away from her throat.

But Lord Hanley had strength on his side. The edge of the blade pressed against Lisette's skin. She felt a trickle drip down to her collarbone.

Suddenly, the knife in his hand crumbled like sand and trickled between his fingers. The swords held by his guards disintegrated, falling away to land between the cracks in the cobblestones. Uncle Rye swore as his sword dissolved in front of him.

In front of the carriage, the traces holding the nervous horses slackened, allowing the pair to dance free. Then the carriage itself withered, folding in on itself.

Everything metal had crumbled — including the nails in her boots, Lisette realized as she pulled away from Lord Hanley and her boot soles flapped open. The horses, already unnerved by the dragon, didn't take the collapse of the carriage behind them calmly. Unable to run forward through the line of people standing in the street, they wheeled and bolted around the wreckage.

Lisette jumped out of the way and scrambled toward the crowd of freeholders. Lord Hanley screamed, "Grab her!" The two nearest guards reached for her, then froze.

Aarat descended to the middle of the street behind the freeholders, the draft from his enormous wings blowing dust and the grit remaining from the swords into the air. The freeholders scattered and flattened themselves against the buildings on either side. Cries of wonder and dismay filled the air from the intersection where the dragon's tail had flattened a cart.

Lisette ran towards the dragon, praying that was the safest direction. If Aarat was sufficiently angry, or just didn't recognize her in time... But better to be a dragon's meal than end up on a long voyage with the man behind her. Horses' hooves clattered on the street behind her. Someone yelled incoherently.

And then she was next to Aarat's gigantic head, the irises in his eyes glowing and swirling as he looked at her. She glanced back to see an empty street. Lord Hanley and his men had run away.

"Lisette." Just her name this time, with no tug on her soul. Steam wafted from Aarat's nostrils. "Take care with your blood. There are mages aplenty in this city, and some would do you harm."

A touch on her shoulder startled her, but it was Remy. Simi jumped from his shoulder onto the dragon's forehead, causing a nearby freeholder to gasp. Lisette only had eyes for Remy.

He pressed a cloth against her throat. "He cut you. I'm sorry. I couldn't set things up fast enough."

Lisette moved one hand on top of his. "That was you, wasn't it? Destroying the metal?"

He nodded. "The original spell transmutes wood to silver — in very small quantities, you understand. I had trouble learning it. My variation was responsible for the destruction of half the school armory." He choked out a laugh. "I did tell you I was a very bad mage, didn't I?"

"You might have mentioned it once." She turned to face Aarat, still holding Remy's hand in hers. "Thank you for your assistance."

The dragon snorted. "It appears I have some scales to balance." He brushed the cat off his forehead. Simi landed neatly on the ground and leapt up to sit on Remy's shoulder again.

The dragon ran down the street, gathering speed until he launched himself into the air again.

Lisette watched him circle above the waterfront. "Aarat is free. Lord Hanley is..." She paused, trying to decide if she needed to worry. "Not here, in any case."

"I think he might be one of the scores Aarat is going to settle," Remy agreed. "I can't imagine that will end well, though the man *is* a mage." He sighed. "And until we can destroy his bonds to the other dragons, he still has a *great* deal of power."

A child ran into the back of Lisette's legs. Lisette reached down and picked up Turtle, closing her eyes and feeling grateful the girl was still alive.

"Auntie Lisette cut my hair!" Turtle told Remy. "See?"

Lisette opened her eyes, trying to decide if she should laugh or cry. Laughter won out.

Remy was nodding with a serious look on his face. "Would you like me to cut the other side off for you?"

Lisette didn't hear the response to that because another arm around her shoulders distracted her. Tiffany kissed her cheek. "Thank you."

"I didn't gut him like you wanted."

Tiffany glanced toward the harbor. "If we ever see him again..."

"Next time. I promise."

"I'll hold you to that." Tiffany looked around and raised her voice. "Alright, everyone needs to go to bed now. It's late and we're all tired." The street had started to clear now all the excitement was over.

"*I'm* not tired," Pot insisted. "I want to see the dragon again."

"Not tonight, love. You can tell your father all about what he missed in the morning." Tiffany herded her brood toward their home.

The uncles took her place. Now that the danger was past, Barlow was wiping his eyes. "Creatures of the deep, Lisette, don't scare me like that ever again." His hug nearly knocked the air out of her.

Behind her, Remy said to Rye, "Sorry about the sword."

"Don't be. I'm just as glad to be rid of it." The pitch of his voice changed. "Don't squash the poor girl, Barlow."

Barlow loosed her, and Lisette stumbled back into Remy. Simi rubbed her cheek on Lisette's hair.

Rye grabbed his partner's arm. "We'll be over in the morning to help fix the shop. And we should probably talk about a few things as well." He cast a worried glance toward the harbor where multiple ships were raising sails. The glow from Aarat's scales was no longer visible. "This is going to change everything."

"Tomorrow, uncle," Lisette said firmly, pulling Remy's arm around her waist. "Happy festival."

Rye smiled. "Happy festival." He and Barlow turned and went back into their shop, hand in hand.

Lisette tipped her head so she could see Remy's face. "I think we were in the middle of discussing where you might leave your staff. If you have a few minutes, I could show you some options..." She tugged him toward her shop, then raised an eyebrow when he didn't move.

"Before we go, I should probably warn you." He winced. "That spell, the one that rusted all the metal away..."

"The one that saved my life."

He brightened. "Yes. Keep that in mind."

Lisette tightened her hand on his. "Out with it."

"The range is a bit unpredictable. I wanted to make sure it went far enough. And your shop was right behind you. I tried not to damage the buildings, but these things are tricky."

Lisette turned her head to look at her shop, only then noticing the door was lying on the ground. "The hinges?"

"And the lock." He looked doubtful. "And I think part of that dragon clock was iron as well."

Lisette tried to keep a straight face as she thought of the ugly dragon clock. "Does it actually look any worse?" She finally let her smile out. "Remy, my family has been trying to get rid of that thing for *generations*."

"Oh."

Lisette pulled him toward the shop, and this time he came along. "We should probably spend some time looking over the damage. Tomorrow."

"Ah, well, that frees up some time tonight, doesn't it?" He leaned to whisper in her ear. "I have an idea or two."

Lisette leaned down to grab the edge of the door. "Let's figure out some way to keep this in place, and then we can go upstairs and talk about them."

CHAPTER 63
EPILOGUE

The rosy light of dawn suffused the street as Lisette stood by her bedroom window, a blanket pulled around her for warmth. Closer to the waterfront, the fires had gone out, though she suspected nothing was left of the duke's residence or Lord Hanley's estate. Aarat had set them both ablaze before he'd soared away. Rumors had flown along the streets, sung out both by criers and street children hoping for an extra coin for the news.

A hollow ache in her chest left her wondering where Aarat had gone. Lisette had felt the dragon fly out over the ocean during the night, and that, too, had been reported loudly in the quarter. This Festival of Secrets would be remembered for many years to come.

Behind her, Remy yawned and lifted his head from the pillow. "Everything alright?"

In the street below, a horse and cart went by — the baker's deliveryman with his baskets of bread. He would also have rolls filled with jam, the food traditionally served the morning after the festival end. Dragons and mages may have warred in the street, but life in the freeholder quarter still went on.

Lisette pulled her blanket tighter. "Aarat's still gone." Lord Hanley had said the city had no defenses once the dragon was freed. For centuries, dragons had flown to the city's aide when ships attacked. Aarat would think twice about helping Harbor Crag again.

"He'll be back. Dragons protect their own. Plus, you still owe him a favor. And there's an egg about to hatch somewhere." Remy sounded as if he was trying to convince himself. He patted the sheets next to him. "Come back to bed. You can help me compose my letter of resignation."

Lisette turned, then. "No more spying? You're sure?"

"I was never very good at it." He sighed. "And I don't want to accidentally pass on knowledge that could help someone replicate this elsewhere."

"Ah." Lisette glanced out toward the harbor again, where fishing boats bobbed on the water. "We'll have to figure out how to free the others." Free them and hope those dragons didn't take revenge on Harbor Crag once they were no longer bound. Though Aarat had confined himself to specific buildings — thus far — so maybe the other dragons could be reasoned with as well.

"I have some ideas." Remy paused. "Things are going to be a bit of a mess here. And if Lord Hanley makes it to the Island of Light, he may gain support." He levered himself onto his elbow with a grin. "Though if the mages are expecting Harbor Crag to be undefended, I think they may be in for a very big surprise."

Lisette let the window covering drop back into place. "I guess we'll just have to find out." She slipped under the sheets next to him, laughing at his yelp when her cold feet touched his leg. "Shouldn't you have a spell to keep my feet warm?"

"Yes, but there's a possibility I might light the bedclothes on fire instead." He shifted toward her under the blankets. "I have a better idea." What followed indeed led to heat and required no magic at all to sustain it.

Just as Lisette was about to drop off to sleep, the ember in her chest twinged. She smiled and placed one hand over her sternum.

The oldest dragon of Harbor Crag had returned.

~

TURN the page for a preview of Shift Happens, where everyone has an animal form and only lucky people never find out what it is...

If you would like to be notified of new releases, as well as receive exclusive short stories and other bonus content, join my free newsletter at https://tmbaumgartner.com/subscribe/.

SHIFT HAPPENS
(PREVIEW)

CHAPTER
ONE

Angela should have brought her gloves.

She hadn't really planned on crouching on the roof of a building, talking down a freaked-out porcupine, and yet it hadn't been completely out of the question either. But no, the black leather gloves, newly washed after the encounter with a very apologetic hamster, were still sitting on the stand by her apartment door. Right where she'd put them so she wouldn't forget to take them to work.

"Darren?" Angela edged a bit closer, roof gravel crunching under her shoes, and tried to look non-threatening, which wasn't all that hard for a short pudgy fifty-six year old white woman. She aimed for the aura of benevolent aunt, but was aware that she sometimes achieved crazy cat lady instead. "Darren, can we talk about this?"

"Just leave me alone!" The voice should have sounded odd coming from a little woodland creature, but Angela had been doing her job too long to even notice any more. "Why won't anybody ever leave me alone?"

Angela's left calf started to cramp up as she held her

crouch. "Look, I'll be happy to leave you by yourself for a while, but first we have to get you back to your human form. What do you think about that?"

The porcupine took a step back from her, quills rattling. "I'm not going to live in a cage in some secret military facility!"

With a sigh Angela knelt on her right knee and stretched out her left leg, massaging her calf. The young guys always brought that one up, as if they couldn't imagine a world where everyone didn't realize how important they were. Still, it looked like they might skip the whole "Why me?" conversation, which was a relief because Angela didn't have a good answer for that one. Everyone had the potential to shift into another form, but most people were lucky enough to never do so. "Darren, what the heck would the military want with a porcupine that doesn't want to leave his room? Let's get you back to human and then we can get you in a class so you can control your shifting and get you on a probation schedule." He seemed like a nice kid. If she could just get him through this crisis, he could go back to writing the web comic his mother didn't understand, and playing the final scenes of *The Last Salamander* with his online guild.

"You're trying to trick me. I've seen *Shift Enforcers*."

Shit Enforcers, Angela thought but didn't say it out loud. "Darren, do I look like some guy on steroids who's going to knock you out? I knit. I do yoga. I have a book club that meets every other week to talk about the latest romance novels. I don't knock people out and put them in magical handcuffs while I chant Latin at them." She took a breath and continued in a quieter voice. "Now why don't you move away from there and we can talk about what to do next." After a long career of talking accidental shifters off ledges usually more metaphorical than this, Angela could tell he was starting to listen. Maybe she wouldn't need those gloves after all.

Silence. His nose twitched. "No cage?"

"Absolutely not. We'll get you changed back, then I'll put a spell on you so you won't accidentally shift. It'll wear off in a week or so, but that will give you a chance to get some training." She scooted back a foot. At least she didn't need to worry about the building being destroyed by the amount of magic released even if he did happen to dive into the concrete below. "Let's move away from the edge, though. I don't want you to end up falling when we get you back to normal size."

He waddled forward on little feet, maintaining the same separation. "What now?"

Angela relaxed. "Now I just need you to think about letting me help you." She probably could have shifted him without his cooperation — his magic didn't feel all that strong, an M7 or maybe M6 at best — but this way would be easier on them both.

"That's it?"

"Yep. It's a little anticlimactic, isn't it?"

"No Latin?" He sounded disappointed.

"I mean, if it makes you feel better I can throw some in." Angela looked at the energies flickering in his core, the threads of both forms spiraling together, and bumped them with a spark of power to get some separation.

"Wait!" The porcupine sidled off to the left. "I'm not going to end up naked, am I?"

Angela smiled. "Were you wearing clothes when you shifted?" At his nod she opened a hand. "Then you'll have them when you shift back." She raised her eyebrows. "Ready?"

"Okay."

She readied the spell to bind him to one form. "Quod erat demonstrandum. Quid pro quo." The net settled over him and she shoved a little more power into it, lighting up the strands. "Veni vidi vi—"

Then disaster struck. With a bang the door to the roof flew open and two cops rushed through guns drawn. "Freeze!"

The porcupine eeped, all spines suddenly erect, and jumped backward. Not, Angela thought later, in an attempt to jump off the roof, but in the startled reflex of a small prey animal. Either way, he sailed toward the edge of a three-story drop and she did the only thing she could do.

She really should have brought her gloves.

PORCUPINE QUILLS WERE a pain to get out. As the emergency department resident dug out forty-seven quills, Angela had plenty of time to think about the significance of the third magical lightweight shifting within two weeks. She tried to decide if the background hum of magic in the hospital felt abnormal or if she was just thinking about it too hard. She'd spent the weekend driving around asking herself the same question without finding any source.

While he worked, the resident quoted his favorite bits from *Shift Enforcers*. Tug. "'Looks like we *steered* that one on a path back to humanity!'" The resident snorted and pulled another quill out. From the compactness of his magical core, he'd never shifted, but from the buzz of his fingers against her flesh, even through the latex gloves, she suspected he was one of the few that could be trained to work magic. Maybe that explained why he was so obsessed with the show. "The 'Salamander's Bones' episode was one of the best. It was the one where they trained him for that mission in Spain where he ran with the bulls and they gored that spy."

Angela wondered if the doctor was aware that steers were castrated. Probably not. She worked on her breathing and tried to tune him out. The local anesthetic was starting to wear off, but there were only a few quills left.

At least she'd managed to shift Darren back and settle the binding on him before the cops had handcuffed her. Darren hadn't even complained about the bald spots he'd been left with, although it was possible he hadn't noticed them yet. In any case, she'd done her job and Darren was safe for the next week or two.

Tug. "'Go *cluck* yourself!'"

True fact: the script writers for *Shift Enforcers* were only allowed to write characters that shifted into animals already tested on camera and approved by the star, Guy Barron. At 5'8" Guy was sensitive about looking too short, and after the first season there were more and more mini-horses, small dogs, and chickens. He'd even passed on the opportunity to film with a dragon shifter who'd been passing through. The world may have lost some spectacular cinematography but the sets were easier to clean up afterward.

Angela's phone rang before the resident could think up another quip. With her free hand cuffed to the rail of the nearby bed, she couldn't raise it to her ear. "You're on speaker, Captain." Maybe that would convince him to be a little more professional. "I really think we need to get a team in to survey downtown to see if there's—"

Her attempt to direct the conversation failed. "What the

hell, Jones? How the fuck do you go out on a simple bitch-n-switch and end up assaulting a cop?"

The resident's eyes lit up at the lingo. They hadn't used that term until after the *Shift Enforcers* writers had come up with it. Until then they'd just called it "talking to a new shifter."

The silence lengthened and she realized the question hadn't been rhetorical. "It was...an accident?"

"You kneed the guy in the balls so hard he's still packing ice around his nuts and it was an *accident*?" Captain Rosenthal's voice got louder until by the end of the question he was yelling, and she could picture his face getting redder and the vein on his temple pulsing. She'd certainly seen it happen enough times to know what it looked like. "Moore and Young never have *accidents*" — he drew out the word — "like that. I don't get calls from the chief of police about *their* conduct on a regular basis."

To be fair, this would only be the third time he'd been called about her in the five years since he'd transferred in, so "regular basis" was a bit of a stretch, but she didn't think pointing that out would help her any. "I'd just talked this guy off the ledge, I mean literally, and those guys ran onto the scene and almost ruined everything. He's lucky I just kneed him instead of throwing him off the building. I'm in the emergency room now." She paused for a moment then brought out the big guns. "This could cause...long term disability."

The resident looked up in confusion at that and opened his mouth, but her look was enough to make him stay silent. He angled his groin further away from her knee and went back to pulling out quills.

While she'd expected to derail the captain's argument a bit by bringing up permanent disability, Angela hadn't expected to silence him completely. She glanced at the phone to make sure he hadn't hung up, but the line was still open. "Captain Rosenthal? Are you still there?" Finger on the disconnect button she paused. She couldn't hear him talking, but if she used her imagination that background noise was labored breathing. "Captain? Can you hear me?" Nothing. After another five seconds, Angela hit disconnect and scrolled through her contact list. The phone on the daytime dispatcher's desk rang. Twelve-oh-five. Candace would be at lunch, the emergency calls automatically rolling over to the main police dispatch center. Angela didn't have the number of the building guard station. Gritting her teeth she dialed again.

Matt Moore's voice had a patronizing edge when he finally answered. "Angie! Hey when we said you didn't have any balls, we meant you should grow a pair not take someone—"

She interrupted. "Are you in the office?"

"What's it to you?"

"If you're in the office can you go check on the captain?"

"Yeah, right, like I'm going to fall for that. He just got off the phone with the police chief. I'm still working on this stupid survey about new incidents that we all have to do because of you."

"Matt, seriously, he was on the phone with me and I think there's something wrong."

"Not happening, Angie. Hey, if you're still over by the stadium can you swing by one of my—"

She hung up and dialed the only other person who might be in the office.

Caleb Young answered right before it would have transferred to voicemail. "What. I'm busy."

Busy doing online training for yet another useless

certificate if the past was any predictor of the present, but she tried to keep her voice level. "Can you go check on the captain? We were on the phone and I'm worried he might have had a medical emergency."

"No way. He's so pissed off right now I'm staying out of sight for the afternoon." The bright ding from a question correctly answered came over the line. If Caleb spent as much time helping his clients as he did following the checklist to get the next promotion, he probably wouldn't spend as much time complaining about his workload.

Angela leaned toward the phone and dropped her voice. "Young. If you don't go check on him right now I swear I will call your wife and tell her exactly" — she split the word up into three distinct syllables — "what you were up to after the last holiday party." Not that Angela knew anything, but she'd heard him trying to fill gaps the next day.

The resident's eyebrows went up but he went back to pulling the last three quills from her wrist. One breath. Two. By the third she knew she'd overplayed her hand and she'd just have to call an ambulance and cross her fingers that she didn't get fired if the captain was just having phone trouble.

"Fine. Whatever. I'll go look."

His chair squeaked, then Angela heard him knock on the captain's door. "Cap? You okay in there... Oh my god!" His voice went up an octave and he was suddenly close to the phone again. "He's lying on the floor and I think he's *dead*!"

"Start CPR," she ordered. "I'll call for an ambulance."

"Wait! What do I do?"

Every year. They re-certified in CPR every damn year. She knew this because she was the one stuck with keeping track of it. Caleb had been with the department for five years, so he'd been through the training at least five times.

The resident put down his forceps and took the phone from her. "I'm going to guide you through this, okay?" He pulled his own cell phone out of the pocket in his lab coat and gave it to Angela. "Call 911 and get them rolling." He bandaged up her hand while talking Caleb, and then Matt a few minutes later, through chest compressions.

By the time they heard the EMTs enter the room ten minutes later and hung up both phones they were sitting next to each other on the bed. The resident sighed. "Sorry about your boss."

He looked so disappointed she patted him on the shoulder, lightly. "Maybe he'll pull through. There was nothing else you could have done."

He looked startled. "I knew that." He stood up and checked her bandage over.

"You just looked so disappointed..." Angela thought back to the point when his shoulders had drooped. "Oh. You thought they would be more like the officers on *Shift Enforcers*. Sorry."

"No, no, it was stupid of me. It's just a television show. If anyone should know how much they make stuff up, I should." He gestured at the building around him. "It's just... when I was in high school I thought that was what I wanted to do when I grew up."

"Why didn't you?" Angela flipped to her other sight. After a lifetime of practice, it was automatic, the physical world fading while the currents and eddies of magic came into focus, letting her see the resident's magical potential. He probably wasn't a powerhouse, but he certainly had enough innate magic to do her job, and he'd had enough empathy to explain what he was planning to do, instead of just treating her like she was an injured hand with a body attached to it. "I think you would have been good at it."

"Thanks." For the first time he gave her a real smile. "I guess I was just too intimidated. I'd never be able to face down a cobra with just a trash can lid and my wits."

READY FOR MORE? Download Shift Happens *now!*

ACKNOWLEDGMENTS

When I found out my 10-year-old niece had read and enjoyed *Shift Happens*, I was a little surprised. While there wasn't anything really age-inappropriate in my first novel[1], the protagonist is a woman in her fifties. I was curious about what drew her in. Was it the humor? The magic system? The writing style?

The answer was quite simple. Dragons. She was willing, she told me, to read anything with a dragon in it. Pro tip: don't ask questions of kids if you aren't ready to hear the brutally honest truth.

A few months later, Kindle Vella launched. I'd never written a serial, but I decided to give it a try. I had just the subject.

So I guess I have to thank my niece for giving me the idea for *Dragon Freehold*, even if my ego still hasn't quite recovered from our conversation.

Thanks also go to my brother Eric, who helped proofread the episodes before I posted them. I don't know if he likes dragons. He might. I've learned my lesson about asking those sorts of questions.

---

1. Except a few curse words. My niece cast aspersions on my sister's parenting ability when she pointed this out.

ABOUT THE AUTHOR

T. M. Baumgartner is a speculative fiction writer who has difficulty following directions. This probably explains why the IRS recalculates her tax refund after she files it every year. At various times she has been a veterinarian, Unix system administrator, software developer, and after-hours book-shelver in a medical library.

Theresa currently lives in Northern California in a house with too many animals. She knits hats for garden gnomes and fails to grow tomatoes despite living in the perfect climate.

She also writes cozy mysteries under the pen name Tess Baytree.

Want updates about new releases? Silly dog anecdotes? Free stories? Join the newsletter mailing list! Go to https://tmbaumgartner.com/subscribe/ or point your phone's camera at the QR code above.

The marketing department here at Speculative Turtle Press is great at tail wagging, but a little challenged by tasks that require thumbs.

If you enjoyed this book and would like to help other

readers find it, please tell your friends and consider leaving a review at your favorite site.

ALSO BY T.M. BAUMGARTNER

As T.M. Baumgartner:

Shift Happens

The Chaos Job (Jackpot Drift #1)

The Chaos Connection (Jackpot Drift #2)

As Tess Baytree:

Death Walks a Dog

Death Tracks the Scent

Death Smells a Rose

Death Trims the Tree